Of Sin & Sanctuary

A Revelry's Tempest Novel, Volume 2

K.J. Jackson

First Edition: September 2017
ISBN: 978-1-940149-25-7
http://www.kjjackson.com

K.J. JACKSON BOOKS

HISTORICAL ROMANCE:

Stone Devil Duke, *A Hold Your Breath Novel*
Unmasking the Marquess, *A Hold Your Breath Novel*
My Captain, My Earl, *A Hold Your Breath Novel*
Worth of a Duke, *A Lords of Fate Novel*
Earl of Destiny, *A Lords of Fate Novel*
Marquess of Fortune, *A Lords of Fate Novel*
Vow, *A Lords of Action Novel*
Promise, *A Lords of Action Novel*
Oath, *A Lords of Action Novel*
Of Valor & Vice, *A Revelry's Tempest Novel*
Of Sin & Sanctuary, *A Revelry's Tempest Novel*

PARANORMAL ROMANCE:

Flame Moon
Triple Infinity, *Flame Moon #2*
Flux Flame, *Flame Moon #3*

Be sure to sign up for news of my next releases at www.KJJackson.com

Dedication

– As Always,
For my favorite Ks

{ Prologue }

Staffordshire, England
April 1811

It had happened to thousands of men before him.

It would happen to thousands of men after him.

The scene, played out countless times in studies rife with cigar smoke. The scene, just like this one, all across England. The scene that would start kindly, cordially, and then descend into demands—ultimatums of honor and sacrifice designed to serve the right of primogeniture. Designed to serve first-born sons.

The grand estates of the country demanded it.

Theo's own scene echoed the ghosts of every last one of those conversations.

He was nothing but the latest fool to be crushed under the custom. Another casualty to the convention of society.

Theo turned from the low flames of the fireplace in the study to Mr. Demetrick, only to find the man standing by the desk, his face impenetrable. Exactly as Theo knew it would be.

"Violet will never be yours, boy," Mr. Demetrick said. "You are a rascal, a rogue, but beyond all of that, you are a third son of an earl. You will never be more. A second son, possibly—there would be a chance, but a third son?" He scoffed. "I will never allow my niece to marry you. I made a vow to her father on that accord long ago."

"Yet, if I could offer her security—"

"Security beyond her own plentiful inheritance? I know of your finances, Mr. Williston. Or the lack thereof." Violet's uncle and guardian moved forward, puffing out his chest as he scratched his robust belly. "It is best to end this infatuation between the two of you before she becomes overly attached to you. You do realize, Mr. Williston, that you only do her harm by continuing this assault upon her time. And as a man of honor, I do not think you wish her any undue distress."

Honor. Of course Violet's blasted uncle would call upon his honor. Nothing was beneath the man at this juncture.

Theo's left fist clenched at his side, as his glare skewered Mr. Demetrick. "Violet may very well disagree with what you have decided for her, Mr. Demetrick."

"Violet does not know what she wants." Mr. Demetrick paused, looking to Mr. Nullter, the solicitor of Violet's estate who stood in the corner, silent.

Mr. Nullter offered Mr. Demetrick an angled nod, his thin voice snaking into the room. "It appears to be appropriate to tell him. It would lessen the debacle about to ensue."

Mr. Demetrick's look shifted back to Theo, his voice brutal. "I do know what is best for Violet. Lord Vandestile has already spoken to me about her."

"Lord Vandestile?" Theo's chest clenched, his fingertips digging into his palm from his tight fist. "But Violet has only met the man once—and at that, she was not impressed with him. She spoke those very words to me."

"Yes, well that can be overcome," Mr. Nullter said. "He would make a fine match for her and her inheritance."

"I told him I would seriously consider his proposal," Mr. Demetrick said.

"He's already proposed?" Theo's head shook. "No. Violet will never fall for him—the man is a notorious libertine."

"The man is a viscount." Mr. Nullter took a timid step forward, aligning himself with Violet's uncle. "Impeccable lines. And he has already made efforts to curb his rakish ways as he pursues Violet."

"And after he gets her?" Theo spit the words out, having to hold his feet in place—hold back against lunging at Mr. Nullter—or Mr. Demetrick—or both of them.

"She will have made a proper match that I approve of." Mr. Demetrick patted his protruding stomach as he glanced down at Theo's drawn fist. "From there, it is up to her to serve her husband. It is no longer my business."

Theo's eyes narrowed at Violet's uncle. "What are you getting out of this blasphemous deal?"

"You go too far, boy."

"Do I? You are willing to sacrifice Violet's happiness at the altar of a title? For self-gain? Against what she truly desires?"

"Happiness is fleeting, Mr. Williston. As is what association you have with her." Mr. Demetrick's thin-lipped mouth turned downward in pity. "Violet is young. Her happiness is malleable. Even if she did buck against being paired with Lord Vandestile, it would have no consequence. As these matters go, I know you understand that it matters very little what Violet actually desires."

"You would do well to release her now," Mr. Nullter said. "That is what we ask of you—of your honor as a gentleman. Do not engage her. Do not encourage her attentions any further."

Theo's look shifted from one man to the other. He knew this had been coming. Knew it since the day he had been born a third son.

But to hear it. To live it.

He swallowed hard, his look landing on Mr. Demetrick. "You cannot control her."

"No," Mr. Demetrick said. "But all of us in this room know who controls her inheritance and how this will end—no matter how you argue against it, no matter how you fight it, Mr. Williston. So please, do the respectable thing and remove yourself from Violet. The longer you stay within reach, the more harm you do her."

"Harm?" Theo guffawed and stepped to Mr. Demetrick, his look challenging with every fiber of his being. "You know nothing of harm, you sanctimonious prig. I may not be the man that you want for your niece. I may not be worthy of her." He forcibly unclenched his fist, taking a step backward as he shook his head. "But someday—someday, she will fall. And it will be me—I will be the one to catch her. I always will be. I will be worthy of her. I will bring her happiness. And you will choke upon your words, old man."

Without waiting for a response, Theo turned and left the room quietly, each step precise, echoing through the hazy smoke suffocating the room. Each step a silent promise, a silent rail against his order of birth and what it meant for his future.

A future he had always refused to acknowledge, but could always see.

A future he didn't want.

A future he had no idea how to change.

~~~

Two Years Later
Derbyshire, England
September 1813

She hadn't thought her life would end like this.

The darkness swooping in, eating her whole.

She had always been meant for much brighter things. Adventure. Laughter. Love. The world at her command. Her mama had always said so before she died.

Not the tentacles of cold death, snaking around her, squeezing the life out of her.

Violet let her breath exhale.

One last time.

The bubbles of air drifted up through the water above her, disappearing into the surface.

She had floated once in the ocean, long ago on a trip to Brighton with her parents after begging endlessly to do so. Dipping under the waves had been so very much like this.

Water above her.

But as once she had lifted herself toward the blazing sun, laughing as she broke free from the water's surface, now she battled away the panic, the instinctive need for breath.

The struggle wasn't even as hard as she had anticipated.
~~~

She kept her eyes open, watching, until the end. More out of curiosity, than out of need to fight against the black.

The last bubble popped above her.

Her eyelids faltered, quivering as they slid closed.

Done. She was done.

{ CHAPTER 1 }

LONDON, ENGLAND
MARCH 1816

Violet flipped the page on her calendar, her fingernail pressing into the wood grain of the desk, sawing back and forth as she stared at the dates, willing them to change, even though she knew she couldn't alter the rotation of the earth around the sun.

Less than a month away.

The *Gala of Three* was approaching far too quickly for the amount of work that still needed to be done. But there was no altering course now—the three-year anniversary of the opening of the Revelry's Tempest gaming house was coming whether she wished it or not.

It would be the most fruitful event of the year. That, Violet was sure of. In the two and a half years that she had run the gaming hall on Brook Street, she knew the numbers better than she knew her own hands. She could now predict, merely by the attendee list, how much coin an evening of gaming would bring to the Revelry's Tempest's coffers.

And the third anniversary celebration had attendees of the highest order set to come. It would be a success. It had to be.

Even if one of her dearest friends, Adalia, wasn't here to help. Adalia had started the Revelry's Tempest three years earlier, just months before marrying the Duke of Dellon, and was the mastermind behind the inventive games the Revelry's Tempest was known for. Adalia was an expert at producing the most bizarre and fantastical moments of entertainment for the crowds. And while Adalia still owned the house, she had given Violet the Revelry's Tempest to run as her own years ago.

As much as Violet wished her here, she was no force against nature. Adalia and her husband were currently sequestered away at Dellon Castle, awaiting the birth of their second child.

A knock on the door thudded into her office and Violet looked up from her desk. "Enter."

The door cracked open and Logan, the Revelry's Tempest's head of guards, poked his far-too-handsome head in. A rush of warmth from the ballroom and the cacophony of gleeful winners and grumbling losers floated into the office. "Lady Vandestile, there is a slight commotion upstairs in one of the private card rooms that requires your presence."

"Cass is not available?"

"Lady Desmond would not be the proper authority in this situation, my lady."

Her eyebrow cocked. Logan rarely had a situation that needed her interference. And if there was an altercation, no one was better at diffusing a fracas than Cassandra, so Logan usually brought most concerns to Violet's dear friend.

"What is it?" Violet stood, walking around the desk to follow him into the thick of the crush that had gathered to gamble that night.

Logan waited until they threaded their way through the crowd to lean down to her as they walked to the stairs in the hall just outside the ballroom. His voice was low—the utmost in discretion. "There is a man that insists that we approve an additional marker to his name."

Violet looked up at Logan, noting his slight limp was more pronounced than usual. She was on the wrong side for him to lean down toward her. "And it would be unwise to do so?"

Logan shrugged as they started up the stairs.

"How much has he already lost?"

"Seven thousand pounds."

Violet coughed, her gut dropping. "Seven thousand pounds? Who would we allow that much credit to—and who would dare to think we would extend that credit even further?"

They reached the top of the stairs and Violet switched to walk by Logan's right side.

Logan pointed to the third door along the hall. "That is why your assistance is needed. He…he is making claims that you will approve it."

Her eyebrows lifted at Logan just as he opened the door to the card room for her.

She stepped into the room, quickly taking in the scene. Two men standing, hands wildly swinging as they shouted at each other. Four women—two of them her most loyal patrons—sitting around the gaming table, chatting, obviously titillated by the ensuing scandal. The dealer leaned back in his chair, a staunchly bored look on his face.

Whatever had just happened in this room was not going to reflect well on the name of her gaming house.

Violet took a step forward just as a third man moving from the sideboard with a full tumbler of amber liquid wobbled in front of her path.

She froze for a long moment. An excruciatingly long moment. So long, it gave the staggering man a chance to stumble forward and throw his left arm around her shoulders.

The stench of brandy—both cheap and expensive—enveloped her.

"There she is. The flower. My little petal." The crux of his elbow tightened around the back of her bare neck as he pointed at Logan with a finger flipped above his tumbler. "She will tell you. Tell you all how wrong you are. She'll approve the marker." He looked at her. "Won't you, Violet?"

Bloody hell.

Theodore Williston, the fourteenth Earl of Alton.

Adalia's wayward turned wastrel brother.

Back from the dead and working on an early grave, if all she had heard of him during the past two and a half years was true.

Violet jumped to the left, shoving off his arm resting on her shoulders.

His support suddenly removed, he stumbled to gain his balance, his drink sloshing onto the floor as his gaze swung to her.

Now that he stood swaying in front of her, Violet could truly take in Theodore's face.

His blue eyes bloodshot, Adalia's brother looked like he hadn't slept in five days. His nose sat crooked—far from the straight line it once was—with a bump halfway down before the slope shifted slightly to the side. A long scar, rippled, like the skin had torn rather than been cut, ran from his left eyebrow down across his cheekbone until it disappeared at the base of his ear.

She searched his face, searched for a remnant of the past in him that she recognized. He had disappeared one day and then had sequestered himself away for so long that she had to hunt in her mind for a solid memory of the past.

His hair. His sandy blond hair was the same. Disheveled, as it always had been. But the same. Cut or mangled, hair grew back. Skin and bone did not.

Adalia had told Violet of her brother's injuries two and a half years ago. But this—his face so marred—she had not imagined.

Logan cleared his throat behind her. "Lady Vandestile, Lord Alton was insistent that you would approve a marker that is far above our limits."

Violet jumped, Logan's sudden voice in the quiet room emphasizing the fact she was standing there like a ninny, staring at Theodore.

Theo. The man she had known since she was thirteen and had made friends with Adalia. The man she had once had fanciful dreams of marrying.

When she had last seen his face five years before, it had been perfect.

No more.

And now she was gaping at him, trying to reconcile what he had become.

"Is your inspection of my current state satisfied, Vee? I am hideous, I know it. You now know it. So let us move onward." Theo pointed to Logan over her shoulder. "Tell him, Vee. Tell your man to allow the marker I need." Theo swayed slightly in a slow circle that threatened his balance.

Brazenly presumptuous, as always. That had not changed.

She glanced about the room, noting all the wide eyes eager for her next move—for her to dole out humiliation. She bit her tongue.

For how she had just gawked at him, she owed him that much—to be spared any more indignity. She conjured her most patient smile. "Lord Alton, can we discuss this in private?"

"Anything you say can be heard by all my new friends here, Vee." Theo's left hand swung out, motioning to the men and women at the table.

Violet glanced to the octagonal card table. By the setup on the table and the pot in the middle, the group had been playing a rather high-stakes game of Loo. A game that was not over.

She looked to Theo. "Please, Lord Alton. Just for a moment in private, please."

He stepped toward her, his left arm flopping along her shoulders again. "Truly, Vee. No secrets here."

His weight shifted, using her for a crutch against his inebriation. A fresh waft of brandy hit her, the smell smothering her. Violet spread her feet wide, bracing herself against the extra weight on her shoulders. Her look landed on Lord Jiften across the room—one of the most dreadful gossips of the *ton*.

She glanced up at the side of Theodore's face.

The bugger.

He was abusing the situation—the room. He knew she wouldn't humiliate him in front of these people. But the unpaid credit he had managed to draw out of Cassandra the last time he visited the Revelry's Tempest had put Violet's bank into the negative for months. Violet had been at Dellon Castle, visiting Adalia, and Cassandra had assumed responsibility for the Revelry's Tempest while Violet was away. Cassandra had felt horrible for the incident, having never even questioned Theodore's ability to satisfy the markers when he had asked for the credit.

Violet would not make that mistake. "I would rather not discuss private matters in public, Lord Alton."

"Public—private—everyone knows everything, Vee." His voice took on a demanding tone. "You know that as well as I. So you can draw up that marker now."

That was her limit. It was one thing to be asked. Quite another to be ordered. "I am afraid we cannot offer further markers to you, Lord Alton."

His head jerked back, shocked for a moment before a strained grin came to his lips. Anger simmered under the smile. "Violet, surely you understand that my sister would approve any marker, since this is legally her house."

Violet stepped forward to duck away from his arm and turned to face him directly. "I actually have no doubt your sister would approve of exactly what I am doing, Lord Alton."

His top lip curled in a sneer. "My hideousness too much for you, Violet? You cannot trust a monster like me?"

The back of her neck flushed. She recognized exactly what he was doing—exploiting her guilt at her earlier boorishness. It was so very easy for her to now see through his manipulations—any man's manipulations, for that matter. Little did Theo know plying upon her guilt wouldn't work.

She opened her mouth to tell him exactly that just as her eyes met his.

His eyes.

The color she recognized from long ago, the cool blue of ice under a clear sky. Bloodshot, but the silver-flecked blue was there. Angry. Overbearing. But also struggling. Raging. Raging against everything in this world.

She recognized that, the fierce depth of the torment. It made her mouth clamp closed, hiding the slight gasp bubbling from her chest.

Without a word, she walked around Theo.

Logan still stood by the door and she paused next to him, going to her toes to whisper in his ear. "Allow him enough to make it through the next hands. But throw as much brandy as you can down his throat. The quicker he loses consciousness, the less money we will lose."

Logan nodded.

Her chest growing heavy with dread, she left the room. Down the stairs to the ballroom, she avoided eye contact with everyone in the crowd as she weaved her way through the hazard and card tables to her office at the back of the main gaming room.

Her avoidance didn't stop the portly Lord Hortman from grabbing her arm as she passed him. Her look whipping to him, she cocked her head upward so she could stare down her nose at him. She was a widowed viscountess and expected the respect the title demanded, but she also owned a gaming house—and that made far too many men audacious with their grabby paws.

"Lady Vandestile, I have been waiting for you to make an appearance this eve in the ballroom—you have been my good luck." Lord Hortman motioned to the French roulette table in front of him. "What say you, red or black?"

She forced a sweet smile at him. "You bring your own luck with you, Lord Hortman."

He laughed an overly hearty chuckle. "The luck I bring is poor tonight, my lady. I need some of yours. Come, you have much to spare."

Violet doubted that, what with the scene upstairs with Theodore. She had an overwhelming suspicion her luck was quickly waning. The smile on her face spread wider, sweeter. "Whatever you see in my face, Lord Hortman—red or black, that is the one to bet on."

He considered her a moment, eyes canny, and then he laughed. "Red it is, my lady." He set his markers down onto the red velvet of the table.

Violet walked away from the table before the wheel stopped. A whoop followed her as she opened the door to her office. Red it was.

Closing the door behind her, both of her hands gripped the doorknob behind her back as the farce of the smile slipped from her face, her head dropping forward. The brass knob a lifeline, she leaned back against the door, gasping for breath after breath.

She could play the part she needed to in order to fill the coffers—play the sweetly flirtatious widow for every idiot looking to part ways with his coin. She could do that to ensure she had complete control of her funds, her life.

But each and every time she had to slap a smile on her face in front of a man, she had to simultaneously swallow back a gag in her throat and instant panic in her chest.

She couldn't let that show. Especially not to another idiot man, just as her husband had been.

Her head lifted, her eyes landing on the calendar on her desk. Even from across the room, she could see the word "Gala" in thick ink, taunting her.

It *would* be a success. It would.

As long as the entertainment fell into place. The Spanish wine shipment arrived from Montes de Malaga. The new games of chance were developed. The right food was chosen to specifically fatten bellies and loosen purse strings.

As long as everything was perfect.

She needed it. Needed to make Adalia proud of her. Needed to finally secure her own future after years of paying off debts.

And the gala would do just that.

Secure her future.

{ CHAPTER 2 }

Violet shoved open the skinny door on the fourth level of the Revelry's Tempest. So hard, it made the door swing inward and knock the side wall.

The bang did nothing to wake the inert mass of the man unconscious on the floor inside.

Three stomps of her boots across the tiny room, and she kicked the man in the ribs.

He jolted upright and his head knocked into a low rafter, sending him back to the floor.

Good.

He landed on his side, still for a long moment. A low groan rumbled from his chest, his hand slowly going to the crown of his head. He rubbed his scalp as he slowly pulled himself up to a sitting position. Resting his forearms on his bent knees, he looked up at the morning light coming in the tiny window first, then to her as his eyebrows collapsed together over squinty eyes. "You put me in the servants' quarters."

Her hands went to her hips, her glare piercing him, her toes aching to kick him in the ribs again. Hard. "You are lucky I didn't toss you into the gutter, Lord Alton."

He blinked hard, his eyes attempting to focus on her. "The gutter hardly seems like the place for me, Violet."

"The gutter is exactly where you should be—the only reason you are not is that you are Adalia's brother."

She took a step forward, her heel stomping hard onto the floorboards. "The last time you were here at the

Revelry's Tempest you ruined my bank for months with your disastrous gaming. And now you have sunk the blasted ship again."

His hands lifted, the butt of his palms rubbing his eyes before he looked at her with a sigh. "Just what is it you believe me to have sunk, Violet?"

"You don't recall?"

"Enlighten me."

"Ten thousand pounds, to be exact. Ten thousand pounds slipping from your fingers."

He flipped his fingers into the air. "A trifle."

"A trifle?" Her voice went shrill. "Forgive me, Lord Alton, but do you not think that is an outrage? Ten thousand pounds—lost?"

He looked up at her, his words sharp. "Forgive me, Vee, but do you not run a gaming house? I would think your outrage at my poor gambling skills is not warranted. That you are accustomed to watching such losses. Especially as the proprietress of said house."

She leaned down slightly, her words sliding through gritted teeth. "Outrage is warranted when it has sent my bank to the edge of collapse. You have no idea what you have wrought, do you?"

He shrugged and then laid himself back onto the floor on his side, his hand rubbing his forehead. "Just what is it that I have wrought, Vee?"

"You weren't losing your money last night—you were losing my money. Money you have no way to pay back. You have put me in a precarious position. My bank is now in the negative, and I will need to borrow money for the gala in a month. And to do that, I need some sort of security for my lender." She paused, a long exhale hissing from her mouth. "Of which, I have none."

His eyes closed as he settled his right hand under his head as a pillow. "That does sound like a predicament you have gotten yourself into, Vee."

She nudged him in the stomach with the toe of her boot. "Do better, you sluggard."

"Why not just ask my sister for more funds?" He didn't bother to even turn his head up to her, much less open his eyes.

"This is not the time to put this upon her shoulders—do you not know carrying this babe has been very difficult for her? I refuse to add anything to her worry."

His eyes popped open, his look jumping to her face. "Adalia is not well?"

"When was the last time you visited her? Wrote her?"

He stared up at her, not answering, yet his look of concern didn't waver.

Violet sighed. "Adalia is well enough, as of now. She is resting. In bed day and night. And I intend to keep her there by, one, not bothering her with any matters of the Revelry's Tempest, and by, two, not reporting her ne'er-do-well brother's latest antics here in London."

"I am a ne'er-do-well now?"

"Yes."

He rolled over onto his back, his hand clasping onto his forehead. His chest rose in an exaggerated sigh. "So what do you want of me?"

"I want you to right the predicament you put me in last night. I need something—anything with a stake that

I can use as a guarantee against a loan so I can make it through the gala in a month."

"A gala?"

"Yes—the *Gala of Three.* A celebration of the three years the Revelry's Tempest has been open."

"That is a particularly obvious name."

"It is a particularly obvious event."

His hand on his forehead slipped over his eyes. "I would think you would have planned the balance of your bank more appropriately, Violet, if this was so important."

She growled and nudged him with her boot again. "I planned my funds out very well—down to the penny. What I did not plan upon was Adalia's oafish brother showing up and losing ten thousand pounds of my money."

He scoffed. "What? Ten thousand pounds?"

"Yes, ten thousand pounds. Have you not been listening to me?"

His hand moved from covering his eyes and he looked at her. "Ten thousand? No. Ridiculous. I would never have done that."

"Never has come for you, then." She poked him in the ribs with her boot. "You did. And it would have been far more had you not drunk yourself into a stupor." Violet paused, drawing a deep breath, striving for calm when all she really wanted to do was jump on top of him and choke him. "So now I ask you again, do you have anything of value—anything I can use as security?"

He shook his head as his fingers went to his temples and rubbed. His eyes closed. "You truly should not have approved my credit, Vee. That was quite careless of you."

A screech escaped her. She leaned down even further to him, hovering above his face. "You do realize I am a breath away from setting Logan upon you, Theo? If you thought your scars hideous before, you will not like the mirror at all when he is done with you."

The temple rubbing continued, his face not even flinching at the threat. "Logan does not scare me."

"He should."

Theo shrugged and then his eyes popped open. "How about the mine?"

"Your lead mine?" Violet straightened a bit, her arms crossing in front of her. "That is worthless. It has been for years."

Theo pushed himself up to sitting once more, his knees bending as he steadied himself. "You seem to have intimate knowledge on the matter."

"I do. Adalia asked me to look at all of the Alton finances years ago."

His hands gripped the tops of his knees as he looked up at her. "Years ago? Why would she have had you, of all people, look at the Alton finances?"

Violet ignored the obvious derision in his comment. Theodore wasn't the first man to underestimate her knowledge of numbers. "It was when you were missing after Caldwell died. When you had abandoned her."

"I didn't abandon her."

She gave a slight shake of her head. She wasn't about to spare him the truth of the matter and she had been sitting on this scolding for two and a half years. "Well, you were not here. She lost two of her brothers to early graves, and you were missing. All three of her brothers gone and she was left with the responsibility of the estate and two nieces. But you were alive, and yet you stayed away for what?"

Her lips drew back in a disgusted line as her eyes went to the low slanted rafters just above her head. She rushed on without waiting for an answer. "For the devil only knows why. So yes, you abandoned her, Theo. She thought you were dead." She looked down at him. "Do you know how alone she was? How scared? How she struggled—scratched every day to keep the Alton estate afloat? Your name. Your title. Not that you cared then. Not that you care now."

His gaze dropped from her. "My sister is a saint. I understand."

"She would be the last person to say that about herself. But, yes. Adalia managed to figure out a way to maintain the estate—your estate—to feed your nieces, to survive. All without your help."

"Done so well, I just should have stayed missing—dead." His head suddenly jerked up, his blue eyes meeting hers. "Did you know they put a gravesite out for me at Glenhaven House? Headstone and everything. Awkward, looking at your own death."

Violet drew a sharp intake of breath.

He was trying to throw her off-balance again.

She exhaled slowly. It wouldn't work. "I don't know what happened to you those many years ago, Theo. Adalia never told me, and I never asked. It clearly was painful. But frankly, I don't care. All I know is you are now a person that is manipulative, boorish, drunk at every turn from what the gossips say, abusing your relationship with your sister, and most importantly, threatening my livelihood."

"No, you're wrong, Vee."

"About what?" Her crossed arms tightened.

He met her glare, challenging it. "About the mine. It is worth something—we have been digging. We have been for the past year. There is a new vein."

"If that was true, Adalia would have told me."

"She doesn't know."

"What do you mean, she doesn't know? She knows every step you take, you have her worried so."

"Yes. Well, she doesn't know this."

Violet shook her head. "Honestly, I don't believe you, Theo."

He shrugged. "Believe me or not. It's all I have." He motioned to the doorway. "So get out and leave me to this floor for a few hours. I have nothing else to offer you, Vee."

He was lying. The bloody idiot was lying.

There was no doubt.

And she was wasting her time even talking to him. He could have his blasted floor.

She turned to move to the door.

"Come and see it then, Vee."

Her boot heels clicking hard on the floorboards, she took three steps to the doorway. At the threshold, her feet slowed against her own better instincts. Instincts she should never trust. Instincts that had been harsh in their failure before.

She stopped, sighing. "You think to show me the mine?"

"If it will make you believe me, then yes. I can show you the vein."

She stared at a top black hinge on the door, debating.

She needed to walk away. Walk away this instant from Theodore. Walk away before he drew her into his madcap existence—just as he had the previous night.

But a mine was a mine, and she had nothing else to secure a loan. She would just need to convince her creditor, Mr. Olston, the mine was worth something, about to produce—and hope he knew nothing of the sad affairs of the Alton holdings.

"Just sign a portion of the mine over to me." Her eyes closed as she said the words against her better judgement. "That will suffice. I will sign it back to you once the loan from my creditor is satisfied. I assume that will be immediately after the gala."

"No."

Her eyes flew open as she whipped around to look at him. "No?"

"No—not until you see it."

"Why? I have no need to see the mine, Theodore."

"Because you don't believe me, Vee. You don't believe there is another vein. And I don't take charity. Not while I have a modicum of honor left in me."

She stared at him sitting on the floor, her tongue pressing on the roof of her mouth. The last thing she had time for at the moment was a weeklong tromp to Derbyshire to poke around an old abandoned mine.

His jaw shifted forward, setting hard. "I won't sign it over unless you see it for yourself, Vee. Unless I prove it to you. Come to Glenhaven."

She held in a groan. Aggravating to no end. Her fingers went to her temples, rubbing tiny circles. What was she going to do without the mine as collateral? She could find a way to raise the funds—she always had. She didn't need the mine.

Just as she was about to say no, Theo's eyes shifted. Shifted from challenge to desperation. The same desperation she saw in his look the night before. The hopelessness he was mired in.

He needed this.

Needed someone to believe in him, if only for a moment.

And he was staring directly at her.

He picked the wrong person.

Wrong on every measure.

Violet exhaled as the reality she was trying hard to deny set in. She was the wrong person—by far—but she was also the only person standing there.

"Fine. I will go." The words rushed out before she could reconsider.

He nodded and then proceeded to stretch back out on the floor, the back of his head clunking to rest on the wooden boards. His eyes closed as his hands settled into a clasp over his belly. "Let me sleep for another hour and then we will leave for Glenhaven."

Violet swallowed a growl as she stared at him splayed out on the floor. His eyes closed, the whole of the matter settled and calm in his mind. His mouth had even relaxed, almost to a smile. If not a smile, a smirk. Definitely a smirk.

The longer she stared, the more annoyed she became. Theo had manipulated her again, the bastard. And she had fallen for it.

Her gut started to burn. It was time someone called him on his lies—forced him to admit his life had become a dung heap. As much as Adalia had tried to right her brother and his way through life since he had returned, her friend hadn't been successful at it. And Violet knew just how desperate Adalia was to have Theodore turn his life around.

Maybe she could help with that. Call him on his bluff about the mine. Force him to admit the mine was worthless and he could not lie to *everyone* he met.

And in the process—even though the mine was worthless—at least she would have a guarantee for the loan.

But if she was wrong about the worthlessness of the mine and there really was a new vein…

Well, she wasn't wrong.

Theodore was bluffing.

She was sure of it.

{ CHAPTER 3 }

Wagons. Carriages. Horses. The fast flurry on the cobblestone street in front of the coaching inn sent the air rushing about Theo, frantic.

His muscles clenched as he resisted the urge to spin in a slow circle with his head bowed, noting every detail of the chaotic street scene around him. Instead, his feet stayed rooted to the ground as he lifted the reins of his horse to the approaching stable boy without looking at the lad.

His gaze was focused on the woman alighting from the carriage in front of him. The woman he had believed to be long lost to the passage of time.

The wool of Violet's plum-hued carriage dress trailed behind her on the carriage step, sticking along the bottom inside corner of the coach's door until she reached behind her and tugged free the folds of fabric.

If he was closer to her, he knew the plum color would bring out the deep shards of purple in her blue eyes—the very color she had been named for. But one had to look close to notice the rogue streaks in her eyes. Color that Theo had noticed the very first day he had met her nine years ago. His sister's new friend. An awkward but pretty young pup.

But that was long before she had grown into a young woman. Before she fully understood the worth of a third son. Before the war. Before his life had been reduced to a ghostly existence, nothing more.

Theo shook his head.

Thoughts of loss and rage and pain would not serve him well at the moment.

He was grateful for the day on his horse—it forced him to be without a full decanter of brandy within reach—and he had managed to mostly sober in the hours since leaving London. He needed to be clear-headed if he was to deal with the formidable force that was one of his sister's best friends.

When they were young, Violet had no margin in her life for behavior that skirted outside the bounds of propriety. A challenge he had always enjoyed toying with. He imagined not much had changed with her. Except for, of course, that she had become the proprietress of one of the most successful gaming houses to exist in the thick of London West End society.

That turn of her life had to have put a slight kink in her armor of propriety.

A curious twist of fate indeed.

His left hand suddenly dropped the leather reins in a spasm, his arm swinging limply to his side.

Theo glanced at the stable boy. Not noticing anything out of the ordinary, the boy had already picked up the swinging reins, tugging on the horse as he turned away.

Theo still wasn't used to it. Two and a half years, and the random loss of feeling in his left arm—the sudden absence of all control in his fingers—still caught him off-guard, still made him feel like a stranger in his own body. It happened sporadically without warning, a remnant from when his left shoulder was out of socket for months.

Staring down at the muddy stones of the street, he lifted his left shoulder, shaking his arm the best he could, willing his fingers into obedience. Ten seconds, and his forefinger twitched.

Longer than usual.

He looked up from the cobblestones by his feet to see Violet turned fully toward him, staring at him. She straightened the small bonnet perched on the upsweep of her chestnut hair, and then took two steps forward, pausing at the rear corner of the carriage. Her blue eyes were slightly squinted, her look flickering back and forth from his face to his left arm.

What he thought he had hidden well, Violet had just noticed.

Because that was his luck.

Hell. He needed a steep tumbler of cognac. The last thing he needed was Violet's sympathy. From her, of all people, he did not think he could take the pity.

Traveling as her companion, Violet's maid exited the carriage behind her and Violet looked over her shoulder to the woman. She spoke words Theo couldn't hear over the noise of the frenzied street, and her maid nodded, moving toward the main door of the coaching inn with Violet's driver.

Waiting until they disappeared into the quaint tan and grey fieldstone building, she turned back to Theo and quickly moved toward him and then stopped, standing before him.

Her dark blue eyes searched his face. "I can see you have sobered since this morning. Truth told, I expected you to fall off your horse at some point during the journey today."

"No pleasantries?"

The right side of her mouth pulled back. "How was your ride?"

"I managed to stay upright. That was as accomplished as it was."

She nodded, her fingers going to the right side of her dark plum bonnet to tug it forward against the low rays of the evening sun. "Clarissa and Mr. Druper are securing rooms for us. Have you stayed at this establishment before in Northampton? Do you have preferred chambers?"

"I usually ride straight through to Glenhaven."

"Without sleeping?"

"Sleep is fleeting, if it is at all for me, so I may as well be riding."

She nodded, her full cherry lips slipping into a slight frown. "I do not mean to slow you. You may feel free to travel on ahead of us. As long as the muck on the roads holds solid, we should be at Glenhaven in two days."

Theo considered the option for a long moment. "No, I will travel with you. I imagine it is the appropriate thing to do in this situation."

"Because dragging me to Derbyshire to see a mine is *appropriate*?" A smile and a sound near to a chuckle escaped her. "I doubt we are bound by any rules of propriety at the moment, Theo. Or is it that you think I am about to turn back to London once I am out of your sight?"

"Would you?"

"I have not changed so much, Theo, from when we were young." She shook her head. "I have committed to coming to see the mine. And I have never been one to fail a commitment."

"No, if I recall correctly, that is exactly who you are."

She nodded, satisfied he respected her word on the matter.

"You are not going to ask me about my arm?" Theo lifted his left hand, mostly to prove it was in working order. "I saw you notice it when you stepped onto the street."

Her look stayed on his face, not dipping to peek at his arm. "Do I need to ask? Whatever it was that ailed you, it seemed to resolve itself." Her arms folded in front of her, her reticule swinging. "Or are you searching for sympathy? If so, you will not receive it from my quarter. I offered for you to ride in my carriage—even with the stench of your latest rout in London haunting your clothes. I do believe Clarissa would have strangled me in my sleep if you had actually taken me up on the offer."

"No, I prefer to ride." A grin that he wasn't prepared for carved into his face. "The air keeps the stench away from my own nose as well."

Violet laughed, and the sound was light, floating into the wind like dozens of tiny bells.

The weight of the air around him lifted slightly at the sound, and Theo looked up past Violet's head to the busy thoroughfare. For the first time in a long time, the urge to want to actually see the world around him struck him.

A mistake, for the very first thing he saw was a blond woman in a dark green cloak moving past the front of Violet's carriage.

No. Impossible.

Not here. Not in the middle of England. Not this many years later.

"I did assume you would have changed clothing before we left London, or is it that—"

Theo pushed past Violet, her words holding no meaning in his ears as he ran past her and the carriage.

He jumped, bobbing above heads and horses, searching for the blond head in the busy street.

The light blond hair flashed in the late day sunlight. A glimpse of green and he sprinted for it, haphazardly shoving his way through the crowd.

But it stayed a block ahead of him. Blond hair. Green wool. Block after block. Glimpse after glimpse. Always ahead of him.

Six blocks he ran, pushing past people and carts, dodging horses and carriages. Six blocks, and he stopped at a crossroad where the masses of bodies and horses had waned to a trickle.

Only a mostly empty street before him.

Gone. The woman was gone. Gone into nothing.

Just as the ghost he knew she was.

But what if she wasn't a ghost?

Reality slipped sideways, and he knew it. But he had also just seen her. He was sure of it. He just missed her. If he searched a little bit harder, he would find the green cloak. Find the blond head.

Back. He had to go back. He must have missed her slipping down a side street.

He spun around and stumbled, tripping over the person directly behind him.

Violet fell to the side, flailing as he rammed into her.

His reflexes lightning quick, he caught her around the waist before she fell into the thick mound of mud on the edge of the street.

Theo righted her, startled at how light she was to pick up. Maybe it was that Violet always filled the air around her so fully that he thought of her as far taller and larger. But she wasn't. The top of her head only reached the middle of his chest and her body was slender.

Turning, he set her feet onto the solid ground of the pavement, holding onto her slight frame until she had her balance. Her fingers gripped his forearms and she stared up at him, her blue eyes wide, her cheeks pulsating pink with every breath she panted.

He glanced above her head, searching the street behind her. No green cloak, no blond head in sight.

Not willing to remove his hands from her body just yet, he looked down to Violet. "You are not going to faint on me?"

"Faint, why?"

"You are clearly not accustomed to running."

"Running blocks at top speed—no, you're right." Every other word she said was punctuated with a quick pant. "I am not accustomed to that at all."

Her head dipped down as she swallowed hard, working to catch her breath.

"Why did you follow me?"

She looked up at him. "Why did you run?"

"I…I…" His words trailed as his look darted about the street.

"Exactly. I blink and you are tearing away from me into the crowd, running like a demon was after you. A madman. Why would I not follow you?"

His gaze dropped to her. "I didn't expect you to chase after me."

"Well, what was I to do?"

"Not chase after me."

"That hardly seemed like the best course in the moment. What if you needed help?" Her fingertips dug into the muscles of his forearms. "You look like you saw a ghost, Theo. Why?"

I did see a ghost.

Not that he was about to tell Violet that. He had to stop seeing them. People he had sent to their deaths.

His hands dropped from her waist and he took a step backward. "I thought I saw an acquaintance that I needed to speak with about a business matter."

Her eyes narrowed as her lips pulled back, her head shaking. "And I am the Queen of the Nile. No one runs like that for a *business matter*, Theo. You do me a grievous insult by stooping to lie about whatever this matter is that sent you scattering into the streets."

He shook his head. "It was of no consequence, Violet."

"It was something, Theo."

"It was nothing." His voice snapped, his yell pitching above the street sounds. "Leave it be, Violet."

She spun from him and started walking away, her kidskin-gloved hand waving in the air. "I knew this was a mistake."

Her footsteps were quick back toward the coaching inn.

It took Theo several seconds to realize she had dismissed him.

It took several more to remember that he liked that about her. She had never stood for lies. And she had certainly never stood for him attempting to evade his way around honesty.

What he didn't like was her walking away from him. Didn't like the erect set of her posture, stiff to the point of breaking. Aside from his sister and brother-in-law, Violet was the first person that he'd had a near to normal conversation with since the war.

In that moment, alone on the street, his stomach still churning from seeing a ghost, the smallest flicker of yearning sparked to life in his chest. He hadn't wanted anything in the past two and a half years. Not food, or wine, or women, or politics, or friends, or purpose. He had been going through the motions of life—barely—and at that, only for love of his sister and twin nieces.

But Violet. He wanted her. Or at least he wanted her not walking away from him in disgust.

His feet started to move before he made the conscious decision to do so. Five long strides and he caught up to Violet, falling in step beside her.

Ignoring his presence, her shoulders pulled back even tighter.

"I saw a ghost that I needed to chase, Violet." His voice was soft, the words harder to admit to himself than to her.

Her gait didn't slow, but she did look up at him. Her blue eyes skewered him so thoroughly he almost stumbled.

She looked away, her gaze going to the pavement before them. "Thank you."

"For what?"

"The truth."

He waited for more from her as they walked, the questions he had instantly braced himself for. *What ghost? Who did you see? Why?*

They didn't come.

His forehead wrinkled as he watched her profile. "You are not going to ask?"

"About the ghost?" She looked up at him. "I have no right to intrude on your demons, Theo. The truth, not a lie, was all I wanted."

He nodded. "You are going back to London?"

"That is a conclusion you have jumped to." She stopped, turning to him. "What I will tell you is that I sat all day in the carriage dwelling upon my actions—what I was doing here, why I was traveling to Glenhaven with you when I have a thousand other things that need my attention at the moment."

"Did you find answers in your ponderings?"

"Yes. And it goes back to when I was sixteen years old and you were at my doorstep." Her right hand came up, her palm flattening against the smooth expanse of the plum fabric over her stomach. "The truth is, I was never able to say no to you, Theo. Not then, and to my dismay, not now."

Theo grinned. "Had I known that then—"

"No, do not make light of it. Those days when you pursued me." She took a deep breath, her chest lifting with the effort. "You were so charming. Exciting. Dangerous. And I adored all of those things about you. You had this unending well of wild ideas and an enthusiasm for everything around you, and I could never bring myself to say no to you, no matter how bizarre your antics were or how close they came to getting me into grievous trouble with Uncle Demetrick. I could never refuse you, and you knew it."

Memories that he had long since forgotten flooded back to him. Violet swimming in the brook in just her white chemise, giggling as she splashed water at him to make him avert his eyes. Her blue eyes sparkling in mischievousness in the light of the torches after he pulled her into the gardens at Glenhaven late in the eve. Her laughter when they raced mares down the long grassy knoll at the south end of Glenhaven. She had embodied all of the finest things in those days—youth, innocence, happiness.

He swallowed hard, the sudden memories choking his throat. After her parents had died, she had spent far too many hours at Glenhaven visiting Adalia in those days. Visiting him.

Her hand slipped off her stomach, settling at her side. "I was so young and you made me want more out of my life than what I thought I could reach for. More than what Uncle Demetrick would allow. I thought…" She shook her head, washing away whatever she was about to say. "But then you just left, Theo. Without a word. Without an explanation."

Theo stiffened, his jawline setting hard. "You moved onward with haste, if I recall. Directly to Lord Vandestile. He was a fine match for a woman with your inheritance. He had the right bloodlines. The proper birth order."

Her head slanted to the side, her dark blue eyes piercing him. Just as her lips opened to speak, a burly man pushing a wheelbarrow full of oats angled himself between her and the building behind her, brushing the back of her skirts. She jumped forward out of his way, her mouth clamping closed on whatever she was about to say. With a quick glance to Theo, she shook her head and turned, walking toward the coaching inn.

This time Theo was immediately step-in-step alongside her.

"You did not answer the question, Violet." He motioned for her to step before him to pass by a cart piled with various hot pies. Next to her once more, he looked at her. "Will you be returning to London?"

She looked to him for a moment, and then her focus shifted forward to concentrate on the coaching inn a block away. "I did not want to get pulled into your world again, Theo, because I still cannot say no to you. And that fault of mine will only bring me woe. I did not want to get pulled into your world last night when you appeared at the Revelry's Tempest asking for that credit, and I do not want it now. But I came for Adalia. I owe her everything, and I thought, in some odd way, this would help her. Help her with her worry over her sole surviving brother."

"That does not answer the question."

"I will stay true to my word. I will come to Glenhaven to see the mine." She looked up at him. "But I cannot be near you if you insist on lying to me. If you insist on manipulating me. For I will not allow that any longer. Last night, you manipulated me into allowing that marker. This morning, you manipulated me into coming to Glenhaven."

"I would not go so far as to say manipulated—"

"You manipulated me, Theo. You blatantly used your past, your scars against me. To play upon my sympathies. And I was the fool to buckle to it. So I will go to Glenhaven, see the new vein, and you will sign over a portion of the mine to me. Then we are to be done with one another."

He shrugged. "If it is the only way."

"It is. But heed my warning, if you think to lie to me, manipulate me again, I will leave immediately and find another way to raise the needed funds for the gala."

"Your plan is sensible—except what if I ask you to stay longer?" A slight grin lifted his mouth. "It is by your own admission that you are unable to say no to me."

Her jaw shifted to the side, an exasperated sigh groaning out of her mouth. She looked up at him. "I will find a way. Somehow, I will find a way."

It was then he noticed it. The glint of steel in her eyes. The mettle so hardened within her, he had no doubt she would leave him behind without another thought.

He had suffered atrocities in the war. But what he saw in that moment in Violet was caused by a scar just as real, just as jagged as the visible one along his face.

He had been so consumed in the last eighteen hours about his own purgatory, he had not considered the possibility that Violet had her own demons to contend with.

What in the bloody depths of hell had happened to her?

{ CHAPTER 4 }

Her boots slipping every third step on the slick grass, Violet walked up the hillside toward the Alton family cemetery. The cold spring rain that had greeted them upon arriving at Glenhaven House had cleared overnight, and Violet had slept in far longer than she had intended.

She had forgotten how well she had always slept at Glenhaven when she was visiting Adalia. Her chambers were tasteful, but beyond that, the entire Palladian designed home with its sleek, symmetrical lines and imposing pediments was a warm cocoon against the wet cool of the midlands.

Whether it was because the place had held Adalia's family and the joy that had surrounded them when they were young, or whether the architects of the original building had managed to design the building without drafts, she had always felt coddled there.

For two years after her parents had died, she had suffered a gaping hole in her life that had just grown larger and larger—and then she had met Adalia. Adalia and her three brothers had welcomed her into their home, and that gaping hole was filled—or at least covered—for a time.

Violet paused halfway up the hill. She could see Theo fully at this angle, not just his head as she could from the stables when she had gone looking for him. He stood as a stone, his head bent, staring at a grey marble gravestone standing up from the ground. Strands of his sandy blond hair fell forward, curling along his forehead. Her eyes traced the line of the scar along his cheek, dropping to the juncture of his ear and jawline. His chin was set hard—even with the distance between them she could see the unwavering steel line of it.

After a moment of debate if she should disturb him, she started up the remaining hillside. She needed to get on with the day, see whatever it was Theo was insisting upon showing her, and prepare for her return to London tomorrow. She could interrupt him for a mere moment, just to let him know of her intentions, and then she would leave him to his reverie.

As she crested the top edge of the hill, her eyes wandered over the gravestones and pointed obelisks. Twelve generations of the Altons were laid to rest here, since the era of the knights when the title and lands had been bestowed upon the first Earl of Alton.

Theo's arm twitched, and she knew he recognized her presence, but he did not look up at her approaching footsteps. Five more steps to him, and she aligned herself next to him, turning to the gravestone before them.

The gasp escaped her lips before she could choke it back.

Theodore's gravestone.

Beloved brother, uncle, friend.

Tears instantly swelled in her eyes.

He wasn't staring at the stones of parents, or the stones of his brothers. Not Caldwell's. Not Alfred's.

His own.

His own gravesite.

Her look whipped up to Theo's profile. His jaw flexed, nothing more.

"It is still here," she whispered.

His ice blue eyes did not lift to her as he nodded, remaining fixed on the stone. He'd had more than two years to have the stone removed, yet there it sat.

Ready. Waiting for him.

What in the bloody depths of hell had happened to him?

Violet inhaled, the air loosening the clamp in her chest. "Why do you leave it?" Her soft words settled into the air, wispy.

Silent, his head shook slightly, the lump in his throat bobbing as he swallowed again and again.

A sudden primal—foreign—urge to wrap her arms around him, bury him to her chest and take away all of the pain she could feel vibrating from him surged in her gut. From where or why the urge manifested, she didn't care to reason upon.

But she held back, accepting that she could only allow herself to lift her hand, the tips of her fingers lightly brushing the scar along his eye. "Is this not reminder enough?"

His head jerked away. Not far, but enough to distance his face from her fingers. "That is nothing compared to what others suffered." His eyes closed. "I leave it because it is where I should be. That I lived…it was not as it should have been."

Her look drifted to the stone. "Lots of things should have been, Theo. But they are not. Is a 'should have' a reason to keep it?"

He shrugged, his eyes opening to focus on his name etched deep into the grey marble. "They will need it eventually. Why go through the trouble of removing it?"

Violet's head snapped backward, looking to him as she blinked hard. *They will need it eventually?*

She stepped in front of him, putting herself between him and the cold stone, forcing him to look at her. "You are alive, Theo. That seems a logical reason enough for the trouble of removing it."

His forehead tilting downward, his light blue eyes centered on her under raised eyebrows. He glared at her, a simmering explosion aching to happen.

Ten beats of her pounding heart passed, and without a word, Theo spun away from her, walking down the hillside.

She was not prepared for this—to learn Theo had one foot firmly in the grave just below her feet. She had thought him angry. Pouty. Flippant. A drunk. An irredeemable rake with no regard to those around him.

But not this.

In the next breath, she hurried down the hillside, sliding along the wet grass with every step. Sliding so much, she flew out of control just as she passed Theo. Her toe snagged on a fat stone and she slipped, falling onto her side. She managed to catch herself before the bodice of her riding habit hit the ground, her left kidskin glove sinking into the mush of the dirt.

Before her body stilled from the fall, a hand wrapped under her elbow, dragging her upright.

Once she had regained her feet, Theo released her. There was the faintest hint of a smile on his lips. The darkness tempered, if not dissolved.

"Do not make light." She slapped her hands together, trying to smack away the mud that had coated her glove. "I never grew into the grace my mother had always hoped for me and I am still as horrifyingly clumsy as I always have been. It is why I belong locked away in a drawing room."

His light blue eyes met hers, his stare piercing. "You have always belonged everywhere but in a drawing room, Vee." The words came out of him, unexpected and so heated Violet forgot to breathe for long seconds.

He bent, breaking eye contact as he made a paltry swipe at the mud on her dark blue skirt, seemingly unsure if he should help her shake off the dirt. "Why did you come out here, Violet?"

Her clean right hand went down, joining his hands to swipe away at the dirt on her skirt. "I needed to find you as I had hoped we could dispense with the business of visiting the mine today."

"In a hurry to see it and be on your way?" His hand paused above the bottom of her hem.

She was. But that was something that didn't need to be said.

Standing straight, he nodded. "We will ride out to the mine now. It is a half hour to the east. Is your maid ready to accompany you?"

"Clarissa has been sick from the carriage ride—the motion of it, she believes." Violet wrinkled her nose. "I assumed you could hear her retching. The smell in the carriage had me near to joining you on a horse yesterday and riding the rest of the way. If not for the rain, I would have done so."

"Then I am glad I could sit a horse properly and avoid that. Shall I gather a maid? I do have one left in the house. I imagine she should have skill enough to ride. Or possibly

Cook. She is the only other female at Glenhaven at the moment."

"It is fine to go without a companion." Violet flipped her fingers in the air. "I already feel guilty for the extra burden we are on the household."

His right eyebrow cocked. "You are positive? I remember how protective you are of your reputation."

She chuckled. "Then you also must remember how you convinced me time and again to dip my toes outside the bounds of propriety." She smacked her hands together one last time and then gave up on removing the last of the dirt. "Truly, Theo, it is just a ride to the mine. We are in the country, and your staff does not seem to have the time to stoop to gossip of the household. As a widow now I find people care very little about my whereabouts and pursuits. I was not even particularly concerned about travelling here to Glenhaven with you. Becoming proprietress of the Revelry's Tempest has inadvertently freed me from so many of the shackles of society." Her eyebrow cocked as she looked at him. "Unless, of course, you have designs to not be on your finest behavior with me."

"I swear to epitomize the utmost in gentlemanly behavior." He inclined his head toward the stables. "Shall we?"

"Yes." Violet started walking, digging the heels of her boots into the soft ground so she didn't repeat her earlier slide.

They were halfway to the stables when a lone figure on a horse came thundering across the sheep field toward them, one hand high, waving at them.

Theo lifted his hand to his brow, staring at the approaching figure. "Who is that?"

She squinted. "Is that—Mr. Nullter?"

Theo looked at her. "Mr. Nullter? Is he still the Vandestile solicitor?"

Her eyes flickered off the maniacally waving man to look at Theo. "You don't know?"

"I have not bothered to keep up on the happenings in the county."

"Yes, he is—the last one left. He also took the position of steward at the Vandestile estate as well. I usually only deal with him through correspondence." She looked back to the elderly man quickly approaching, riding far faster than one his age should. His horse leapt the low stone fence. "He is one of the few that stayed on after my husband's death. Valiantly so, I might add."

"Valiantly?" The word spit from Theo's mouth, half a question, half a sarcastic statement.

Just as she was about to inquire at the derision in Theo's voice, Mr. Nullter reached them.

"My lady, it is true, you are here. My lord." Mr. Nullter yanked his horse to a stop, nodding to Theo as he quickly jumped from the saddle. "It is more than I could have hoped for."

As agitated as he was, Violet had to keep her hands from reaching out and steadying the older man as he bounced with excitement. "Mr. Nullter, however did you learn I was here at Glenhaven?"

"The coaching inn at Northampton—Mrs. Bentworth was travelling from visiting her cousin in London, and she saw you leaving the coaching inn just as she arrived.

She inquired as to your destination with the owner." Mr. Nullter's thin, weathered hands twisted the leather reins, his frenzy sending his words to speeding. "You are a sight for my old eyes, my lady. It has been far too long since you have been at the estate. I came directly when I heard you were here—I left before dawn, before Cook had breakfast ready—and with all that needs to be prepared, but that you are here is a sign that cannot be ignored, my lady."

"Wait, Mr. Nullter, slow down," Violet said. "What needs to be prepared? What has sent a wild rabbit under your hat?"

Confusion deepened the thick wrinkles on his face. "My lady, did you not receive my letter?"

She shook her head. "Letter?"

"The new viscount. He has finally made his way to England. There is a ball celebrating his arrival in two days, and you must attend, my lady."

Her hand flew to her chest. "The new viscount has finally come? But it has been a year since they found him in America, and he appears now? Why? I thought he had no interest in the title."

"I do not know the reasoning, my lady. He is an American, and they are a different sort, as I understand it. Regardless, he has finally accepted his birthright and is travelling to Vandestile Manor as we speak."

A swath of relief swept through Violet. Relief she had longed for, ever since her husband had died nearly three long years past. "That is excellent news, Mr. Nullter. You will not need to suffer my inept interference in the estate any longer."

"Inept? No, no, my lady. We both know that is a humility you should not own for what you have suffered—and for what you have managed since his lordship's death." Mr. Nullter's free arm swung a wide arc in the air. "But no, we will not dwell in the past. Everyone you know will be at the ball, my lady—they have already started to arrive. That you are here in the area—well, you must come. It is a wonder it happened so. It is your duty as Lady Vandestile to meet the man. To welcome him as the new viscount."

Violet swallowed a groan. Her life had been haunted for too long by her "duty" to the Vandestile title. She set her sweetest smile onto her lips. "While I would thoroughly enjoy the honor of meeting this American, Mr. Nullter, I am afraid I am due to leave back to London tomorrow. You will give the new viscount my best wishes?"

Mr. Nullter's wiry white eyebrows crinkled. "You came to Derbyshire without intention to stop at Vandestile Manor?" He shook his head. "But you must meet the man, my lady. It is only proper."

"I had not planned to come to Glenhaven as it was." She glanced at Theo. "This was an unexpected trip I needed to make—for my friend, Adalia, the duchess. I needed to come to arrange a business matter with Lord Alton on her behalf."

"Yes, of course, I recall the duchess is a fine friend." He nodded, looking between Violet and Theo. "But it will not do—your presence in the area and then obvious avoidance of the ball. It is rudeness beyond imagining."

"Truly, Mr. Nullter—"

"I do believe you can afford an extra two days, Lady Vandestile." Theo interrupted her, his ice blue eyes twinkling.

"No, I do need to get back to London." She strained to keep her feigned smile in place. "There is still so much organization needed for the gala, not to mention the weekly events until then. And the necessity of this matter here at Glenhaven has already taken so much time."

"Yet you said yourself Lady Desmond was perfectly capable of handling the Revelry's Tempest while you were away." Theo nodded, having already made the decision for her. "I do not see what harm an extra two days will make. I will even accompany you on horseback to London to make the return journey faster than travelling in your coach."

Her smile pulled tight, morphing into a near grimace as she skewered Theo with a look. "That is not necessary, Lord Alton. I will be leaving in the morning."

"My lady, if I may say so, I have always held tremendous respect for you," Mr. Nullter said, the reins twisting in his hands. "For both what you brought to the Vandestile estate with your inheritance, and all that you have done for it in the ensuing years since your husband died. The only reason the estate has survived intact was because of you."

Mr. Nullter took a step toward her. "Your attendance would put a much-needed sheen of respectability upon the ball after the…unpleasantness of the past several years. There will be certain expectations put upon the new viscount, and as an American, I do not believe he is prepared for what is required of him. He is not of English soil, does not understand the responsibilities upon the title, nor does he know how many people depend upon the estate for their livelihood. I only wish to begin in the proper place with him, and your assistance would be greatly appreciated in that matter."

"A sound argument, Mr. Nullter," Theo said, his gaze directed at the man.

But Violet saw the side-smirk on Theo's face. A smirk intended for her.

Blasted idiot.

She looked at Mr. Nullter, the serene smile finding its place back on her lips. "You do have a valid point, Mr. Nullter. But I think even more important in welcoming the man to his new position would be for the nearest earl to attend the event as well. Another man with a title available to the new viscount for the many questions he must have. And also to, as you said, put the proper sheen upon the event." Her sweet smile stretched into glee as she glanced at Theo. "It appears that important responsibility should fall upon Lord Alton, as he is so conveniently close. Don't you agree, Mr. Nullter?"

Mr. Nullter nodded emphatically, as she guessed he would. "I do, my lady." His look went to Theo. "Your invitation was delivered a week ago, but as you were not in residence, we did not believe you would be available."

"Oh, but he is available, I am most assured." Violet's smile widened, her gaze going to Theo.

Her words were rewarded with a scowl.

"In fact, I believe the only way I will be able to attend the ball is if Lord Alton is able to join the event as well."

Mr. Nullter looked between the two of them, confused. "Well, that does not seem necessary, my la—"

"Oh, it is very necessary, Mr. Nullter." She cut Mr. Nullter off, her look burning into Theo. "I can only attend if Lord Alton does. It is especially important to the business I need to conclude while I am here."

Theo's scowl darkened for one long second, and then he snapped out of it, an easy smile overtaking his lips as he looked to Mr. Nullter. "I will attend, Mr. Nullter."

"Thank you, my lord. As you yourself came into your title unexpectedly, I do believe the American will appreciate your reflections upon the matter."

Violet's look whipped to Mr. Nullter. She had never known the man to be anything but respectful, but his comment bordered on rude. One did not point out the fact that a title was inherited only because of unfortunate family tragedies.

Theo's smile didn't falter. "You have what you came here for, Mr. Nullter, so you will now be off to Vandestile Manor. With haste."

Mr. Nullter bowed his head slightly. "Yes, of course, my lord. If I could just stop by your kitchens and—"

"We will see you in two nights, Mr. Nullter. That will be all."

His weathered face crinkling, Mr. Nullter nodded, quickly turning and lifting himself onto the saddle of the horse. He looked to Violet. "Shall I have a room prepared for you at Vandestile Manor, my lady?"

"That is not necessary, Mr. Nullter. I am here with my maid, and as Lord Alton is an old family friend, he has opened his home to us while we conduct our business." She said the words with simple authority, leaving no margin for Mr. Nullter to question the propriety of her presence at Glenhaven House. "I do imagine there is already an overabundance of guests at the manor, so we will not add our presence to the mayhem."

"It is indeed full, my lady. Very good, we shall welcome you back to the manor in two nights, then." With efficiency, he nudged his horse onto his earlier path across the field. He did not veer toward the main house.

"That was rude." Forearms clasped over her ribcage, Violet watched the retreating figure.

"It was."

"I meant you, Theo. The poor man hasn't eaten since yesterday, and you effectively kicked him off your land with not a bread crumb."

"So what if I did?"

Her look swung to him. "So you were raised better than that. Your sister would have your head on a platter right now."

His blue eyes met hers, the cool depths turning frigid. "There are things you don't know about that man, Vee."

"And there are a thousand things I don't know about you, Theo. But what I do know is that Mr. Nullter was always very kind to me."

"Yes, well, a large fortune always accompanied you."

"What do you mean?"

He stopped, looking her up and down, and sighed. "Nothing, Vee."

He swiftly stepped past her, walking toward the stables. "Let us go to the mine."

{ CHAPTER 5 }

Violet stared up at the grey sky, now a tiny square of light at the top of the dark shaft of dirt and stone. Her look shifted to the rough ladder she had descended. Twenty-seven rungs. This secondary, exploratory shaft on the far edge of the old tunnels was not terribly deep. But it was still below the earth—well below the surface.

The cool dampness was the first thing she noticed as she moved below ground. A slick layer sticking to her skin, coating her neck. The scent was the second. Dirt, darkness seeping into her lungs, and a slightly sour smell.

What had she been thinking, coming down into a mine? That there would be a gently curved marble staircase to descend down? A hand rail? Lilacs in the air? A nice roaring fire at the bottom?

Her eyes dropped to the rough beaten wood of the rung at eye level. This secondary shaft didn't even have an intact pulley system in place, much less a wheelhouse.

Just a ladder.

Deep breath. Deep breath. Deep breath.

"I did not think you would actually want to come down into the mine, Violet." Theo had leaned down behind her, the breath of his words tickling the bare skin of her neck.

She spun to him, poking her finger into his chest. "Then why in the devil did you make me come down here?"

"To annoy you." The devilish grin was full on his face.

"You have nothing better to do?"

"No. And I was curious to see how far you would come before crying off." Theo's low voice echoed around the rock and into the long tunnel behind him.

"Theo, if this whole expedition is a farce, I will have you tied to a spit and—"

"No, Vee, no." His hands flew up, palms facing her. "This is real. I swear it."

She looked past his shoulder, eyeing how quickly the dark tunnel descended into deep blackness. Squelching the urge to turn around and climb out of the hole, she motioned toward the dark abyss. "Then let us do this, and do this quickly. I am here, so show me the vein. Make me believe you."

He gave her one nod, the glint in his eye unreadable. Lifting the Davy lamp, he moved into the darkness, the lantern offering flickering streaks of brightness against the surrounding rock of the tight tunnel.

Theo had to bend over as he moved or risk bumping his head into the rock ceiling every third step. Violet mimicked his posture, even though the top of her head was in no danger of brushing the stone, or even the low wooden beams every six feet. As they moved deeper into the shaft, three splotches of mud landed on her head, dripping through the strands of her hair until the wetness sank onto her scalp. She instantly regretted leaving her bonnet above ground with the horse.

"I am impressed, Vee," Theo said, not stopping his movement into the tunnel.

"Impressed with what?"

"You never would have done this five years ago—never would have even considered the thought."

She stared at the wide expanse of his dark jacket. "Why not?"

He glanced back over his shoulder, though his feet kept pace. "You were far too proper. A mine was the last place you would have dared go, especially with your skirts dangling above me on a ladder."

"Yes, well, as much as I cling to propriety, propriety has not clung to me. My life, in fact, has conspired greatly against me on the matter in the last years. Being in this mine is the least of what I have sunk to as far as respectability is concerned."

Her hand went out, touching the slick wall of rock as she shifted to the right to make it through a narrow portion. The dampness of the stone sank through the kidskin of her gloves to soak her fingertips. She cleared her throat. "And may I remind you, you promised to keep your eyes averted as I descended. Tell me you did not break your promise in the first minute of this excursion."

"I did not. My eyes were properly affixed on stone. Except for the once or twice I had to glance upward to make sure you made your way down the ladder without issue." The smirk in his voice dangled as bait, but she chose to ignore his teasing for the benefit of getting in and out of this mine as quickly as possible. She could always scold him later—above ground—on the matter.

The tunnel narrowed even more, and Theo's wide shoulders started to brush the sides of stone with every step.

His body blocked the light from the lantern in front of him, and the darkness of the tunnel began to close in around Violet. Her heart started to speed, every manic thump trying to override the logic in her mind that she was safe. "I don't like this, Theo. These walls. There is so little room to breathe."

He lifted the lantern higher, and a few trickles of light fell past his shoulder to her. It helped—marginally. "That feeling is natural the first time down here. Man should not be below ground such as this—yet here we are, nonetheless."

"No. I truly do not like this, Theo." Violet could not hold the tremor from her voice.

He glanced back, nodding, but still he forged forth. "Then talk to me, Violet. It helps."

"About what?"

His shoulders lifted in a shrug that blocked some of her precious light. Light she needed to concentrate on.

"I know," Theo said. "Tell me what Mr. Nullter meant when he mentioned the 'recent unpleasantness.'"

The hairs on the back of her neck spiked. She was instantly wary that the one thing that had consumed so much of her life in the last two and a half years had followed her into—of all places—an underground tunnel. She opened and closed her mouth three times, undecided on what to tell Theo. Finally, she settled on simple. "He was referring to the time after my husband died."

When she didn't say more, his steps paused for a second and he looked back to her. "Adalia mentioned it was a hard time for you."

"What did she say?"

He resumed walking. "That it was a difficult situation you were in and there were debts. Nothing more."

"Yes. Malcolm exhausted my inheritance rather quickly in our marriage and then decided to live on credit. So there were the debts." Violet inhaled a deep breath, the cool dampness sinking heavy into her lungs. "But not just my husband's debts. Debts he had somehow managed to sign to my name."

"Without your consent?"

"Without it."

Theo nodded, his head creating a bobbing shadow. "So you could not just refer the creditors to the estate for payment—or nonpayment."

"Exactly."

"I assume if it was difficult the sums of the debts were staggering."

"They were."

"So that is why you took over the gaming house?"

"Yes." Violet offered the one word with her voice low, threatened, as it always was whenever she dwelled too long on the state in which Malcolm left her.

They veered to the right, branching away from the main shaft into a corridor that was only half the width of the tunnel they had been in. In front of her, Theo had to turn sideways to make it through.

The thumping in her chest grew more frantic.

"You managed to clear all the debt on the estate—not just the ones signed to you—didn't you, Violet? That is why Mr. Nullter is so enamored with you—fawning over you, even."

She blinked hard, eyeing the back of Theo's neck. How had he discerned that in a five-minute conversation? "I did."

"Why? Those were debts you did not owe."

"I had to." She took a steadying breath. Beyond Adalia and Cassandra, no one knew what she had done, much less why. Her friends had fully supported her in the endeavor—even taking over during the times when she had crumpled and not been able to move forward herself. "I had to satisfy the debts signed to my name, but it became more than that. It was about what he did to me—beyond the debts."

She turned sideways, mimicking Theo as she shuffled through a narrow cut-away in the rock. Dirt and debris fell from the wall as she brushed by.

She looked down into the darkness swirling about her feet. Should the walls of a mine tunnel crumble like that when brushed?

"What did your husband do to you, Vee?"

Violet jumped, looking up to Theo. He'd stopped a few steps in front of her and stood staring at her, his eyes slightly squinting, though the shadows on his face afforded her no clue as to why.

How long had she frozen in place?

She gave a quick shake and started forward. "Malcolm destroyed my world—everything around me, what I was accustomed to, who I socialized with, what I cared about. My life was beautiful once, but it was a carefully crafted illusion. And the worst part is that I didn't recognize it as such. Not until long after his death. Not until I understood fully all he had done—the betrayals. What he did…it went deeper than the money." She paused, clucking her tongue.

Theo turned and started moving forward again.

She followed, her words still matter-of-fact. "But when Malcolm was alive, when he was with me, I loved that illusion. I loved my life. I didn't want to see anything else—acknowledge that life wasn't beautiful. The paint is cracked on most masterpieces—but I didn't want to see the cracks…

so I just plain didn't. I glossed over them. That was my mistake. My cowardice to own."

"Ignorance is not cowardice, Violet." Theo's words echoed along the stone, low and measured.

"It is when one clings to the ignorance instead of accepting a reality." Her toe stubbed on a rock and she had to catch herself on the tunnel wall. "Regardless, after he died, after I could think again—think without my thoughts jumbling and tangling into a rat's nest in my mind—I decided I was not about to let my late husband determine whether or not my life was destroyed. That would be my own choice. And with the Revelry's Tempest I discovered I had means. Means to not only pay off the debts that were crushing me, but to also right the wrongs he had wrought on others."

"If you couldn't control him in life, you could control him in death?"

Her lips drew inward and she nodded at the back of Theo's jacket. "Yes. Something akin to that."

The tunnel came to an abrupt stop and Theo halted, turning back to Violet. "Here, this is it." He held the lantern up to his right, illuminating a gaping hole in the stone wall she hadn't even noticed.

She stepped close to the lantern, glancing into the rough hole. It started halfway up the wall, the opening about half as tall as her and only the width of her shoulders wide. Her look darted from Theo's chest to the hole. He would fit through on his hands and knees if he slithered through, but just barely.

"I am not going to crawl in there, Theo."

He chuckled. "And I would never ask you to, Vee." He motioned into the hole with his left hand. "There's no need to, just look. You can see it from here." He moved the lantern into the hole, stretching his arm long through the opening. The metal base of the lantern bumped along the bottom of the hole until it reached the other side of the tunnel and illuminated an open chamber. "It's there, on the far wall. You can see the color variation, the line. The wall of dark orange and the wide swaths of grey, almost black and reflective, running through it. That is the new vein that we found."

Moving her head close to his, Violet peered into the gaping hole in the rock. It took her eyes a moment to adjust to the dim glow of the lantern, and then she saw it. A mass of orange rock cut directly in half with a jagged line of shiny black. "Oh. I see it."

"Oh? That is all you have to say?"

She looked at him, her forehead bumping into his. "It is underwhelming, Theo. It is rock." She pointed into the hole, her eyes searching. "Truly? That is what you brought me down here to see? This is it?"

"That rock is the key to the next generation of the Alton line, Violet." His voice grumbled. "And may I remind you, the key to the collateral you seek."

"Then why is no one extracting it?"

"I don't have the funds, Violet. I told you that."

She stood straight, taking a step back from the hole. "I mean no disrespect, Theo, but this is lost on me. It is rock, rock that I could not discern from the gravel on my garden paths. And you knew that—you knew that I didn't need to come down into the mine to witness it myself. Except you wanted to drag me down here merely for your own amusement. I can see that quite clearly now."

"What did you think it was going to be, Violet? A line of glittering stones?"

"I don't know." The thundering of her heart exploded into a rapid frenzy, and her hand went flat onto her chest, trying to hold it slow. "But you were insistent, like you always have been, and I have admitted to what little capability I have to say no to you."

"You think to put this fully upon me?" He drew his arm with the lantern out of the hole, standing straight, annoyance making his every motion a wild jerk.

Free of the hole, the lamp lit the tunnel once more, reminding Violet of how very close the walls were to her. How the rounded stone above her was hovering, near to collapse with the merest breath.

Not that she truly believed Theo would bring her into a tunnel that was about to collapse.

But it was.

She was sure of it.

It was about to crash down onto her head. She leaned back, her body propped up by the stone wall as her palm went to her forehead and she squeezed her eyes shut.

The light flickered—she could see it through her closed eyelids.

This was the moment. It was falling. Coming down on her.

Thousands of stones to crush her.

"Violet, what are you doing? Drama such as this is Adalia's forte—not yours."

She couldn't answer him, could only shake her head, the back of her upsweep grinding into the wet rock.

The light shifted again.

"Violet. Look at me."

She cracked her eyes open.

"What is happening?"

"I—I don't know." Her look drifted off of his face to the stone at his left. It moved. She blinked hard, her eyes darting to all the dark corners surrounding them. "This tight space. Is the wall moving, Theo? Is it getting closer to me?"

"What? No. Don't be daft, Violet. This tunnel is solid."

She found his face in the shadows. "It is. Don't you see it? It's getting closer, Theo—just look." She pointed to the far wall, her finger thrusting wildly in the air.

Theo looked to his left. When his gaze returned to her, concern had replaced the annoyance in his eyes. "What is happening to you?"

"This tunnel—it, it is so tiny. I don't—I don't like spaces like this, Theo."

"Why did you come down here then, Violet?" His voice dipped, his words slow, almost as if he was afraid to startle her.

"I didn't know I would react like this. I told you on the way through that first tunnel. But you kept moving and I thought I would be fine, but I am not fine. I am not fine, Theo." Her voice pitched into a shrillness that echoed deep into the tunnel. "The walls are moving and they are going to crush me and crush you and I am going to run out of air and—" Her words cut off, her gasping breaths stealing any last shreds of reality she had grasp of.

Theo grabbed her forearm. "Let us move. Let us get to the surface."

Her head dropped forward, her chin bumping onto her chest with every gasp as she searched for her feet. Why wouldn't her feet move? She couldn't feel her legs, much less make them move. Yet she was still standing. She shook her head. "I cannot. I cannot move my feet, Theo. I cannot—cannot move through there again."

His left hand released her arm and slid around her back. "Then forgive me for how I am about to make you move, Vee. But I need to get you above ground." He yanked her into his torso, pressing the front of her body flat against his.

All Violet could see was blackness. The black of his jacket. The sudden glimmer of white from his linen shirt. She had the sensation of moving.

He was moving her. Moving her through the tunnels, around the twists and turns.

Were her feet moving? No. She didn't think so. Her fingers found fabric, muscle to dig her nails into.

He squeezed their melded forms through the tight passages in the rock, both of their bodies scraping the stone walls.

But he was fast. Or maybe she had lost all sense of time and place.

In the next instant, he had stopped and set her gently to her feet. Solid ground under her, she could feel her legs again, feel her toes.

He bent to the side, setting the Davy lamp down on the floor of the tunnel, and then he grabbed her left shoulder, steadying her as he withdrew his left arm from around her body.

His right hand still on her shoulder, he stepped back, allowing space between them as he violently shook his left arm.

Violet swayed and her shoulder blades skimmed against wood. Wood—not stone.

He grabbed her with both hands before she tilted too far and fell. He spun her in place, and she opened her eyes to find they were at the base of the main ladder.

His voice was next to her ear, his breath heavy on the skin of her neck after the exertion of carrying her through the tunnels. "Just the ladder now, Vee. Just a few steps upward. You have to climb. You cannot depend on me to keep you upright."

She could barely hear him, barely make out his words as a brutal wave of terror hit her, sending her body into a violent shake.

"Dammit, Vee, I need you to climb. I am right behind you."

She couldn't. She couldn't move. Her mouth opened with a strangled whisper. "But—"

"No. You have to climb, Vee. Your legs, your arms moving. I cannot chance you falling. I will be behind you—directly behind you—but you must hold onto the rungs—no matter what."

No matter what?

She craned her neck to look back at him, forcing words through the panic crushing her chest. "What—what would happen?"

He growled, his mouth pulling back in an exasperated line. "My arm—it gives out—and if I lose grip, if I fall, you will fall—and I cannot chance that." An angry hiss expelled from his lips. Several heartbeats skipped past before he spoke again, his voice defeated. "So hold onto the blasted rungs, Vee, please. Keep your feet about you."

She nodded, turning back to the ladder. "You will be behind me?"

"Yes."

"You will not fall away from me?"

"I will damn well try not to."

She sucked in a long breath of air and grabbed the rung in front of her. He got her this far. She had to do the rest herself.

"That is it, Vee. Both hands. Now your right foot."

Her right foot a lead anchor, she lifted it, her thigh shaking from the strain. She dropped it, the arch of her boot landing on the bottom rung. She gasped as all feeling left her body.

And then something warm. Theo pressing himself against the length of her back. "I am right here, Vee. Directly behind you. And you can move. I know you can."

Her head dipped downward, and for the life of her, she had never done anything as difficult as forcing her left foot up onto the next step of the ladder.

Her left boot clunked onto the wooden rung.

"Good. Now the next. Don't think, Vee. Just move. Up with your hand."

Violet did as ordered. Step after step up the ladder, she could not move without his demands, the next movement directed into her ear. But the orders worked. Theo's voice prodding her upward. Upward into the air. Into the land she belonged in. The one with birds and trees and lakes and fields and rivers. Upward.

The first breath of fresh air hit her lungs and she almost collapsed at the sheer relief of it.

Two more steps, and she swung herself over the ladder's top rung and onto the ground. Real ground with dirt and grass in it. Her fingers dug into the soil, her arms quivering as feeling flowed back into her muscles.

She looked over at Theo, her face contorting in horror as his left fingers—on the only hand currently attached to the ladder—slipped off the side rail just as he stepped onto the third rung down.

For an achingly slow second, he flailed, his right arm swinging in a circle, grasping at balance. His left foot slipped off the rung

His body froze in midair, completely still for a breath, until the whole of him started to tip backward.

Her body dead weight, Violet couldn't move, couldn't help—only watch in terror as he fell away from her.

A vicious growl, and Theo twisted his body as his right foot fell off the ladder, his right fingers managing to snag the side rail just above the top rung. He grunted as the momentum sent his body slamming hard into the side of the shaft.

But he was hanging. Swinging. Not falling to his death. That was all Violet cared about.

He hung for a long moment, his body a swaying pendulum. Another grunt, and he swung his left leg upward, catching the heel of his boot onto the ground next to the shaft. Straining, he contorted the rest of his body upward, following his foot.

The bulk of his weight heaved onto solid ground, and he loosened his hold on the ladder and rolled away from the opening. He landed on his back inches from Violet's feet. His eyes closed, he gasped for breath, the back of his right forearm slung over his forehead.

Blood rushing back into her legs, she nudged him none-to-kindly with her toe. "Theo, you just scared me half to Hades."

"So sorry to have vexed you, Violet."

She unclenched her fingers from the ground, the fear that had gripped her from being below ground now paling in comparison to watching Theo almost fall to his death. She watched his chest rise and fall with quick breaths, the instant surge of anger at him for that scene morphing into concern. "Theo, what was that? You said your arm gives out—but that—it was well beyond that, it went dead. What is wrong with your arm?"

His right arm above his eyes shifted upward as he cracked his eyelids to her. "Not exactly the shining armor hero that was necessary in that situation?"

"Hero? No, Theo, you got me out of there—I frankly don't care how it came about—you got me out of that coffin." She shifted onto her knees and her fingers went lightly to his left bicep, still limp by his side. "Why did your arm give way?"

He jerked, rolling away from her touch and scrambling to his feet. "It's damaged. Damaged like the whole of me." His voice seethed through gritted teeth.

She stared up at him. "But—"

He spun away from her, storming toward his horse. "Let us get back to the house." He didn't bother to turn back to her with the words.

Mouth agape, she watched as he grabbed his reins, swinging up onto his horse using only his right hand.

He was off, his horse disappearing into the woods before she could shake herself into movement.

She sat there, her body still trembling. Minutes passed before the quaking eased and she was convinced she could depend on her legs to carry her again. Slowly, she found her feet and walked over to her mare.

Theo hadn't even waited to assist her onto her horse.

She tugged the leather reins from the branch they were secured to. With a sigh, she tucked one around the pretty brown mare's neck.

No bother.

At this point, she'd been alone long enough to be perfectly capable of mounting a horse on her own.

She didn't need Theo.

Didn't need him at all.

{ Chapter 6 }

He needed that book.

Where in blazes had he left the damn thing?

Theo shuffled through the bottom two drawers of the heavy walnut desk. His great-grandfather's desk, or so his four-year-old mind remembered. He had only overheard his father telling his eldest brother that fact—weighing upon Caldwell the importance of the desk.

Why had the desk been so important? If Theo had stayed in the room that day, instead of wandering off, maybe he would possess that fact. But those words of his father's had been for Caldwell. The eldest son. The heir.

Not the third son. The spare of the spare.

He slammed the drawer closed, irked it didn't bang as loudly as he had intended.

Leaning back in his chair, his hands gripped the edge of the desk as he surveyed the shelves in the study, looking for a crevice he had set the book into amongst the ledgers.

He had misplaced that leather-bound book more times than a man should and still have any right to expect it to be found.

A knock on the study door thudded into the room.

Before he could bark away the person on the other side of the wood, the knob turned and the door opened.

Thompson, his butler and one of the last four servants he kept on at Glenhaven, didn't appear. Instead, of all people, Violet stuck her head into the room.

She wore a simple blue muslin dress, her chestnut hair smoothed into a loose chignon—far different from the debacle it had become at the mine when he had last seen her.

He braced himself as she stepped into the room, shutting the door behind her with a distinctive click. Not quite a slam, but a click that held a note of a forthcoming deluge. Still, silent air just before a storm.

She stepped to the center of the room, her dark blue eyes pinning him. "Where have you been, Theo? You left me out by the mine alone. Heaven knows what could have happened to me. When I arrived here, you were gone. When I woke this morning you were still gone. For the last day I was left to twiddle my thumbs for goodness—"

"I didn't leave you, Violet."

Her hands planted on the curves of her hips. "What?"

"I didn't leave you. I circled back and followed you from the mine to the estate. I would not abandon you in the woods, Violet."

Her hands flew upward. "But you would abandon me here at the house?"

He looked to the black marble fireplace mantel and shrugged.

She didn't respond to his avoidance, didn't say a word. Only silence echoed in the room, harsh, louder than she could ever yell at him.

He forced his look back to her. "I was irate and I didn't want to explain myself to you. I didn't want to explain what happened."

"So explain yourself now."

Explain what? That he had an appendage that was often useless? That he could barely now function in society? That he was not the man that he once was—not by far? That where once he was strong, now he was weak? That his life had deteriorated, day by day, year by year, since he had removed himself from her world five years ago?

His chin nudged forward, his mouth tight. It was his turn for silence.

"Explain, or I leave, Theo."

"The Vandestile ball is tonight."

"Yes, and I didn't want to attend the affair as it was—you very well know that fact. Mr. Nullter will just have to accept my deepest regrets."

Theo stared at her. Her cheeks were flushed pink above the determined set of her chin.

He had been an arse, disappearing like that. He knew it. But he also knew he didn't want her to leave. This place—Glenhaven—was so much easier to be in with her present. He had recognized that strange fact the first day they arrived. The weight of the estate—of the responsibility—hadn't hit him as harshly when he had stepped through the front doors with her by his side.

Violet spun, walking to the door.

And now she was about to leave.

"It was out of place—my arm."

Her feet stopped, but she didn't turn around.

"My left arm was out of place—removed from the socket—for a long time, months, and it was ripped about often enough in that state to ensure constant pain. That is why it does not work now. Why it randomly loses all control."

"Months?" Her body tensed, her head dropping slightly forward. Even from across the room, he could feel the air around her spike in defense against what he said.

"You do not want to hear this, Vee." He attempted to keep his voice even. "Believe me, you do not want to know. Let us just be done with the conversation."

Her shoulders lifted in an exasperated sigh and she turned around to face him. "You think to determine what is appropriate for my ears?"

"I still retain enough remnants of gentlemanly inclinations to know this is beyond what any lady of society should hear."

"When do you imagine it was, Theo, that I became such a delicate flower that I cannot hear the truth of what happened to you?" Her arms folded across her stomach. "Was I a delicate flower at sixteen, seventeen, eighteen? No. You never would have shied from telling me anything in those days. Do you think I am naïve to the fact that the world is a brutal place?"

"If you are not naïve to the realities of what happened to me, Vee, then your life has taken a tragic turn from all that I had hoped for you."

She stiffened. "It was torture, then?"

He nodded.

"Is that what your scars are from?" She pulled her right hand free from her left arm to point at his eyebrow. "The one on your face? The one on the back of your hand?"

He started. His face he could do nothing for. But he thought he hid the scar along the back of his hand well. He met her blue eyes. "The face, yes. The hand, no."

"How? What happened to you when you disappeared after Alfred's death? Adalia never told me."

Theo flinched. He rarely heard the name of his second brother uttered. The middle brother, the peacemaker, the smart one—Alfred's death at the hoof of a horse had broken Theo, broken Caldwell, broken Adalia in a thousand ways none of them would ever understand.

So he had run. Run from what he couldn't have with Violet. Run from Alfred's death. Run because he wasn't strong enough for any of it.

He was well acquainted with his own cowardice, but he wasn't about to admit it to her.

His look slipped from her face to the bookshelf next to her. "I disappeared to do one of the only things I could. What was expected of me as a third son in a time of war. Service to the crown."

His gaze travelled back to her face. "The scar on my hand happened soon after I landed on the continent, courtesy of the first man I ever killed. The torture happened years later—a gift in-kind from our dear Boney." He gave a slight shake of his head, the side of his mouth curling. "I had come home to finally assume the title and was in London but for a breath when they captured me at the docks. I had knowledge that Boney's men—the Band of Vipers—wanted to pry from my head. Names, locations they were intent on getting me to betray. So they held me prisoner—here, on English soil—for months. Months of torture, beatings. Months of filthy blades carving my skin. Months of red-hot pokers searing into my flesh. Shall I continue?"

The edges of her eyes cringed as though she could see the blades flashing before her eyes. "That was the mess Adalia got tangled into? That was when she and the duke found you?"

"Ada told you what happened to me?"

"No. She said very little about the events. But the random fragments that she did share with me make much more sense now. She did say it was a miracle you were alive. A miracle that you survived."

He sighed, his shoulders lifting. "Yes, if you consider a body riddled with scars, a mind that will offer no peace, and this blasted arm that dies on me without warning, survival. I was left weak, Vee."

"There is strength in survival, Theo," she said softly, her arms tightening around her waist.

He stared at her. How she had said the words, he wasn't sure if they were meant for him or herself.

"Yet I find no glory in the weakness I live within. No matter the cause. Especially when I needed to be strong to get you out of that mine." He exhaled a hiss, his head shaking as his look moved away from her. "I knew this could happen. I knew my arm could give out. I never should have made you go down there."

She took a step toward him. "You are aware I could have refused at any time to go down there, Theo? Yet I did not."

His head tipped back to stare blankly at the ceiling as his fingers ran through his hair, scruffing the back of his head. "I just wanted someone else to see it—to witness the possibility of what is down there."

"No one else has seen it?"

His gaze dropped from the ceiling to her. "Not since my mine foreman died down there. He blasted in to what you saw. On the way out to tell me, he dropped dead at the base of the ladder."

Her hand flew up over her mouth, covering a gasp.

"Yes. And now the workers refuse to go back in—they say it is cursed." His look went to the fireplace. "It does not help that they haven't been paid in months."

"You have not paid them in months?"

"No. I failed them. Failed the estate. I had them working on hope. I was working on hope."

"Well, that is just irresponsible, Theo."

He looked at her, his voice dry. "I am aware, Violet. I have been attempting to figure this out for the family for the last two years—how to scrape this estate back into profitability. That new vein was my last chance. And I have failed. I am not my eldest brother—I have not been able to convince any possible investors that I have even a modicum of Caldwell's intellect—that I have a new vein waiting for exploitation. I have tried, but I am not the man my brother was. So there the mine sits. Empty."

"True, Caldwell was intelligent. But he was also trained since the day he spoke to become the next earl." Violet stepped forward, setting herself onto the edge of the wooden chair at the opposite side of the desk. She teetered, barely balanced, barely committing to sitting.

He would take it. As long as she wasn't walking out the door.

"Why do you not ask the duke for funds?"

Theo gave an emphatic shake of his head and then shrugged. "Ill-placed pride? The man has already done more for me than any brother-in-law has a right to ask. I cannot go back to him for charity. I need to do this on my own, Vee. Can you understand that?"

She nodded. "I do understand—probably too well. I would not have fathomed understanding two years ago, but now—yes. Yes, I do."

She slid back along the seat of the chair, her hands settling into her lap as she stared at him. "This is odd."

"What?"

"Growing up, whenever I was here at Glenhaven—this room was Caldwell's domain. It is odd seeing you behind the desk."

"It is still odd sitting behind it. I usually avoid it."

"Yes, well, you look much the same as he did in those days."

Theo's head cocked slightly to the side. "How did he look?"

"Like the weight of the world was upon him. Like he had three younger siblings to care for—to raise. Like he had inherited a four-hundred-year-old estate that he had vowed to do right by." A stray curl of chestnut hair slipped from her upsweep, and she tucked it behind her ear. "But he wore it well. Probably because when I met him, when I came here with Ada for the first time, he had already been the earl for twelve years. So who is to say that two years after inheriting the title he didn't look like you do now?"

Theo shook his head, his eyes closing as he rubbed the back of his neck. "There was never a time that Caldwell did not wear the title well."

"Tell me again why no one is working on the mine."

His eyes cracked open to her. "I've exhausted all of my possible funds, Violet. I cannot pay the workers. And they won't go down there."

"So find other workers. Find the funds. Surely you can source them from some connection."

"I have tried. It didn't work."

She slapped her palm on the edge of the desk, the clap making him jump, eyes wide.

"Then try again." She leaned forward, pinning him with her blue eyes. "And again. And again. Try until it does work. You owe this to Caldwell. You owe this to Adalia—to all the work she did to keep the estate afloat."

Theo instantly bristled, his shoulders pulling back. "Take care in blithely tossing about judgements, Violet. Maybe you should try again."

Her body snapped backward. "What does that mean?"

"It means that maybe you should attempt to not be irate with half of the world's population. It means you refuse to look at any man with anything but polite disgust, at best. I saw it at the Revelry's Tempest when you mingled with the crowd. I saw it with every man we encountered on the way to Glenhaven." A tight smile curled his lips. "Oh, you hide it well, make no mistake. The fools choose not to see it. But it is there just the same. I see it—the disgust, the hate."

Her head jerked back with a violent shake of her head. "I do not. Besides we are not talking about me, we are talking about you. About how your sister scraped and salvaged everything to keep the Alton name above reproach—"

His fist slammed onto the desk. "She opened a blasted gaming house."

"Better that than admit the entire Alton estate bankrupt." Her hand still on the desk curled, forefinger left straight to point at him. "Adalia saved it—for you. For you, Theo. You. And you are letting it all go for naught. You are giving up."

Her forefinger curled into her palm, her fist thumping onto the wood. "And I want to know why."

{ CHAPTER 7 }

Theo stared at her, his breath suddenly heavy in his chest.

She had no right.

No right to come into his home and demand this of him—challenge him on giving up.

Fool woman.

She met his stare, not wavering from the daggers his eyes shot at her. Blast her. She never would have challenged him like this when she was sixteen. She would have bowed her head at his anger. Meekly gone about her way.

And he would have gone about his business, holding on to his anger. Always holding on to his anger—hiding it from the world, but clutching it tight. Holding onto it because it was the last thing he possessed. The last thing he controlled.

Because if he didn't hold on to his anger, the alternative was too grim.

The alternative was to take his rightful place under the headstone outside.

"Why, Theo?" Her stiff countenance didn't break, but her voice softened, cracking on the two words.

Damn her. He needed her anger to fuel his own. Anger he needed to avoid the truth.

Pulling his fist slowly from the desk, he glared at her. He tried to hold the anger, hold it in a ball in his gut, but it evaporated, dispersing into a thousand intangible shards with her two quiet words.

He slumped backward in his chair. "I was not born for this, Violet. In charge. Fighting for the estate. Fighting for something I want. None of that was ever for me."

"Why not?" The hard glint in her blue eyes softened.

"Because I learned long ago I would never get what I wanted. Birth order alone determined that."

"When? When did you learn that?" Her palm flattened on the desk. "Caldwell, Alfred—neither would have ever made you feel like less."

Hell. He had thought to never tell her.

But she needed to know. For as much as she was demanding to understand, she needed to know this.

He took a deep breath, holding it in his chest for a long moment before exhaling. "You said I was rude to Mr. Nullter."

Her face contorted in confusion, a frown overtaking her mouth. "You *were* rude to Mr. Nullter."

"Yes, well, he was there. He was there to drive me off." Elbows on the arms of his chair, Theo entwined his fingers as he settled them on his stomach. "Mr. Nullter and your Uncle Demetrick were the ones to decide I did not rank high enough."

"What—what are you talking about, Theo?"

"Before I left for the war—before I left *you,* Vee. You had a fortune, you were beautiful, docile, charming, intelligent, and a title was what you were due. That was what your uncle had decided, and Mr. Nullter was his old friend. Which was why Demetrick had him serving as the solicitor of your fortune—when at the same time he was already the main solicitor of the Vandestile estate." His gaze centered on her. "Those two bastards were the ones to decide that you would wed Lord Vandestile. Mr. Nullter knew he needed a fortune of your size to keep the Vandestile estate from crumbling under the viscount's destruction."

"What?" Violet's jaw dropped. "But I—I had never even met Lord Vandestile when I was with you."

"No, you had actually, I remember it. I remember you gave him not even a glance at the introduction, much less retained his name. But that was a minor concern for them, your wishes. I, on the other hand, was a major concern. They needed to remove me from your life, and your uncle was very adept at doing so."

"Uncle Demetrick—no—he never would have done such a thing."

"Yet he did. He controlled your trust, Vee. He swore he would not release one shilling to a third son with no hope of the title." His top thumbnail pressed into his knuckle, the skin turning pink. "Your uncle impressed upon me how cruel it was for me to continue to vie for your affections when I would soon have you in poverty. How cruel it would be of me to make you have to decide between love and money. Mr. Nullter stood in that room and observed the whole debacle—even piped in on occasion—a rabid dog salivating."

She gasped. "No, Theo."

"Yes."

"So you…you just left?"

"Yes."

"You didn't even think to give me a chance to decide on my own?"

His tongue jabbed hard into the roof of his mouth as he considered her. "Would you have chosen me over the money?"

Another quick intake of breath—not quite a gasp—lifted her chest as she shifted backward in the chair, her hand falling from the desk. She opened her mouth, then stopped before words escaped, her look going to the dormant fireplace for long seconds. "I do not know. I was so young—we were so…so…so new, even though we knew each other for years. I didn't know at that time what we would become." Her gaze travelled back to him. "And then there was never a chance to find out."

"Because I left."

"Yes. You left. Alfred died and you left. And my heart broke for you. All I wanted to do in those days was comfort you. But you left without a word directly after the burial. You never even let me talk to you—and I tried again and again to find you alone. And then I waited—waited for word from you. Waited for you to come back to Glenhaven."

"My brother died the day after your uncle demanded I leave you be, Violet." His fingernail digging into his knuckle drew a drop of blood. "So I did not even think on it—couldn't think on it. I just knew I was done. I was done with Glenhaven, done with everyone—done for good."

"But should you have been? Who knows what I would have chosen, Theo? You made the choice for me."

"I did." He leaned forward, his jaw tightening. "I left because I didn't want to force an ungodly choice such as that upon you, Vee. It was not a fair thing to do to you. I had nothing to offer you. So yes, I made the choice. And I would have done it a thousand times over to save you from it because it was the honorable thing to do."

She stared at him as she nodded slowly, considering his words. "Valiant, of you. Or so I think you would like me to believe." Her eyes narrowed at him. "But is it possible you left because you believed I would not choose you?"

He sighed, his fingers unthreading and moving to grip the arms of the chair as he shifted in his seat. "Does it matter?"

"No." Her lips drew backward on one side, her voice defeated. "No, I suppose it does not."

She scooted forward, starting to her feet, but then stopped, sinking back down to the edge of the chair as her look pinned him. "You have never fought for anything you wanted, have you, Theo?"

He scoffed. "Of course I have. Put a blade, a rifle in my hand—I know exactly what to do."

"But this?" Her knuckles rapped onto the desk. "Something in your soul you truly want?"

"This…" His hand swung above his head around the room and then fell to his side as he sighed. "I don't know how to fight for something like this. The estate, the mine, the title. I was never allowed this, Violet. When you knew me when we were young, I always was trouble, I always said yes to everything because I had no responsibility to anything of importance—that was why I was so carefree—there was nothing expected of me. The most I could see in the future was the military—to die in honor for the crown. I was not allowed aspirations. And your uncle very succinctly verified my fate for me." His eyes met hers. "There has never been anything to fight for."

"So you don't know how to fight?" She grabbed the edge of the desk, angling herself toward him. "You learn. You don't break. You don't bow. You fight. You learn how to fight and make your life what you want."

He met her look, the vehemence in her blue eyes startling him, but not swaying him. "Why? Why bother?"

"So you can breathe. So you can wake in the morning and want to move from your bed. So you can smile. Laugh on occasion. So you can make life just a touch easier for those around you. So you *mean* something."

His eyes dropped to the center of the desk between them. "Those things are lost to me, Violet. And my will to fight vanished long ago."

"You think to hide behind what happened to you?"

He shrugged. "It is not yours to judge."

"No. But bad things happen. I know they have happened to you." Her words took on a hard edge. "But how long can that be your excuse for being an arse? For wasting your way through life? For pushing your sister away at every turn? For turning what little is left of the fine Alton name into a mockery?"

His look lifted to her. "Tell me what you truly think, Vee."

Her mouth clamped shut, her lips tight at his sarcasm. A long breath passed before she spoke again. "I think I just did. Do with it what you will."

Theo met her glare head-on.

He had tried to save himself once from this woman. A woman who could consume him—body and soul—if he allowed it. And he had done a fine job of it.

For a time.

But then she had gone and kicked him on the floor of the Revelry's Tempest. He had looked up, seen her face, and there hadn't been a moment since that time when she was not in his mind, devouring him from deep within.

She pushed away from the desk, silently turning from him and walking to the study entrance. Opening the door, she paused and glanced back at him. Disgust marred her delicate face. One quick sweep of her eyes about the room, and she exited, the door closing softly behind her.

He collapsed back into his chair and exhaled a long breath.

Absurd. Absolutely absurd. He now possessed the very thing that had driven him away years ago—a title—and little good it did him for the boor he'd become.

Little good it did him against the growing derision in Violet's eyes.

{ CHAPTER 8 }

"You stayed."

Violet jumped, her fingers ripping out the weed she had just clamped onto. Craning her neck, she looked over her shoulder to see Theo at the arched entrance to Glenhaven's conservatory.

He walked into the conservatory, stopping at the far end of the plant bed she was working on. In buckskin breeches and dark boots, he was free of his tailcoat, only his dark waistcoat contrasting against the white of his linen shirt. "Your intention must be to attend the ball tonight at the Vandestile estate?"

Not bothering to stand from the short stool she was balanced on, she dropped the weed in her fingers onto the pile of wilting leaves by her feet and looked up at him. "Yes. I decided I can offer one last responsibility to the Vandestile title, and then I do believe I can free myself."

He nodded and his eyes quickly scanned the overgrown plant bed in front of her. "You do not need to be doing that. I have—had—a gardener."

She brushed her hands together, flicking dirt from her gloves. "Well, I have pulled thousands of weeds in here with Adalia over the years. And I actually enjoy it. This place became my home, my family after my parents died." A lump formed in her throat and she struggled to quickly clear it. Her hand swept out over the tips of the many rose bushes. "When was the last time Adalia was here? She would be distraught to see the overgrowth."

His gaze left her face, fully surveying the large room and the eight neat rectangular plant beds filled with a wide variety of roses. "It has been a year, at least. She came to move some of them to Dellon Castle that she wanted to cross-pollinate with. She had the plant beds cleaned and trimmed then."

Violet nodded, spying another close-by weed. She leaned forward to dig her fingers into the dirt and grasp the root before plucking. "I was always envious of this room when I visited. It was like swimming in a bottle of the most heavenly perfume."

Still at the far end of the plant bed, Theo cleared his throat. "I have given up, Vee. You are right. I could not find an easy path forward, so I stopped. I just stopped moving at all. And I…I need to reconsider that."

She froze, the weed in her grasp only half wiggled from the ground as she awkwardly twisted to look up at him. "What? Truly?"

He stared at her, his jaw flexing. He had said it once, and she wasn't about to be granted a repeat of his admission.

Once was enough for her.

"Theo, that you said that…" She stood, peeling off her gloves tucking them into the pocket of the dirt-streaked apron she had tied around her waist. "I was going to tell you this morning. But then our conversation in the study turned for the worse and I decided not to." She paused, her head tilting to the side as she questioned herself. "At least not immediately. But then again, I would have told you… eventually."

His eyebrows lifted in slight exasperation of her rambling. "Tell me what, Vee?"

Brushing her hands on her apron, she walked toward him. "I am still not positive I wish to tell you at this time." She stopped halfway along the rose bed and met his eyes. "But it is not right that I know this and do not share the information with you."

His right hand curled into a fist, cracking his knuckles. At the sound, he instantly straightened his fingers. "There are lies?"

"No, not lies." She flipped her fingers in the air, waving away the absurdity. "Discoveries. While you were gone yesterday and last night I went over your ledgers. It was actually why I had come down to the study earlier this morning. To grab several more to peruse."

"You went through my ledgers?" His voice went hard.

"I invaded your privacy, yes—but I have also seen these accounts before, at least the ones that existed before you assumed the title."

"How?"

"Adalia asked me for my help when you were missing and she was attempting to hold the estate together. She knows I am adept at numbers and can manage to look at page after page of entries without tiring. So I did not think it too much of an intrusion yesterday. I have gone through all of the ledgers—except the newer ones—several times over in the past."

"So you decided to just invite yourself to do so again?"

"You said no one was working on the mine because of lack of funds so I decided to try to discover a way forward for exploiting the new vein. Favors you could possibly call in—associates Caldwell or your father once helped that may be open to loans." She gave a slight shake of her head.

"But I made a grievous error, or rather, I missed a rather important entry when I went over the ledgers for Adalia—or quite possibly the name meant nothing to me at the time."

Theo took several steps toward her, closing the distance between them. The anger that had spiked in his eyes when she admitted to rifling through his ledgers had already dissipated. "What in heaven's name are you talking about, Violet?"

"You have a substantial loan out to Baron Telliton that was never repaid. It was years ago—long before Caldwell died, and I don't imagine you looked back into the records that long ago. Baron Telliton gave him the note ten years ago, and it was only listed once—there was never any notation to collect—which was why I missed it."

"Baron Telliton? I do not know the man."

She smiled. "But I do. And I know for a fact Baron Telliton is a slippery eel. He visits the Revelry's Tempest often, and he has attempted to get out of every note he has ever been issued by my bank. The crux of it is, he is actually rather wealthy. He just prefers to borrow and not pay the debts if he can manage it." Her smile grew wider. "Oddly enough, if one actually calls him upon a note, he will pay it willingly. It is just that he manages to eschew most of them. He is slippery, that one."

"The bastard."

"Or a cunning gentleman, which is what I prefer to call him so he keeps losing at my tables. His is not the worst practice, if slightly dishonorable." Her mouth quirked to the side as she gave him a tart glance. "He does, at least, have the actual funds to support his debts—which is better than half of the *ton*."

Theo's eyes escaped upward to the glass dome of the conservatory. "Yes, your insinuation is taken and admitted to, Vee."

"Cognizant of you." She stared at the line of stubble along his jaw—almost brown in color instead of blond. "You have not asked."

His look dropped to her. "What should I be asking?"

"How much the debt is worth."

"Tell me."

"I know nothing of mines and how expensive it is to open up new tunnels around that vein, but will fifteen thousand pounds do as a start?"

He stilled, staring at her as a slow smile crept onto his face. "Truly? That was what the note was for?"

"It was. It may take Baron Telliton time to gather the necessary funds for repayment, but from what I know of his finances, I do believe he can do so."

Theo rushed to her in two steps, snatching her into the air and swinging her around in one madcap motion.

Shock, and then instant laughter filled Violet's lungs as her world went spinning. Six spins, and Theo set her down on the mossy brick pathway between the plant beds, her skirts fluttering about her legs. His hands didn't move from their clasp around her waist.

"How are you this…"

"Astute?" she guessed, laughter still bubbling on her lips.

"I was about to say calculating...intelligent... cunning—but I didn't want to offend you in the slightest in this moment and I wasn't sure which word was right."

She laughed. "I'll take intelligent."

His face sobered. "But I must pay you for my losses first."

"No. These funds are much better spent getting the mine operational. As long as my loan with Mr. Olston is approved—and it should be with the mine as security—I shall be fine for the gala." She grinned. "Be assured, of course, that when the mine is profitable, I will be the first in line demanding you pay off your losses in full."

"And you will get that payment." The smile slowly carved back into his face. "Truly, Vee—those many years ago you never even gave hint to having all of this craftiness behind those blue eyes of yours."

"I did not need to be smart those many years ago—I was an heiress, so it was preferred that I was not." Wedging her arm upward in between them, she flicked out a finger to poke his chest. "But that didn't mean I didn't possess the abilities."

"You hid them well."

Her lips drew inward and she leaned slightly against the clasp of his hands on her lower back. "I hope you did not think me a simpleton. I was young and participating in the game—the cat and mouse of it all—the best I could."

"No. Never." He looked down at her, the mirth in his eyes darkening. "It is just the duplicity of it—we all hide things we do not want others to see."

"Hiding?" She grinned. "And just what are you hiding at the mome—"

His lips dove downward, meeting her mouth and cutting her words. Hard, demanding—but with the buzzing excitement that had taken over his body. Excitement that had lit up his eyes when she had told him of the note—the same excitement in his eyes that she remembered seeing when she was eighteen and he had convinced her to sneak into the side gardens with him.

Dangerous. Impulsive. Scandalous. He was everything she attempted to avoid at eighteen.

She cared then. She didn't now.

His kiss deepened, his tongue slipping past her throbbing lips—lips that betrayed her instant surrender to his touch. Instant surrender to his hands, his body, the solid mass of him. He wasn't soft—he never had been.

It had been so long since she had allowed a man to touch her. She lost herself in the kiss, the world swirling around her, bringing her back in time. Back before the time of her husband. Back to when Theo kissed—truly kissed her like this. When she was young and without a care and he would kiss her so hard her toes would scrunch, a sweeping fire lighting every nerve in her skin.

She could feel her body going limp. Every second that his tongue traced the swells in her mouth, slid along the line of her lower lip, she lost another sliver of control.

Control she could not afford to lose. Not again.

"That is what I was hiding at the moment." A nip on her swollen bottom lip and he pulled away, his ice blue eyes intense. "I don't know what to do with you, Violet."

"What to do with me?" Hazy from the kiss, her look fluttered to him.

"You make me remember." His eyes closed for a long second, his head shaking. His eyelids cracked to meet her gaze. "That is why I wanted you to come to Glenhaven. The mine, yes, but you—you make me…remember who I was. Remember how I could be. And it—you—are tangible. An anchor. Something to hold onto while I'm flailing, every minute, every second of my cursed life."

The last wisps of fog evaporated in her mind as his words hit her. Their breath, their bodies still entwined, she realized how very close she had just come to losing control.

To losing herself.

She couldn't disappear again. Lose herself to something she couldn't control.

"I cannot be your something to hold onto, Theo. I cannot." She wedged her arms out from underneath his—out of captivity—and then pawed behind her to free his hands from her back. "I am happy I found Baron Telliton's entry in the ledgers. Happy for you. But I cannot—I cannot afford you any more of me."

She jerked a step backward, scrambling. "Please excuse me. I need to prepare for the ball."

Instantly, Theo released her and she stumbled around him, making her way through the conservatory and into the cool confines of the house.

Away. She needed away.

Away from Theo. Away from what he had just made her feel. Away from what she realized she would need to give up in order to feel that cruel, magnificent tingle invading her body, begging for more. Begging for release.

She could not afford herself the pleasure of that again.

Not again. Not ever.

Not at the price it would demand.

{ CHAPTER 9 }

Violet smoothed the fine cerulean satin along her side and over the curve of her hip. Her gaze following the drape of the gown to the floor, she flipped the toe of her white slipper out. Clarissa had done a fine job during the last day in lengthening the gown Violet was borrowing from Adalia. The pair of Adalia's satin slippers were a touch too small, but she would survive.

Not a single thing to cause her not to attend the Vandestile ball. No sudden illness. No clothing mishaps. No bolts of lightning.

Why had she so foolishly agreed to this? She had nothing left to prove to these people. Nothing left to give to the mighty Vandestile name. She had a new life far away. A life she could control. A life she was happy with.

Of course, the last time she had seen these people, she had thought her life was perfect as well. She had thought she was happy. And that reality had quite viciously turned on her.

Straightening her spine, Violet stepped to the side, peering out the window that abutted the front doors of Glenhaven.

Clarissa had run to fetch Mr. Druper and the carriage, and Violet didn't want to make her maid have to run into the house to collect her as well. She already had Clarissa running ragged as it was.

"You look exquisite."

Violet hopped a tiny step, startled by Theo sneaking up upon her for the second time that day. Looking up the stairs leading into the foyer she found Theo walking down to her. "Thank you. The gown is one of your sister's. I commandeered it for the purpose as I did not imagine I would need a ball gown during this excursion to Glenhaven."

"You will represent the Vandestile history well. They are sure to cower at your satin-clad toes." He stepped onto the marble floor and Violet's gaze ran over his clothing. Still in buckskin breeches, he was as far away from full dress as possible.

"You are not going to accompany me to the ball?"

His head tilted to the side as he considered her. "I did not think you preferred my company beyond what was necessary until we are back in London and I sign the note of guarantee."

"Oh no, Theo. You do not saddle me with this event, only to squirm out of attending it yourself."

His hands came up, palms high in defense. "I was merely thinking of your comfort. That you would not want to be forced with me into a coach for three hours each way."

Her right fingers curled, her knuckles landing on her hip. "No, you were thinking of *your* comfort."

"Possibly." Theo grinned. "But truly, Violet, I did not think you wished to have me nearby."

"Why would I not wish that?"

"Because you said as much in the conservatory." His hand rubbed along the back of his neck, tousling the ends of rogue strands of hair. "Because I do not live up to your standards."

"Standards?" She took a step toward him, meeting his blue eyes. "You misunderstand why I cannot…" She shook her head. "I do not have standards that you do not meet, Theo. Not at all. But I do have things I want for you. Things I want for Adalia. I want you to fight for the Alton name. For your family. For the legacy you were given and must pass along. I want you to become the man I knew you would be five years ago—with or without a title."

His lower jaw shifted to the side as he nodded, his gaze dropping to the floor between them. His look lifted to her, the ice blue in his eyes uncannily warm. Hot, even. "And you? What do you want for you, Vee?"

"Me?" Her eyes shifted to the stairs to avoid his gaze as her left hand lifted, flattening on the bare slope of her chest above the lace trim on her bodice. It took a long second before she could force herself to meet his eyes. "For me…for me, in this moment, I want you to hold my hand through this, Theo. I want a friend of old, someone I can trust, to prop me up before these people and ensure I do not break in front of them. They are rabid for it. Rabid for one last scandal they can embroil me in."

A half smile came to his face, wicked. "Then you should fight for what you want, Vee."

She laughed.

He held his hand up, grin stretching across his lips. "No need. You will never have to fight to have me by your side. If you help me with my cravat, instead of waiting for Thompson to painstakingly tie it, I can be ready to leave in five minutes."

She exhaled, relief flushing through her body. "I would like that."

"Then we will go, meet the new viscount, and be done with the name of Vandestile for good, if that is what you wish—except for the small fact that you are Lady Vandestile, of course."

She smiled, her eyes sparkling as a chuckle came to her lips. "Yes, except for that particular bothersome issue."

He nodded. "I will not be long."

~~~

Theo glanced out the coach's window at the main walk into Vandestile manor, the pathway lined with blazing torches. The heat of the warm spring day had not dissipated with the sun setting, and several couples loitered, making their way slowly to the tall arched doorway.

His look veered back to Violet's profile.

She hadn't made the slightest motion in three minutes, not since she had floundered as he was exiting the carriage, grabbing the tail of his coat and pulling him back inward. Mr. Druper had immediately closed the carriage door, and they had sat, Violet worrying her bottom lip, staring at the front door for far too long.

"You were glowing an hour ago, Violet."

It took a long second, but she managed to drag her stare away from the window and look across the carriage at him. "And I am not now?"

"No. Every step those horses have taken here has ripped a tiny piece of that glow from your eyes. I fear I will have to walk back on the return to Glenhaven and collect all the scattered pieces for you."
~~~

"If you are attempting to bolster my confidence so I will enter the party, Theo, that is a dismal start, telling me I don't glow."

His head tilted to the side with a slight shrug of acknowledgement. "Glowing or not, Vee, you are beautiful. That has not changed. Do you know what else has not changed?"

She lifted her eyebrows at him.

"Everyone inside." He pointed to the front door. "They are the same as always—all of those people in there. They are still humorous, boorish, smart, dumb, rude, polite, judgmental, charming—the gamut of all personalities. They do not change, the lot of them. So you know exactly what you will be walking into."

Her head swiveled back to the side, her look intent on the torches near the door. "Yes, and that is why I am cowering. They have not changed, but I have—and that is unforgivable in their eyes. I know exactly how they will skewer me, skewer the choices I have made, the constant barbs about the Revelry's Tempest. How Malcolm turned the estate into shambles. None of it is a secret."

"You—cower? I hardly believe it possible, Vee."

Her gaze swung to him, wry disbelief evident in her violet-blue eyes. "I have become that crusty of a widow?"

He grinned. "You have become a force. There is a difference."

"Well, once I was a fool—I thought, believed down to my soul, that my old life was perfect. My husband. My home. And none of it was." She inclined her head to the front door. "This home was the lie I lived within for years.

And if I go in there, I have to contend with what a fool I was. How blind. What I was reduced to at the end."

"Have you not been back here since you opened the Revelry's Tempest?"

"No, not since—" She swallowed an audible gasp, her head bowing. She gave herself a slight shake, her gaze returning to the front facade of the neoclassical building. The full moonlight set the smooth white stones of the manor into a glimmer. "Not since Adalia took me from here and brought me to London. I dealt with all Vandestile matters by messengers, or Mr. Nullter travelled to London."

Theo stared at her, his eyes narrowing. Something dark—brutally dark—had just washed over her, swallowing her whole. A sadness, a pain he could not name, but recognized just the same. The same type of pain that had threatened to bring him to the bowels of hell time and again.

He cleared his throat, setting a wide smile onto his face. A smile that reached his eyes, even though he had to force it. It was always about the eyes. The eyes could always fool—or just as easily betray the falsehood.

He held the smile for a moment before he was sure he could maintain it. "Well, then this moment seems like a fortunate time to step foot in there again. Contend with this building when it is alive with people, when you cannot peel back the layers to see the dirt of the past. When that dirt cannot consume you."

She looked at him, her eyes wary. "I wanted to believe that I had left all this behind. It was past. But I haven't, Theo. This has just been another lie I have been telling myself. And I am uncannily good at living in falsehoods."

"So it stops tonight, Vee."

"Can it?"

He motioned with his head to the house. "It is a building—stone and mortar—it is not more, unless you choose to make it more."

Her lips drew inward, and a frown dropped her chin. She didn't believe him.

He reset his smile, crinkling the edges of his eyes. "Tell me, Vee, what do you do at the Revelry's Tempest when you must deal with an idiot—no, let us say a slew of idiots around a table? What do you do right before you approach them?" He leaned forward to grab her left hand and clasp it between his palms. "Close your eyes. Imagine a tableful of imbeciles. Imagine a tableful of me soused, five times over, all rambling for your attention."

The smallest smile breached her lips as her eyelids dropped closed. Her chest lifted in a heavy breath. "Five foxed yous? I straighten my spine. Smile. Become impenetrable."

"Exactly. *That,* you are very good at. You excel at it—I have seen it firsthand. So that is what you shall do in that ballroom."

Her long dark eyelashes opened to him.

He released his clasp on her hand and squeezed her knee through her satin gown. "Spine straight. Smile in place. Let no one in. Let no one disparage."

"You say it as though it is easy."

He shrugged. "It is and it isn't. It is a character to slip into. And that—being someone else, is easy."

"It is being yourself that is hard?"

A true smile lifted his eyes as he chuckled. "If I had an answer for that, Vee, my life would not be in the current state that it is." He pointed to the door. "You are ready?"

"Yes."

Theo exited the coach, assisted Violet down the carriage step, and within minutes they were past the columns at the entrance to the Vandestile ballroom. Lined on two sides with Ionic columns that created long alcoves stretching the length of the space, the two-story-high room boasted gold gilding on every possible surface, tinting even the air into a yellow hue.

He glanced down at her. Not surprisingly, she had fortified herself amazingly well during the walk inside. Her posture impeccable, the grace with which she moved—soft smiles and nods to all acquaintances, immunity to any whispers as she passed—was admirable. A mistress in her own land once more, whether she believed it or not.

Violet could slip into a character faster than anyone he knew.

He could have used her during the war.

The thought struck him without warning—random and callous and jarring.

A dark strike to his heart, sending it pounding out of control.

Not Violet. Not her.

"Theo?"

A covert poke in the side of his ribs.

"Theo?"

He started, looking at her. She stared up at him, confusion in the violet shards of her eyes. Had she just been talking to him?

"What is it?" She angled herself slightly in front of him, hiding her concern as her voice dropped to a whisper. "Is it your arm?"

He stared down at her, centering himself in time and place. It took several blinks before he could answer. "No. My arm is fine. It is nothing."

Nodding, she stepped back to his side. She surveyed the ballroom from the nook they had settled into by the French doors leading to the gardens. The soft, regal smile had returned solidly to her lips.

He followed Violet's sight line around the ballroom until a flash of light blond hair piled high with a single sparkling black ostrich feather caught his eye by the far door into the dining hall. Hair at its finest. Hair he recognized.

No. Blast it to hell. Not here.

His body tensing, he shook his head. He wasn't seeing her. Not again.

The face attached to the blond hair was obscured by the height of the man next to her, and then the blond hair disappeared through the open door and into the dining hall.

"Oh." Violet looked up at him. "My uncle is in attendance."

Hearing Violet's voice but not her words, Theo ignored her, taking a step toward the dining hall. Violet's sudden hand on his forearm stopped his motion.

"Theo?"

He looked back to Violet. Her eyebrows were arched, perplexed.

His head swiveled, searching the crowd, searching for the blond hair. It was gone. Another ghost. Dammit. What the hell was happening to him?

"Theo?" Violet's whisper commanded his attention.

He looked at her, unable to focus, unable to draw himself back into the moment, his body still aching to sprint across the ballroom to find the blond hair.

Understanding flashed across her dark blue eyes. "A ghost?"

He shrugged.

She quickly glanced around, the lines on her forehead nervously creasing before her look landed back on him. Her hand slipped from gripping his arm. "Do you need to pursue it? It is fine if you do. I will survive alone."

She bolstered a smile onto her face. A smile he could see right through. A smile that didn't come close to her eyes.

He dug his heels into the perfectly shined floorboards. "There is only one thing I need to pursue at the moment, and that is to be by your side through this adventure we find ourselves in, Vee."

She exhaled, relieved. "I think you will regret saying that."

"Why?"

"I don't think you heard me." Her look veered from him to across the room as a serene smile settled onto her face. "My uncle is in attendance. I apologize. I know how you regard him and I did not know he would be here as his health is so poor." Her smile belied her words, so light and unaffected she should have been talking about butterflies and roses. "I would have warned you earlier had I known."

"I did not know he was still alive. I have heard nothing of him for years."

"That is because he has held tightly to this world in the privacy of his bedroom. I have several nurses taking care of him at the Vandestile dower house."

His eyebrows cocked as he glanced at her. "You have been taking care of him as well? He lives off of your generosity?"

"Yes. His access to credit disappeared with Malcolm's death. He had apparently used the connection to my inheritance and my husband quite excessively, with nothing to back his debts."

"Where is he?"

"By the door to the drawing room. I only caught a glimpse of him past the dancers, as he is slumped in his chair."

Theo nodded, taking a sip of the claret he held. "His presence is not a bother. I will simply leave your side while you greet him."

"I would prefer you not."

His smile stretched thin as he kept his eyes on the bobbing feathers adorning the heads of the dancers in the middle of the ballroom. "Your preference is not my concern on the matter, Vee."

"I know what he did." She glanced up at him, the graceful smile still adorning her lips. "It is unforgivable, and I wish I knew at the time what he had done—the position he forced upon you. If I had…" The smile faltered for a moment until she straightened her shoulders, and it instantly reappeared. "I do not condone what he did—I have been beside myself about it since you told me. But it is past. And everything that has happened since that time

I cannot undo. Nor can he. But he is old and feeble. And I hope he regrets his actions—if he has not already done so."

"You look upon it in a much kinder light than I do."

Her eyes drifted back to the couples dancing in the middle of the ballroom. "I simply cannot afford to have his actions filling my brain. I have far too many other things to worry upon."

"Such as refortifying your bank for the upcoming gala?"

Her smile turned into a pointed grin. "Yes. Although that worry has been eased somewhat after what I saw in the mine—assuming you were not just showing me random rock."

"The vein is real."

"I believe you. Though I am still irate at you for losing my money and putting me in this precarious position. And that is why I am about to make you accompany me across the room to greet Uncle Demetrick."

Theo seethed out a long breath. "I don't think you fully understand my hatred of the man, Vee."

"No, I think I do. And for him to see you by my side will be the best revenge in this instance."

Theo's look flew to her. "I thought you magnanimous on the matter."

"I cannot cut off support to the man for the feeble state he is currently in. But I am not above doling out a whit of revenge, Theo. I wish I was above it, but I am not. So think your worst of me."

A bright glint of determination flashed in her eyes. "I want Uncle Demetrick to see me with you. I want him to see us approach, my hand in the crook of your arm. I want him to see you set your hand at the small of my back. I want him to have that image in his mind for the rest of his days."

Staring at her sudden ferocity, it took Theo a long moment before he jerked into action, offering up his left elbow to her. He bowed his head to her. "Then let us make our way across the room."

The serene smile settled back onto her lips, but a peculiar glow was now shining in the deepest violet slivers of her eyes as she looked up at him. "Yes, let us. Together, Theo."

~~~

Her teeth dry behind her lips, Violet sipped claret from the delicate, gold-rimmed glass, her mind drifting from the conversation with Lord Folton. The unique opaque twist stem of the crystal had long ago made it her favorite in the Vandestile glassware collection. That her lips were touching it again, with gaiety surrounding her, was odd.

She had thought to never be in this place again. Never to have to face these people again. Many of them the very faces that had plagued her after Malcolm's death, demanding payment of debts. That they all now stood in the ballroom together, congenially, sent a distasteful streak of bile up her throat.

But the whole of the evening hadn't been nearly as terrible as she had imagined.

Of course, none of these people knew exactly what happened two and a half years ago in a room just above this
~~~

dance floor. This ball would have taken a terribly different turn if that were common knowledge.

The entire reason she had managed to step into Vandestile manor—had managed to face this crowd—was standing four feet behind her, hovering without being overbearing, ready to save her at a moment's notice.

Theo.

She had travelled to Glenhaven on a mission of pity. A mission of repaying an unrepayable debt to Adalia. She was going to make Theo turn his life around. Find a path forward.

Instead, she had found herself staring down a past that would not yield. Learning the real reason Theo had left those many years ago. Returning to Vandestile manor. Both things she had long since dismissed to be forever in the past.

Past she had needed to revisit, whether she admitted to it or not.

Her heart, which had collapsed so brutally onto itself two and a half years ago and had hardened so much since that time, was slowly starting to crack. The smallest slivers opening up to the world.

She had come here to save Theo.

But she was the one being saved.

She heard his chuckle behind her, could feel his eyes piercing the back of her head, and the hairs along the back of her neck spiked.

He had surprised her more than once in the past days. And that he had come here to Vandestile Manor—when it represented the very crushing of his young dreams—merely to hold her hand, support her through this, had been the most generous surprise of all.

"What will your initial plans be after London?" Lord Folton's attention shifted from Violet, his question directed at the new Viscount Vandestile that had moved to stand near them.

Violet exhaled the breath she had been holding in the pit of her lungs after Lord Folton's look left her chest. The man had commandeered her a half hour ago and he had not let her escape the conversation since that time. As a widow she was accustomed to this—men approaching her as fair game for a quick tryst. Yes, Lord Folton was most attentive. Yes, he was generous with his compliments. Yes, he was attractive—almost sinfully so.

But the barriers she had erected two and a half years ago were thick, and no common gentleman was going to breach them.

Hoping her smile wasn't reflecting how tired she was just three hours into the ball, she turned her attention to Lord Vandestile. An American, with the expected brute and gait accompanying him, the man was now quite soused, reeking of whiskey, of all things.

Poor form, if she were to judge. But what could be expected of a hardscrabble American being plucked out of his homeland and dropped into an English ballroom? She rightfully couldn't blame the man for indulging, even if he was dangerously close to swaying out of control and landing upon her.

"London?" The American took a heavy step forward, interrupting the circular sway he was immersed in, his shoulder almost ramming into Lord Folton.

Lord Folton lifted a hand, grabbing the viscount by the upper arm to help steady him. He shot Violet an apologetic look. He had, after all, encouraged the man to stay in the vicinity with his question. "Or perhaps you do not plan on London so soon, Lord Vandestile? Though it would behoove you to take a spell to familiarize yourself with society in London, I imagine. Best to be done with it before parliament ends, and all."

"Tell me, Lord Ooot—Otton—Ollie." The viscount's red-rimmed eyes swung to Violet and he leaned forward, his look dropping lecherously to her chest. "How do it work here? I inherit the title, I inherit the woman, yes? This Lady Vandestile looks ripe to me." He pointed with his finger, making a circle about her breasts. "Seems right fair to me I inherit her as well. She is now my property, correct?" His finger lifted from her chest to point at the ballroom ceiling. "Upstairs, little lady, you know the room? The biggin one on the left?"

Luck was on her side, for Violet had frozen in place the second his leer had hit her bosom. She had braced herself well enough that his words drew no reaction from her, her smile only hardening into place.

Not so for Lord Folton.

He gasped, coughing as he stepped in front of the American to shield Violet. "I say, sir, this will not do—you cannot—"

Violet grabbed Lord Folton's forearm, hoping to intervene before his next words blew the whole evening into mayhem. "Truly, Lord Folton, I take no offense. I am sure Lord Vandestile is accustomed to much freer expressions in America and has not been fully prepared for—"

"Lady Vandestile, may I steal you away for a moment?" Theo snatched her hand from Lord Folton's arm, tugging her sideways and away from the two men. "Mr. Nullter had an urgent question about the proper tablecloths before dinner is served—something about spilled wine. He needs to see you at once."

Before she could turn her head away from Lord Folton and the American, Theo had her shuffled halfway to a side entrance leading to the main hallway. She attempted to keep up to his long strides, nodding politely at people as they passed and trying to make their exit from the ballroom look as natural as possible when she was clearly being dragged from the room. She had needed Theo to keep her from scandal, not cause it.

Theo didn't stop once they had stepped into the hallway, instead leading her up the stairs and down the corridor past the many suites on the third level. He opened and peeked into three chambers before he found an empty room and he stepped into it, his fingers still in a solid clamp around her wrist.

"Mr. Nullter is in here?" Violet asked as she stepped into the room.

Theo released her arm, reaching past her shoulder to close the door behind her.

It wasn't until he moved to the side and turned up the wick in a sconce for more light that she realized which room they had landed in. The bathing chamber. The copper tub sat in the middle of the room, heavy, the metal gleaming in the flickering light from the sconce.

It stole her breath.

"What—what are we doing in here, Theo?"

"You needed to be saved. I could hear it in your voice." He turned back to her, looking down at her, his breath so close she could feel it rippling across her forehead. "I am giving you a moment of respite before that impenetrable facade of yours cracks."

"I was about to crack?"

"I hope not." He took a sudden step backward, leaving a cool draft between them. "I apologize. Maybe I misunderstood. I did not mean to interrupt you and Lord Folton. He is a fine fellow. You deserve a man such as him."

Her head still spinning from being rushed up the stairs from the ballroom, she centered her gaze on him. "I do?"

"Yes. A man that can hold proper conversation and laugh. A man that can charm with genuine intention. I saw it in you tonight, Violet—that glow that you always used to exude." He nodded to himself. "Folton is the standard of a man that you deserve, Violet. A man that can bring that out in you."

His look shifted from her and he spied a short cart at the side of the room holding a decanter of amber liquid and two glasses sitting atop a silver platter. He walked over to it, the heels of his boots clicking on the wooden floorboards. Pulling the stopper on the decanter, he then lifted it, sniffing the contents. "What aberration is this—whiskey, of all things, in a bathing room?"

Violet blinked hard at the sudden change in topic. "Mr. Nullter said he—the American—demands it in every room."

Theo shook his head in disgust, flipping a glass over and pouring a dram. He tipped it back, swallowing it in a quick motion before pouring an even healthier nip.

His hand wrapped around the rim of the glass and his forefinger lifted, pointing at her. "A man with funds. A title.

Manners. A man like that can make you happy, Vee. Take your worries away. That is what you need."

Her eyes narrowed at him. "So now you know what I need?"

He met her look. "I probably recognize it better than you do, Vee."

Her lips drew inward, staring at him as he took a sip of the whiskey.

Maybe he did recognize what she needed. But he had no clue as to what she wanted.

"You were right, Theo."

"I was?" His eyebrow cocked as he lifted the glass to his lips.

"I do hate men."

He choked, sputtering his drink mid-sip. "You—you hate men?"

"I do." Her white-gloved hand drew upward, absently smoothing the front of her cerulean gown over her abdomen. "Rather, I should be exact and say I do not trust men. Adalia and Cass are the ones that say I hate men. And you. You said it as well. You recognized it in me. Regardless, I cannot seem to overcome it. I can lie about it, put on a pretty facade, but I cannot rid myself of it."

"That is a sweeping statement to admit to."

She shrugged. "Sweeping or not, it is true. And my interactions with that American downstairs only substantiated my belief that men are not to be trusted."

Clearing his throat, Theo set the half-full glass of whiskey onto the cart. "I missed something terribly important. What did I interrupt down there, Vee?"

"The new Lord Vandestile thought it appropriate that he inherit the lady along with the title, and then proposed we go upstairs."

"I will kill the bastard."

She waved her hand in midair, stopping him before he took a step to the door. "You will do no such thing. I am a widow in an unusual position as the proprietress of a gaming hall and I am propositioned like that at least weekly, Theo. The American was just much crasser about it. Besides, Lord Folton was more than ready to come to my defense."

"There—proof that Folton is the right man for you."

"No—proof that men can't be trusted. I know very well that Lord Folton was conniving his own way to a proposal. Hopefully, he would have managed more couth with the matter."

His jaw flexing, his hands curling into fists, it was taking a great amount of control for Theo not to storm past her. But he held still, staring at her.

Something was far more important to him at the moment. What it was, she wasn't sure.

He opened his mouth, his voice raw. "You said it before, days ago, but was it a lie, Vee? Do you trust me?"

Her head snapped back. She answered in the same breath, before considering her reply like she normally would. "You…you I do trust for some reason, Theo. It is odd. I never questioned it. It must be because I knew you from long ago, before…"

"Before what?"

"Before my husband."

He nodded, his look calculating. "But when you are with men—at the Revelry's Tempest, or tonight—you are gracious, yet you are stiff and I don't think they notice that in the slightest." The statement came slow, as though he was considering each word with the utmost care.

"No, men are usually too busy looking downward at my chest. Or staring at my lips. They see what they want to, and I allow it. It is easier for all."

"How is that easier?"

"As long as I am charming and docile with the opposite sex, my coffers are full. I am not causing scandal. But I am not an idiot or a martyr. It is not good business to toss daggers at half of the Revelry's Tempest clientele."

"That seems cold—that you have honed a sweeping dislike of men."

"I know the reality, Theo. My circumstances offer me no margin to like or dislike them. But trust? No. That is something I cannot afford."

Silence fell upon them for long seconds. Theo stared at her, his cool blue eyes still assessing her. She didn't care for it. Didn't care for his probing, for his peeking under layers she would rather leave in place.

"Why are you so keen to offer me up to some random baron, Theo?"

"What?"

"Lord Folton."

His fingers ran through his hair, setting the rogue blond tendrils haphazard. "Folton is a fine man. He would make a respectable match for you."

She nodded, her eyes slightly squinting at him. "If he is so fine, why did you so eagerly pull me away from him?"

His jaw shifted to the side, his look hardening. "You know why, Vee."

"Do I? Why?"

"Your hand was on his arm. It will not do. The gossips will explode."

"I held the crux of your arm time and again tonight and you were not concerned on the gossip."

He heaved a sigh. "Fine. I saw you touch him and I reacted. Without thought. Right or wrong or be damned to whatever man you deserve. I reacted."

She took a step toward him. "My hand was on his arm and you could not stand for that?"

"No. You touching another man. It is not something I care to witness, Vee. It's why I disappeared five years ago."

She took another step forward, collapsing the space between them. "But it was an innocent touch, Theo. I was attempting to calm Lord Folton. Nothing more."

"In your eyes, yes. In my eyes..." He stopped, shaking his head. "In my eyes I have great difficulty not breaking into two any man's arm you happen to touch."

Her eyes went wide, searching his face. "You think of me as yours, don't you, Theo? Completely and utterly yours."

The heat in his look was unmistakable. "The answer to that is not something you want to hear, Vee. I recognize that. So I will not admit to it."

She nodded. He was right, she didn't want to hear that. Didn't want to be his property, his toy.

But she did want him to touch her.

Heaven help her, she did want him to kiss her again. She wanted him to turn the spiking tingle rolling down her spine into an uncontrollable fire. He made her feel, and after walking through hours of numb civility a floor below—of nods and smiles and polite agreement to any of the bland subjects being spewed upon—she wanted real like never before.

In that very moment, she realized when he had kissed her the day before he had ripped her out of a cocoon of numbness she hadn't even recognized she existed in. With Malcolm's death, she had thought she had given up all pleasures of the flesh for forever. Pleasures such as that only led to heartache—to betrayal—and she had no allotment left for more heartache in her life.

But then Theo had gone and kissed her. Sparked to life all she thought dead within her—things that should stay dead.

She had run from the conservatory because she needed that spark to stay dead.

But it had only taken one evening with Theo at her side—protecting her at every turn, staring at her like he wanted to devour her skin from head to toe, keeping her sane, not allowing her to cower—to realize what he had sparked to life was not about to be extinguished without satisfaction.

Her body needed it.

Needed *him*.

She took one final step to him, her breasts brushing gently across his jacket.

No more space between them.

Meeting his light blue eyes, she drew air deep into her lungs, her voice dropping to a whisper. "Why, after all this time, Theo, do you still not believe I would choose you against all others?"

{ CHAPTER 10 }

Hell. He was in hell.

Violet standing right before him, bloody well propositioning him.

A test. This had to be a test. She was testing him. Toying with him, because she could. Because he deserved it. Because he had revealed far too much.

She was his. She always had been. She always would be. Whether she knew it or not.

The instant her hand had landed on Lord Folton, he had morphed into a raging oaf. He deserved whatever she had in store for him.

Theo drew his hands behind his back and clasped his fingers tightly together, his knuckles near to snapping. As long as he didn't touch her, he wouldn't break. Wouldn't fail her test.

Her azure eyes wide, twinkling in the light of the sconce, she looked up at him with far too much knowledge the last five years had given her. Touches of innocence lost in blue eyes that recognized well the benefits of carnal pleasures.

She knew exactly what she was doing.

Damn her.

She had claimed she didn't want to be the one he held onto, his sanctuary. But here she stood, a bloody buoy in a sea of raging waves tormenting his body.

She shifted slightly, her breasts dancing along his chest. "You have no answer?"

"What, exactly are you asking of me, Vee?"

Her head slanted slightly to the side, contemplating him. "Belief." She nodded, more to herself than him. "That you have enough belief in yourself to give me what I need in this moment."

"Am I a fool if I believe in what you are offering me right now?"

"You think me a farce?" She leaned ever so slightly into him, her left hand lifting, her fingers soft feathers trailing along his upper arm. "You think me standing before you, alone, in a locked room is something I would risk—with a house full of gossipmongers not but feet away—if I did not mean my words, Theo?"

He drew in a breath, her delicate scent of lilacs filling his lungs. He couldn't take her any closer. Her hips any nearer and she would brush against the unmistakable symbol of how badly he wanted to touch her.

Her hand dropped away from his arm, her eyes widening at him. "Unless…unless I mistake this. You do not want me."

Her foot lifted, taking a step backward.

He would have none of it.

Behind his back, his entwined fingers ripped apart and his right arm wrapped around her waist, his left hand deep into the thick of her hair at her neck, his mouth crushing hers before her toes landed on the floorboard.

She was sweet, then tart, tasting both of the claret and the jellies from below. Her hips drew toward him, her abdomen pressing against his rock hard member, leaving no doubt as to how very much he wanted her.

In a slight but pointed motion, she swiveled her hips against him. A smile curved her lips under his kiss, her words a whisper in his mouth. "I did not mistake this."

He couldn't tear his mouth away from hers long enough to reply, could only drop from her lips to taste her neck as his voice rumbled slowly from his throat. "No, you did not, Vee. Far from it."

Her fingers slipped into the back of his hair, clutching him to her neck. He travelled downward, reaching the slope of her breasts. Below his chin, he dipped his thumb behind the lace edging of her dress, searching, her skin pricking under his touch. He tugged the fabric downward, freeing her nipple to the air for the slightest moment before he captured it in his mouth.

The bud hardened as he sucked, teasing it, his teeth raking the delicate skin.

She gasped at the touch, not in surprise, but in pure gratification. A soft mewl lifted from her throat on her exhale as her fingers dug into the back of his neck.

The sound startled him for the merest second and he had to remind himself that for as much as he saw her as she once was, she was no longer a virginal eighteen-year-old. Married for two years, she would be well versed in how her body reacted to being touched.

He tugged down the other side of her gown, moving to her right breast and forcing it into hard, taut submission.

He wanted her slow. Wanted time to worship her body. Yet her hips were insistent, thrusting forward against his cock through their mounds of clothes, writhing against him.

She pulled back slightly, her white gloves falling to the floor as her fingers dove between them, unbuttoning and stripping back layers of his clothes. Tailcoat. Waistcoat. Cravat she had painstakingly tied on the journey here.

And then her hands dropped, unbuttoning the flap of his trousers. Her palm brushing against his ready-to-burst cock.

For a second, he froze, rattled by her forwardness.

She had been married. He had to remember that. Experience. She had experience, and she damn well knew what to do with his trousers.

A soft moan from her as his mouth was on her breast was one thing, but this—this was beyond. She was fast at it, for blasted sake. This was her having intimate knowledge of stripping off a man's trousers time and again.

The thought sent a shot of rage through his body, so visceral he had to curb the insane need to toss her to the ground and make her his—the need to erase every last touch that bastard of a husband put upon her.

Slow. Slow. Slow.

She would never feel anything from him but the pleasure she wanted—pleasure she begged for.

He lifted his head, capturing her mouth with ferocity just as she freed his shaft to the air. Her soft hand went tentatively to the tender skin on the head, encasing it with delicate precision.

His breath drew in sharply at the shards of exquisiteness ripping through his body. Her hand dropped, squeezing, stroking, and he allowed himself one full second of indulgence, of heaven coursing through his veins.

He pulled from her lips. "Not so swift, Vee." The demand escaped in a harsh growl.

Her hand tightened on his cock.

Hell. She needed it. Needed it more than he did if that was even possible.

Give her this. Give her this and then they could slow. The next one he gave her he could have as his own, her body clenching around him, her naked skin dragging against his.

His hands moved down the sides of her gown and pulled the fabric upward, finding a path to the bare of her thighs above her garters. His right hand, swirling, running upward along her inner right thigh, made her motion still, her body sway, and he had to clamp his left arm around her waist to keep her from tipping.

He found the mound of her, parting her folds to his fingers, and she bucked slightly, the first deft swipe of his thumb sending her into gasps.

"Th—Theo—" Her words cut off as she gripped him at the neck with one hand. Curling into him, she kept her right fingers wrapped around his cock, but all motion from her ceased, her body only able to ride his hand, arching into his strokes.

Her nails dug into his neck, a gasping scream building from her chest as the crux of her throbbed, hardening under the circles of his thumb.

His fingers slipped back and dove inward, two fingers breaching her body, sending her into spasms. He quickened the pace of his circles, his body straining, muscles on fire as he fought against his own control that threatened to snap.

Her hold on his cock constricted—an excruciating challenge against his will to hold fast from exploding. But in the next instant her hand left him and reached up to paw, grasp at anything she could hold onto as a scream racked her body, her limbs shuddering. Pounding wave after wave pulsated through her folds as she came, her body quivering with every breath she attempted.

He had never witnessed such beauty. And he was not done.

Before she went limp, Theo spun her around, keeping his hand deep in the crux of her. He moved her hands to grip the curled top edge of the copper tub as his fingers continued their assault, slow, methodical, an intermission to breathe before the next storm.

She bent at the waist, still gasping, her eyes closed. Theo aligned his body to her back, his lips landing on the side of her neck as he pushed rough words from his throat to her ear. "You're going to come again, Vee. And this time around me. Your shudders are mine. Your screams are mine."

He shoved the rear of her skirts upward, draping them around her middle. His thumb swirled in her folds, starting to speed again as he looked down to the round swells of her creamy white skin.

"I am yours." She turned her head to the side, opening her eyes and looking up at him. "I am all yours, Theo." She arched with the motion of his fingers flicking her nub, gasping as she tipped her backside up to him. Ready for him.

Heaven help him.

He set the tip of his cock at her entrance.

A scream.

But not a scream of pleasure.

Hell.

Another scream, terror incarnate, and Violet shoved off from the copper tub. She slammed violently into him, sending both of them tumbling backward.

He landed flat on his back, catching Violet on top of him, their limbs tangling.

"The tub—the tub—the tub—" Her ranting sped, her feet scrambling, shoving her away from the copper tub.

She couldn't untangle from Theo fast enough to escape across the floor, and some terror gripped her even harder. Her limbs flailing, hitting him, hitting the floor indiscriminately. Escape. She was looking for escape. Desperate for it.

"Violet—Vee, what? What is it? Did I hurt you? I—"

"No, no, no, the bath—" She gasped a breath and then her words tumbled, furious. "I saw it and I ignored it but I didn't think I would touch it and then I opened my eyes and I was looking down into it and I was touching it and I…I…"

Her voice cut off as she rolled herself off of him, effectively untangling their limbs. She jumped to her feet, scrambling to pick up her gloves with hands that shook so violently they could not grasp the fabric.

Gaining his feet with a quick glance at the bath, Theo stepped between her and the copper tub, blocking the sight of it from her. Quickly buttoning his trousers, he then grabbed her arms, pulling her upright and away from her gloves on the floor as he tried to still her frantic motions.

She fought him so he leaned down, setting his face just before hers. "I don't understand. What is happening, Vee?"

Her eyes darted about, a rabbit in a trap. "It is—I have to get out of here, Theo." Her words stuttering, she attempted to squirm away with little success. "I thought I could handle it but then I remembered and it's too much, Theo. Too much. I cannot. I cannot. I have to get out."

Theo looked over his shoulder at the copper tub. Nothing was amiss. It was empty. A standard bathing tub with nothing of note about it. A quick scan of the rest of the bathing room told him the whole of the space was bland, nothing at all out of the ordinary.

But what had just attacked Violet with a vengeance was not ordinary.

He quite clearly needed to get her out of the there. To get her out of Vandestile Manor.

Ignoring her swatting hands, he bent, sweeping up her gloves and his clothes with his left hand and then wrapping his right arm fully around her, enveloping her into his body.

To his relief, she didn't fight him. If anything, she suddenly realized the haven he provided and she curled into him—no doubt would have crawled inside of him if it were possible.

Within minutes, he had managed to partially shove on his coat while ushering Violet down the rear servants' stairs and to the stables where the coach was holding. He sent Mr. Druper in to fetch Clarissa, and then settled Violet into the carriage.

Her shaking had not ceased.

And a tremble of his own had started. He moved to the bench opposite her, his legs wide, capturing her between them as he leaned forward. "What the hell was that, Vee?"

"I—" She glanced out the window, her eyes landing on the rear of the manor. The full moonlight set the white stones of the building into an unearthly glow. Her head shook. "No. I cannot."

"You damn well can." He grabbed her knees through her skirt, his fingers digging into her skin, squeezing harder with every word. "I have just imagined a thousand different scenarios in the last five minutes, Vee. All about what happened to you in that room. Who hurt you so badly that you would react like that. What horror you endured. And now I only need to know one thing—who do I need to kill?"

She gasped, her hand clutching onto her throat, her face contorting in panic. "Me—it is me. Only me."

"What?"

Her trembling fingers dropped from her throat, falling to her lap. "I—I am so sorry, Theo. I am mortified on so many levels it is too ridiculous to even comprehend."

"So start." His grip on her knees eased. "Tell me one of those levels."

"I am a failure." Her head shook, her eyes closing as her voice escaped small, timid like he had never heard it. "I always have been and I failed you."

"What madness are you speaking, Vee?"

"What I offered upstairs, I could not deliver. I apologize."

His hand instantly retightened on her knees. "I could care less about that, Vee. What I care about is the reason that you slipped into insanity on me."

"I am not insane." Her fingers lifted, rubbing her temples. "I am a failure. As I said. Or maybe I am insane."

"And touching a bath told you that?"

Her eyes opened to him. "It was not just any bath, Theo. It was that copper tub. That room."

His head dropped, bowing for a long moment as he attempted to rein in fury he had no target for. Composed once more, he lifted his look to her. "What happened in there, Vee?"

She closed her eyes as her hands dropped, her right palm flattening against her belly as though she needed to hold herself upright. Taking a deep breath, she held it for far too long before she expelled it. A tear escaped from the corner of her eye with her exhale.

Just as Theo was going to prod her for more, she shivered and then opened her mouth, her voice wispy, haunted. "That was where your sister found me two and a half years ago after Malcolm died. After I realized… everything. It was in the autumn. The cold had started to seep into the days. Not the short spurts of coolness in the summer. The cold that teased at gripping the land, holding it hostage into the bitter winds of winter."

She opened her eyes, her head tilting backward as her look fixed on the far top corner of the coach in apparent attempt to stave off tears that welled. "I didn't want the cold anymore. Hated it. So I had the bath filled. That copper tub. Cook and Flanders helped me fill it. They were the only two left in the manor. And the stairs—so many. Up and down. Bucket after bucket. Pity. Such pity in their eyes. They wanted to stop, but I would not let them. And I made sure it was the warmest water. I had it filled so full, that when I got in, it flowed over the top rim, flooding the floor. I can still hear it trickling down, droplets splashing."

She paused for a long moment, another lone tear slipping down the left side of her face, traveling slowly over her cheekbone, catching a glint of moonlight through the open window of the coach.

Her fingers shaking, her hand on her stomach pressed inward as she took another long breath and her gaze dropped to Theo's face. "That was the day I gave up."

He knew exactly what she was telling him, but he didn't believe it.

Not Violet. Not the one woman he knew to have a backbone of steel. To fear nothing except for dark corners deep in mines.

"Violet—"

"I gave up. There was just so much…pain. And every day I would wake up, and I would tell myself that it would get better. It would ease. Every day I did that. Every day. Every single day. Every minute. It would get better. But it never did. It only got worse. And I lost those words. I could no longer utter them. Lie to myself. Then the cold came."

She lifted her hand, swiping at the tear crested on her cheekbone. "So I sank into the warmth of the water. And that was it. I was done. I thought I would have to fight it. Fight the water. Fight to stay down. I even put iron fireback plates on my chest. But I didn't need to. I didn't fight it. Didn't at all."

Her voice trailed, her eyes slipping closed again.

Theo gave her the moment, the space.

He waited in silence for long minutes until he caught sight of Mr. Druper and Clarissa walking down the path to the carriages.

He gently squeezed her knee. "Except that was not the end."

She opened her eyes to him, a sad smile etching into her face. "Adalia is a remarkable friend, Theo. Did you know that?"

"I do."

She nodded. "That was the very day she arrived at the manor. The very minute. I had gone under. Let the water into my lungs. I was in blackness. In nothing." Her mouth closed as she swallowed hard. "And then I was naked, curled onto my side on the floor next to the tub, hacking out water, bile—everything. Adalia was above me, soaked from head to toe, slapping my back with such ferocity she would put your darkest rage to shame. She was so angry at me."

Theo smiled. That sounded exactly like how his sister would react.

"Adalia knew what I did. But she never said so. Never betrayed her thoughts on the matter beyond her initial anger. And she has never spoken a word of it. Never admonished me for it. She just helped me step forward. She collected up Cass and together they became my fortress against the world. My cornerstones. They made me move on from this place—on from everything."

He heaved a sigh. "And I was the one to encourage you to come back here."

A sharp rap came through the carriage door. They both looked out the open window.

His eyes averted to the side, Mr. Druper stood outside the carriage. "Clarissa has been retrieved. She would prefer to ride on the outside again, my lady, unless it is necessary for her to ride inside with you."

Theo moved his hands from her knees, sitting straight on the bench cushions as he looked to Violet. She shook her head.

He glanced out the carriage window. "She is not needed, Mr. Druper. We are ready."

A quick nod, and Mr. Druper moved to the front of the carriage. The horses started forward at a crisp pace, curving along the long path around Vandestile manor. Theo watched the building aglow with moonlight and mirth retreat as the reality of what Violet had done sank in.

"I thought I was ready to come back here, Theo." Violet's sudden words surprised him, drawing his gaze to her. "It is not your fault for encouraging me to come—you could not have known how I would react. *I* did not know how I would react. I believed I would be fine. I thought all of this was in the past—I *knew* it was in the past. And I was fine, until…"

"Until you touched that copper tub."

She nodded. Her hand on her stomach balled into a fist, dropping to her lap. "I knew which room I was in and I thought I could handle it. I just didn't anticipate touching the tub—gripping the edge of it." Her cheeks flushed, her hand starting to shake. "And it came at the exact time—what we were doing and what I was feeling and then I was touching the tub and it was all—it was all just crashing down around me again."

A violent tremble spread through her body. Theo's chest clenched, his heart fracturing for her, for what she suffered. It cut deep in his body—the oddest feeling he almost didn't recognize, for he had long since hardened himself against feeling anything when witnessing pain.

But her pain—what she had been driven to. Hell. He could not watch her face—see her memory of the horror—and stay stoic.

Nor could he make anyone pay for it.

Anyone that needed to suffer for this was long past dead.

So he did the only thing left to him.

He moved across the carriage, sitting down next to her, and drew her into his arms.

She resisted for the merest second, and then collapsed against him.

Every tremble, every quake from her body ran into his chest—solid—a rock quelling the onslaught of waves rolling off her body.

This, he could do for her.

Take the remnants of her pain. Be her sanctuary.

He could take all of it as his own if it could free her.

{ CHAPTER 11 }

Violet looked down, poking with the toe of her slipper at a weed between two bricks in the pathway of Glenhaven's east garden. It was an early spring weed, trying to establish itself before any other plant could get to the business of growing. The light of the full moon, now low in the sky, reflected off the bright green tip, offering the weed no place to hide.

She considered bending over to pluck it, but after tossing about in bed for an hour, her body was still too tense to sleep, much less bend with ease. Her muscles screamed, aching from the force in which she held them rigid, battling the trembles in an attempt to keep them at bay.

Her memories would never be kind to her.

Punishment for what she had done.

She had been a fool to think she could sleep after arriving back at Glenhaven.

She stared at the weed. Only two more hours of darkness and then she could put the whole of the disastrous night behind her.

"Are you not cold?"

Theo's voice came quietly from the darkness and Violet turned, her arms tightening around her waist, pulling closed the slight gape in the front of her robe.

Theo stepped to her from the shadows of the pathway lined with hollyhocks. He had either tossed on clothes haphazardly, or he had never undressed from the night. He was still wearing trousers and his linen shirt, the white cloth opened into a deep V cut in the center of his chest.

Clear of the shadows, he stopped with a healthy space between them—neither pressuring her with proximity, nor far enough away to suggest nonchalance.

She waved her hand in the air. "The cold—the cool of the night… it is a reminder. I don't mind chill now—truthfully, I seek it out when I can. It cleans my mind."

He nodded. "I didn't mean to interrupt." His finger lifted, pointing at the windows along the third level of the house. "From my chambers I saw you come into the garden and I wanted to make sure you were well."

"You thought I was to do something stupid again?" she snapped.

"No." He stilled, his look searing into her. "That never entered my mind. Should I be worried, Vee?"

"I have been to that hell once, Theo. I don't intend to ever go back."

His eyebrows cocked.

She forced her shoulders to relax, to quell her defensive hackles. Theo had been nothing but a gentleman, offering only compassion and understanding after what she had confessed to him in the carriage. There hadn't been the slightest sliver of condemnation in his eyes. He was the last person that deserved her ire.

She took a deep breath to get her voice under control. "No, you don't need to worry. I…I just have never told another soul about what happened. I do not wish you to think me a candidate for Bedlam. Or to think that a silly party at my old home would bring me to my knees. I am not that person anymore."

He nodded, his clear blue eyes catching the moonlight, making them glow in the shadows as his gaze centered on her. "I understand, Vee. I do. Everything changes. *Everyone* changes."

From anybody else, she would have found his words suspect. She would have feared being patronized, of being watched like a hawk in wait of her breaking. But from Theo—she believed him. The way his eyes had closed slightly—his own pain allowing him to recognize hers.

"Thank you."

He gave her one nod and then motioned to the pathway through the beds of hyacinths, the florets sending wafts of their heady fragrance up into the air. "Walk with me?"

"Yes."

He stepped next to her, his hands clutched behind his back as they started to stroll slowly through the garden beds.

Fifteen steps in silence, and Theo's voice cut into the crisp air. "My sister, what she did for you."

"Adalia saved my life."

"Yes." His steps stayed even, but his words paused as he looked at her. "Are you here to save me, Vee? To repay my sister?"

She turned her face toward him, meeting his look. "Yes."

"Hmm." The sound came out in a grunt. "I didn't think you would be entirely honest about it. Nor answer so quickly."

Her gaze swung forward, watching the line of far-off oaks along the edge of the woods rustle in the breeze. "It is the truth. That is exactly why I agreed to come to Glenhaven with you. Though gaining the mine as a guarantee makes my life easier, of course. I thought to save you—or at least get you to take some sort of responsibility for your life. Responsibility for the havoc you create."

"Such as ruining your bank?"

"Yes. Adalia has been fraught with worry over the state you have been in the past two years. And your latest foray into London didn't help matters at all."

"I see."

She stole a glance at his profile. He was looking down, staring at the herringbone pattern of the brick pathway before them. His jawline had tensed, his mouth tight.

She stopped, grabbing his arm to halt his motion. "That is why I came to Glenhaven, Theo, to have you take responsibility for what you did at the Revelry's Tempest. But it is not why I stayed here past our visit to the mine. I could have easily left to reside at Vandestile Manor until the ball."

She turned fully to him, staring at him until he met her eyes. "I stayed here at Glenhaven because of you, Theo."

"I was worse off than you imagined?"

"No. You were you. Just you. Not the London imbecilic drunk lying on my floor. Here at Glenhaven, you are you. Scarred, yes. Weary, yes. I didn't expect to find it, but you are still that man that I once thought to hang the moon and stars upon. You still have a fire burning inside of you. Hope inside of you. I didn't see that in London. But I do here."

"Do not think me more than that drunken louse in London, Vee, lest you be disappointed."

She shook her head. "I don't think so. I know you. I know you can do this, move on, rebuild the estate—do anything you want."

He sighed, his eyes darting away from her gaze, his look fixating past her shoulder. The blue of his eyes darkened for a heartbeat, and then suddenly lit up, a crooked smile lifting the right side of his face. "This. Do you remember this spot, Vee? It is the first place we kissed."

Her head swiveled around and she spotted the wrought iron bench his look had landed on. A slight gasp and a wicked smile came to her lips. "No, it wasn't the first—it was the second."

"The second—no, I distinctly remember it. We were on that bench. You were wearing a peach gauzy dress that your chaperone would have berated you mercilessly for wearing had she seen it."

"Miss Lipstein."

"Yes, she was the one. Oh, how she hated when she lost sight of you when I was around."

"The poor woman." Violet chuckled. "She was just doing her duty. She was scared to Hades she would have to report to my uncle that her charge was in dire need of a trip to Gretna Green due to a swollen belly."

"So yes, you were wearing that flimsy dress and you enticed me into the garden."

"I enticed?" Her eyebrows arched. "Your memory does not serve you correctly."

"No, it was you doing the enticement. I am sure of it. And I kissed you. Our first one."

A smirk came over her face. "Did I never tell you I actually stole our first one?"

"What?"

"I kissed you when you were asleep in the library one evening. You had been out all day riding with your brothers. You were a mess. Hot, sticky, dirty, completely disheveled. Lying on the settee with one leg slung over the side rail, the other long onto the floor. I stumbled upon you and I could not resist. I snuck up upon you and kissed you."

He laughed, a devil grin overtaking his face. "And did I never tell you I was feigning sleep in the library? But I couldn't move and make it be known once I realized what you were doing."

"What?" She thwapped him in the chest. "You rascal."

"You temptress." He caught her hand in midair as she started to swat him again. He stopped it, holding it in the air just above his chest as his look pinned her, his eyes heated. "That one in the library was yours, Vee. Mine—mine was on that bench. That first kiss with you and I was never the same."

"You weren't?"

"No. Never." His eyes clouded. "For good or for bad, I have thought about it thousands of times. How moments of desire—of perfection—such as that, so small, so short, define us. How they set us down unimagined paths. How years later, the draw to them—those small moments—is still ruthlessly hard to deny."

"So why do we try?"

"To deny their existence or to make more?"

"Both."

Theo shrugged. "Society? Propriety? Scandal?"

Her lips pulled to the side in a crooked frown. "That—the excuse of respectability—is a pretense that no longer holds weight on my reputation. At one time propriety was everything to me. My world. But no more. I lost it the second I took over the Revelry's Tempest. As much as I have fought for it, pretend I still have it—I am a widow that runs a gaming house. Propriety is gone, lost to another time that I will never have again. And the odd thing about it…"

"Yes?"

"It doesn't matter. Not now. I don't care about it, and it doesn't care about me. Tonight at the manor reminded me of that. There is no reason to hold onto vows of the past. Hold onto the life I once led. Not anymore."

His grip around her hand tightened and he pulled it to his chest. "I want to kiss you, Vee."

"I think you should."

He released her hand, his fingers diving to the nape of her neck, tangling in the hair she had freed from her upsweep to hang down her back. Dragging her to him, his mouth came down hard, soaking her up, crushing her as though she were the last drop of water in a desert. His tongue breached her lips, exploring, asking, and almost immediately demanding so much more.

Instant fire in her veins. Instant pleasure that she knew she couldn't trust. Pleasure that made her believe—made her believe things she shouldn't in a man. Trusting that very pleasure had blinded her once before, bringing her devastation.

Her head warring with her body, she pulled back from Theo's lips, her hands catching his face between her palms, her voice breathless as she met his eyes. "I had forgotten how it feels. To be held. To be adored. Tell me this is real."

"This is real."

"Tell me you are not lying to me, even if you are, Theo."

"Why would you think that?" His fingers tightened on her neck, his eyes locking on hers. "This is not a lie, Vee. This is me, wanting you. Wanting your body, your thoughts, your soul, like nothing I have ever wanted before."

"I don't know if I can go down this path again." Her eyes closed as she inhaled a trembling breath. "A game—is this a game for you, Theo? Am I merely the conquest that you were denied long ago?"

"You were never a conquest, Vee. You were the woman I loved. Still love. I realized that after only one day with you."

Love? She swallowed hard at his words, her eyes squinting shut. Not the word. Not the lie.

"Open your eyes to me, Vee."

She tried. No success.

"I can stand here all night, Violet. Look at me."

She tried again, her eyelids cracking to find his stare searing into her, taking her breath away.

"Heaven help me, I am going to make you feel this, Vee. Kiss you. Touch you. Have your body sink onto mine. But I don't want to convince you. You have admitted that you cannot say no to me. But I don't want that. I need you to want this. Want this as much as I do." He shook his head as his look dropped, the cords along his throat shifting as he swallowed hard. His gaze lifted to land on her. "If you don't, then—the devil take me—tell me now. This is the no you need to speak. The no I need to hear."

Her eyes opened fully to him. "Do you want me say no, Theo?"

"It is the last thing I want."

She stared at him for a long breath, mesmerized by the agony the threat of a no brought forth in the blue of his eyes. The fire. The honesty. Theo had never been anything but honest with her. "Then, yes. Yes, I want this. There are no copper tubs in sight." A smile curved onto her lips. "There is only you and me, and that bench behind me."

He laughed, his mouth on hers before it ended, sending the soft rumble from his chest into her mouth. Lifting her slightly, he took three steps, and the back of her calves bumped into the front curve of the black metal bench.

Stretching her toes to the ground, she touched the bricks of the path and spun them around. Her lips pulled from his mouth, moving downward along the stubble lining his neck, the pricks of the stiff hairs plumping her lips. She dipped lower into the open V of his shirt, his skin tasting of salt and only partially quenching her thirst. Her hands went low, unbuttoning the flap on his trousers.

"Sit. I need you to sit, Theo."

Her tongue traced circles on the expanse of his skin, and his chest lifted in a deep breath that shook his torso. "I am at your command, Vee."

Her lips stretched wide in a smile against his chest. "I like that answer."

He dropped from her, yanking off his shirt as he sat. His eyes found hers, the fire in them scorching the air between them. "You are the only one I would ever dare offer those words to."

The ferocity of his words made her pause. The value of them intended for so much more than just this one moment in time. She nodded, her fingers slipping to untie the knot on her robe. The belt fell from her grip, the silk of her robe opening, baring herself to him.

She stood for a long moment, letting his eyes run over her body, the heat of his look, of his hunger, teasing her core into frenzied craving. She moved forward, her right knee slipping along the outside of his thigh, the cool metal of the bench pressing into her shin. Following with her left leg until she fully straddled him on the bench, she settled her hands along the warm slope of his neck. "Then I will strive not to abuse the power."

His right hand reached up, gripping her by the base of the neck as he pulled her down to him, his lips voracious on hers. This kiss held no exploration, no tease. Only demand.

For all he had said she could command him, his body ceded no control.

His pinky went under the top back of her robe. "Let it fall, Vee."

Instant acquiescence, she moved her arms, letting the fabric strip from her body. The cold air enveloped her torso, spurring it into attention, into feeling more intensely the heat of his fingertips as they travelled along her body, sweeping into curves, pressing into muscles. Wherever his fingers went, her skin burned under his touch.

He dragged his mouth from hers and invaded her neck, moving quickly down to her left breast. Her head tilted back, her eyes closed as he took the bud into his mouth, his teeth raking the delicate skin.

Her hips drove forward, seeking him out. Finding him. The full of his member, hard and pulsating for her. She shifted, running her core along the length of him.

This. This was what she needed.

"Damn, Vee. You do that and I will have no strength for you." His hand dipped down between them, his fingers finding her folds, stroking.

"Yes." She shifted back slightly, her look dipping to him as her hips maintained their circular siege. "But this is what I want, Theo. Now."

A sudden ferocity took over his face and he exhaled, lifting her and setting her long onto his cock without a word.

It stole her breath and she had to clutch his neck, her head hanging over his shoulder. The sheer size of him filling her sent her gasping for breath.

His fingers wrapped around her hips and pressed into her backside. He lifted her.

"This? This Vee?"

A moan was all that could form in her throat. No words could make it past the storm of nerves swirling in her body. No sense of anything but the length of him moving up into her, and withdrawing, again and again, every stroke a strike on the blast precariously near to explosion.

He kept his rhythm, his onslaught, even as his body began to struggle against itself, his muscles straining. "Hell, Vee, yes. Yes."

The words filtered through the haze in her mind.

No. Not yet. Not yet.

Her body fighting to maintain rhythm, fighting to stay connected to him, she superseded every base instinct and pushed herself upward onto her knees, removing herself from him.

The instant void of him struck her, making her gasp. Her eyes closing, she tilted her face to the sky as she ignored the abandonment she had just forced. Ignored every nerve that was still on fire, waiting to be sated. She dropped her hand in between them and wrapped her fingers around Theo's straining cock, starting to stroke.

He instantly grabbed her wrist. "Why did you pull from me, Vee?"

She swallowed, trying to find ballast in the storm of her body. "You are—you are about to come and that is what you do—how it happens. You have to pull free." Her face stayed upward, her words floating into to the sky.

"What I do?"

"Men do."

"Not most men." He yanked her hand off of him and gripped her hip bones, lifting her and centering her above him in one quick motion.

Her look jerked down to him.

His voice hard, he looked up at her. "Whatever you think you know, Vee, forget it. I want to be inside you. You—your body wrapped around me. Pulsating around me. If you want me to pull out just before to protect against a babe, I will. But not until you have come. Not until I am a hair away from it myself."

Her eyes went wide. "I—I never had the choice."

"Everything is your choice."

She nodded. "This. I want this. You."

He pulled her down onto him hard, filling her to the hilt.

Twice more he lifted and lowered her before he stopped. "You are holding back."

"I…I am not."

He reached up to grab the back of her hair, forcing her to look down at him. "You are, Vee. What are you afraid of?"

The answer slipped from her lips without thought. "This—wanting this."

"Come hell or heaven, you already have it, Vee." His voice was brutal virility. "So tell me what you want."

She met his eyes, unleashing every desire she'd ever had to squelch. "Deep, Theo. I want you deep. Deeper. Deeper. Hard."

He thrust up into her, reaching far into her depths. Consuming her. He slid out and drove upward again. Again and again and again. Every last nerve on her body exploded, her body clamping down upon him, contracting, pulling him even further into her.

The waves rushed in a fury, suffocating her. And in the middle of the turmoil, he swelled deep within her, his body violently shuddering as his arms clamped around her with a growl.

He came. Deep inside of her.

And it was right.

Right.

It finally felt right.

{ CHAPTER 12 }

Her body meshed to his, her chin draped over his shoulder, Violet grasped onto the seconds as their chests rode back and forth with heavy breaths. Even as their panting slowed, she held onto the moment, held onto him—her arms clasped hard around his back—offering only the slightest cracking open of her eyes to the night air.

Scars.

Her body stilling, her eyes flew open. A horrendous mess of scars, up and down and across Theo's back. Long, short, skinny, circular. Too many to count. She had seen the ones on his chest but she hadn't imagined this. She had never felt them through his layers of clothes. But there on his bare back—a horrific display of torture.

Hiding a gasp, she stiffened slightly, her chin drawing away from his shoulder, and the ridge of a rough scar brushed against her neck, just one of the many she had seen marring the front of his body. Far too many to contemplate. Far too many to imagine the pain of.

Her heart constricting, her lips were instinctively drawn onto the ragged line of raised white skin along his shoulder—once smooth, now mangled.

His shoulder jerked slightly from her lips.

"No." She said the one word softly, tightening her hold around his back, not letting him escape her.

He leaned away. "My scars are hideous, Vee. You shouldn't be exposed to them."

Her head jerked up so she could see his face. “Hideous? I shouldn’t be exposed to them? You intend for me to never see your skin, Theo?”

Her eyes pinned him as she shook her head. He responded with a cold stare.

Violet was undeterred. “You intend for me to never see the lines of your muscles?” Leaning forward, she lightly kissed the center of his chest. “Never to touch the cords of strength running through your body? Never to set my lips upon the pathway down your belly?”

A harsh chuckle escaped him. “I should have kept my shirt on. You make this increasingly difficult for me, Vee.”

“I do nothing of the kind.” She said the words into his chest, her lips making slow circles along his skin, both perfect and scarred. “I cannot take certain parts of your body and disregard the ones that have been marred.”

“No, Vee.” His hands lifted to her shoulders and he pushed her slightly away.

She popped up, her eyes wide as she found his face. “You are serious?”

His mouth pulled into a terse line. “I don’t want you to have to witness my scars, Vee. I—”

“Stop.” Her right fingers went onto his lips, cutting his words. “Theo, your body is amazing—a miracle. Your body managed to survive all of these.” Her left hand trailed down the ragged scars on the right side of his chest, the pads of her fingertips caressing each of the bumps. “To survive all of these. To bring you to this moment in time. To bring you to me. The scars are just the price of that. They do not diminish the strength of your body. They are proof of how strong you truly are.”

Her fingers slipped down off of his lips and then moved to cup the side of his neck. She pulled herself close to him, her nose nearly brushing his as her words came soft against the stone set of his jaw. "So you will not hide them from me—ever, Theo. You will let me touch them. You will let me kiss them." Her head dipped down, her lips brushing the round scar on the edge of his left shoulder. "You will let me do whatever I see fit with them. Because they are a part of you."

She moved inward along his shoulder, setting her lips on the next mangled line of skin, her voice cracking in a whisper. "And I think now—now maybe I have right to intrude on your demons."

Theo stiffened under her, his fingers suddenly digging into her back. "Demons?"

Violet lifted her head from his shoulder, pulling away. Cold snaked between the heat of their bodies, but there was nothing for it. She had dipped into this daunting well of the past and was not about to turn away from it now.

Her fingertips went lightly onto his chest, pointedly tracing a long, curved scar. What had torn his skin, she couldn't imagine—didn't want to imagine. Yet she realized the need in the moment. She needed to ask. And he needed to tell her.

"I need to know something, Theo. Anything—something—of you that you do not tell me. What happened to you in those years since we last knew each other? Give me something to make this real—something to trust. Something real of you. Something that makes me believe you won't disappear on me."

"Disappear on you?" His eyebrow cocked as the hard line of his jaw softened. He lifted his hand, tucking back a lock of hair that had fallen along her face. "You say you trust me, Vee, but is that a lie?"

"No—I do trust you." She looked to the side, staring at the smooth curve of the top bar on the back of the bench. "But this is where I lose myself, Theo. I trade this—passion, feeling—for rational thought. I have been an idiot before. I have been humiliated before."

"Your husband?"

She nodded, not able to look at him.

He reached to the left, grabbing her robe from the bench and then setting it about her shoulders, tugging the sides of it forward to ward off the growing gap of cold between them. "He is why you don't trust in my intentions, even in this moment?"

Her look slid to meet his blue eyes. She nodded.

His voice dropped to a growl. "What in the hell did he do to you, Vee?"

She took a deep breath, expelling it after a long moment. "Aside from spending every last coin of my inheritance and leaving me in a heaping mound of debt—all of it, without my knowledge?"

His arms slipped under the fabric of the robe and around the sides of her, pulling her closer to his body. "There is more?"

Before he could flatten her against his bare torso, she curled forward to rest her forehead on the dip along his breastbone. Hiding. She couldn't tell him this to his face. Couldn't watch the pity form in his eyes. Couldn't bear to see him think her a fool.

But he had right to know—she couldn't expect him to trust her with his past if she wasn't willing to do the same.

She inhaled, buoying her words as her fingers folded into tight fists resting on his abdomen. "Malcolm told me he loved me every single night he was in residence at Vandestile Manor with me. He would take me to bed and make me feel it. And because he did that—because my body would feel it, I trusted him. I was blind to things I should not have been. Blind to lies. I believed him when he said I was the only woman he would ever desire. The only woman that knew who he truly was. The only woman that could please him. The only woman that would ever hold his heart. I believed all of it—never questioning the money, never questioning his love, never questioning his long disappearances. Then he died and within days the creditors came pounding on my door. Two weeks later, his mistresses appeared at Vandestile Manor—three of them—together, a band of vicious malkins, demanding I settle his debts with them as well. In my home. His mistresses."

"Bastard." The muscles in Theo's stomach clenched, hard rocks beneath her fists.

"I am not stupid. I know how common mistresses are amongst the ton. But that wasn't us. It couldn't happen to me. My life was perfect and my husband loved me and only me." Her head shook against his chest. "He had told each one of them he loved her. They told me that—told me to my face. And I knew they were telling the truth—I could see myself in each one of them. That was when I realized he never loved any of us. I was just the unfortunate one that was fool enough to believe him—a humiliation like no other."

"Double the bastard."

"That—listening to those women—that was when true devastation fell upon me. Everything I ever believed of my life was a lie." Her fingers uncurled, stretching to flatten along the hard lines of Theo's stomach, needing to hold onto the stability of him to ground herself. "Those—those were dark days—that was when Adalia found me."

"What he did, his lies—that was his failure as a man, Vee. That failure is not yours."

"But I believed him." She kept her face hidden, burrowed into his chest. "It was so easy to believe him—to *want* to believe him. To never question. To shut my eyes. As long as I was satisfied and happy and I heard the right words, I believed in his carefully constructed world of deceit. That is what he gave me as a husband—a sinfully wonderful life wrapped in lies. But he never gave me more than that. Nothing of himself. Nothing real. I knew nothing of him but his lies." She paused with a deep sigh. "And that is how I lose myself. How I lost myself. I am incapable of finding ballast enough to recognize truth from deception."

She stopped, having to drag air into her lungs. Her next words escaped as she exhaled, more to herself than to Theo. "It—being with a man, believing a man—is something I swore I would never do again because I cannot trust myself to discern truth from falsehoods."

His fingers along her lower back flinched with the words, the pads of them pressing into the muscles lining her spine.

Silence was the response. Long breaths, his chest rising and dipping under her forehead.

"This one." His left hand moved to squeeze between them, just under her downturned face, and his forefinger ran along a thin, ridged line of white puckered flesh spanning his ribcage. "This one came from a French colonel that had just sent a sword through the first one of my men to die on the continent. My man that died—no, he was more of a boy, Phillip was—he was young and had a sweet face that could charm the stoniest of women. He spoke flawless French. After we had identified her, Phillip had been the one to approach the colonel's daughter on her way back from the market in the village next to their encampment."

Violet lifted her head, pulling back from his chest as she stared at the scar.

"Phillip bumped into her every day for fourteen days before she was swayed enough to pay him any mind. She had thought him just a traveler, or maybe a local boy. He charmed her. Brought her sweets. Until eventually, Phillip was invited into their house. A month went by, and he managed to collect correspondence on attacks and plans of armaments from the colonel's house, sneaking into the man's study when he wasn't there. Until one day when Phillip didn't show up at our rendezvous point to pass along the information. The boy was always on time. Always. So I went to the colonel's house and made it into the study just as the man was driving a sword straight through Phillip's chest."

Violet's eyes lifted to find an iron mask etched onto Theo's face, holding hard against memories brutally painful to recollect. Though he was still, under her fingers Theo's skin throbbed with every heartbeat, the horror manifesting in the blood pounding through his body.

"I watched the boy drop. He was a little brother to me—a spy, yes, and we knew the danger—but he was the youngest of my men and I had to watch him drop. Watch the blood flow from him. It came so fast. I stood, frozen, a statue. I could not move. Could not go to him. Could not defend myself. Then the colonel turned to me, his sword arcing. I was dead—should have been dead—save for his daughter pushing me out of the way. But his blade still sliced my ribs and I went down. At her interference, the colonel screamed, lunging at his daughter. It was the last thing the man did. She killed him. That girl, her hair in braids—young and innocent—with one quick jab of a dagger up into his neck, killed him. Her own father. Callous. Before he even hit the ground, before he took his last breath, that girl walked out of that room, never looking back."

He closed his eyes, the only crack in his facade of stoic calm. "It was then that I realized the world had gone mad. A world I didn't understand. I was trained for espionage. But even with that, I was not trained, not equipped for death—real, true, brutal, messy death. I didn't understand it, but I knew I had to figure out a way to survive it. So that was the moment—when I was lying on the floor, bleeding, watching the last breath of Phillip—that I stopped feeling. After Alfred's death, after leaving you, that was it. I could take no more. That was the last time I allowed myself to care about anything. It was easy to become merciless, cold—all because I lacked the ability to feel."

"Theo…"

His blue eyes opened to her. "Until I was splayed on the floor of that room at the Revelry's Tempest and I looked up, and you were kicking me, Vee. That was the moment that something in my chest moved again."

His left hand lifted, moving up to cradle the side of her face. "I know I cannot put the responsibility upon you for being my anchor—for being the reason I am coming alive once more. It is something I cannot burden you with. But I needed you to know why I don't want to let you go. Why I don't want you to let me go. I am not going to disappear on you, Vee. I am not going to lie to you. This is real."

Her breath lodged in her throat, her head nodding before words could form.

He had done exactly what she needed—given of himself. As painful as it had been, he had done it.

Her hands went to the sides of his face, her right forefinger aligning with the scar cutting away from his eyebrow. "Thank you. I did not realize how very much I needed that."

He closed his eyes at the touch of her hands, his chest lifting in a deep breath. When he opened his eyes to her, a soft smile had lifted the corners of his mouth. "And I do not ask this of you now, Vee, as it may take you ages to truly trust that I am not about to vanish or demand control over your life or take your money. But the moment you say you are ready, I intend to marry you, if you will have me. Even if it takes until we are eighty and we can no longer walk or hear or even see each other, I will wait."

"Theo—"

"No. Unless your next words are 'I am ready,' then I need no more words on the matter, Vee. I am an inordinately patient man."

She smiled. "Patient? That was not one of your qualities years ago."

"Yes, well, I have learned a few things since the innocence of youth, Vee."

"Yes, you have." Her head tilted slightly to the side as she studied him. "And I may need to depend upon that very thing, Theo."

{ CHAPTER 13 }

"You have been glowing these past two days since you have returned from Glenhaven, Violet." Cassandra walked into the office at the rear of the Revelry's Tempest ballroom and sat down in a ruby-hued upholstered chair across from Violet.

Violet looked up from the contract with the magician set to perform at the gala, unable to contain a smile at Cassandra's words. "It shows so easily?"

"You are humming as you are looking over the performers' contracts. I have never known you to hum in this room." Cassandra's eyes narrowed. "For that matter, I don't think I've heard you hum since you were eighteen. Maybe in the garden I have heard it once or twice—but that could have just as easily been a songbird."

Violet chuckled at the teasing. "I must clamp down upon my smiles. Not a person is going to take me seriously if I evoke the silly blush of a young miss."

"Well, I enjoy it." Cassandra waved her hand in the air, her normally soft voice excited. "Go ahead and hide it from others if you must, but I hope it does not wane. I would have you humming and happy over somberness any day of the year. If I had known this would be the outcome, I would have dragged Theodore to your feet a year ago when he was here and duped me out of those markers while you were away visiting Adalia."

"I don't know if that would have worked a year ago. But now…" She paused, her smile turning serious.

"Humming seems to be a very attainable task since my trip to Glenhaven."

"I had thought never to see it, so I am happy for it."

Genuine happiness for her shined in Cassandra's eyes, so much so, that Violet could not hold her secret any longer.

"He wants to marry me, Cass."

Cassandra's head jerked, a frown overtaking her face. "When did this happen? What did you say?"

"At Glenhaven. Before we left. I did not answer him."

Cassandra sat straight, scooting forward on the chair. "And you are just telling me of this now?"

Her right cheek scrunching upward, Violet's lips drew inward. "I know. I am sorry. But I had to let it sit in my mind—it had to be mine alone for a few days. I was not sure how to react. You know my past. You know how this would be the last thing I would ever consider again."

Cass leaned forward, her eyes earnest. "But it is Theodore."

Violet nodded slowly. "It is Theo. And that is all the difference."

"So…what next?"

"I do not know."

Cassandra sighed, her head shaking. "Well, this will require further discussion—and at length, but at the moment, we do not have that time as the creditor and his associate are in the drawing room."

"Mr. Olston?" Violet's eyebrows drew together. "He is a half hour early. And he brought an associate?"

"Yes. A female. It was a bit awkward as his arrival interrupted my meeting with Logan. We were discussing the four additional men he has hired for security on the night of the gala."

"The four—they are well trained?"

"To my standards?" Cassandra pointed at herself. "Yes. As to Logan's standards—let us just say he is going to be working with them for long hours during the next two weeks."

Violet collected the smattering of contracts strewn in front of her into a neat pile, setting them on the edge of the desk. She picked up a leather folio and stood. "I will go down and meet with Mr. Olston, then."

"Good luck, though I doubt you will need it. Mr. Olston does find you fascinating—that is probably why he is early. It is almost embarrassing to listen to him gush on about you." Cassandra nodded at the contracts on the desk. "Did you manage to get the set of three leopard cubs from the Tower Menagerie? I am most excited about them."

Violet tapped the papers as she walked around the desk. "The keeper said it was odd—wanting a set of three. He wanted to charge a premium for borrowing more than two."

"But it is a third anniversary gala—of course we need a set of three. Everything will be in sets of three."

"Which is what I told him. It is quite obvious." Violet's eyes went to the ceiling with a shake of her head as she walked past Cassandra. "The man proceeded to look at me like I had suddenly started talking with a forked tongue."

"Shall I draft a letter to the keeper explaining the necessity?"

"Yes, if you would. You are much more delicate about these matters when it comes to reasoning with smugness such as his."

Cassandra chuckled, standing to move around the desk.

Violet paused at the door. "Did Mr. Olston mention the name of his associate?"

"Mr. Olston mumbles, which is why I am sure Mr. Walt gave me a look of panic when he announced their arrival. It may be Lady Tiple or Toplan or Teppton—or something of the like. I would ask for her name again."

"So curious." Violet nodded, straightening her simple blue muslin dress as she moved through the doorway and toward the exit of the ballroom. She set her shoulders straight, steeling herself for negotiations. Why Mr. Olston would bring an associate she had never heard of to the meeting was unnerving.

Regardless, it was time to convince Mr. Olston she would be able to satisfy a ten thousand pound loan within a month. She had never dared to extend herself this far into debt and it unnerved her.

But there was no other option.

She needed this gala over and done with. Then…then she could consider the matter of marriage. Consider the merest possibility of it.

~ ~ ~

Barely able to contain his gait, Theo strode across the ballroom at the Revelry's Tempest, dodging the empty gaming tables, his boots clicking on the wooden floorboards.

He had learned in the past two days since they had been back in London that Violet spent an inordinate amount of time in her office off the back of the ballroom. So much so, his worries about her working too hard would be founded if he also didn't know how easy it was to persuade her to take a break.

On the desk.

In an upstairs withdrawing room.

Against her bookcase of ledgers.

He smirked to himself.

Violet was masterful at taking breaks. And he was masterful at convincing her to take them.

If only he could persuade her to spend her nights in his bed. She had steadfastly refused since they had arrived back in London. She maintained she needed to keep a sheen of respectability about her reputation, and popping in and out of her lover's townhouse did not fit particularly well with that objective.

Cassandra suddenly appeared in the doorway of the office, peeking out into the ballroom. "Oh, Theodore. It is you. I heard footsteps."

Of all his sister's friends, Cassandra was the most striking—with her dark, almost black hair and porcelain skin—and also the quietest. His sister had always contended that Cassandra was the exact opposite of quiet when alone with friends. But Theo had only experienced Cassandra as the painfully quiet one, so much so that one rarely knew she was in the room. As far as he understood it, she had married

Lord Desmond at a young age, and her husband had been in India for the last five years.

Theo pointed past Cassandra's shoulder. "Is Violet here?"

"She is, but not up here. You must have walked by her in the lower drawing room."

"The door was closed." He started to spin around.

"She is meeting with Mr. Olston, the creditor."

He turned back to Cassandra. "So I should not interrupt is what you are telling me?"

She offered a half smile, almost nervous. "I do think patience might be in order."

His eyebrows cocked, his head shaking. "I have been attempting to draw upon my patience more than usual as of late."

"Violet?"

He nodded.

"She has been extraordinarily happy since returning from Glenhaven." A beaming smile took over Cassandra's face. "I might guess it is because she has secured with you the mine as a guarantee for the loan, but I actually think it has much more to do with you, Theodore. So I am grateful for the smile you have put on her lips."

Theo looked at Cassandra, studying her face, her warm brown eyes. That was the largest amount of words she had ever spoken to him. "Thank you, I think." He looked back over his shoulder at the doorway. How long would Violet's meeting last?

"Are you about to slip?"

Cassandra's words were so soft spoken—as she always had been—Theo had to replay the words in his mind several times before he was sure he heard them. He looked back to her. "What?"

"Are you about to slip again, Theodore? I have watched you—just the same as Violet and your sister—descend from the man we all knew five years ago into the despicable cod head that has acted in no better regard than a brooding, embarrassing boor during the last two years."

Theo blinked hard, his head shaking as he looked her over again. Cassandra was the quietest woman—he would have guessed she had never uttered most of the words she had just used. Of course, she was incredibly close to Adalia, and his sister had never learned to curb her tongue. His own—not to mention Caldwell and Alfred's—fault, as Adalia had parroted all of them since she had begun talking.

"Do not just look at me with buffoon idiocy." Cassandra stepped away from the office doorway, stopping in front of him. "Do you intend to slip again? Or are you going to attempt to be the man that Violet needs? You have apparently done well at the task in the past fortnight, I will allow you that. But I fear it is fleeting and will not continue. According to Adalia, your path has been…arduous, misguided since the war."

Maybe Cassandra had always been incredibly quiet because she was incredibly rude. He glared down at her. "That is hardly your concern, Cassandra."

"It is my concern, as I need preparation time."

"Preparation for what?"

"Should it become necessary for me to help Violet through the downfall. I am not as bold as your sister is, Theodore, and I will need time to prepare."

"You are not making any sense, Cassandra."

She sighed. "Adalia always knows what to say to help people move past an emotion in the moment. To move their minds to other things. Words like that do not come as easily to me—especially in a demanding situation."

"Demanding—as in I fail Violet in some fashion?"

"Yes. Exactly. So I would like time to prepare myself."

Theo threaded his arms together over his chest. "You don't need to prepare a blasted thing, Cassandra. I love Violet."

Cassandra's head jerked backward. "You do?"

"Yes. And I'm doing my damnedest to be the man she deserves."

"Theo?" Violet's voice preceded her turning the corner from the hallway into the ballroom.

Theo spun to the entrance.

A smile broke wide on her face at seeing him. "Good, you did not leave. I saw you walk by the front window and I heard the front door close, so I was not positive if you stayed or not. I was just meeting with the creditors." Walking into the ballroom, she stopped next to Theo, looking to her friend. "Cass, will you please finish with them? I told them you would be down. All seems in order. Mr. Olston did not fluster at all on the amount. I looked through the terms of the credit, but I would appreciate your keen eye upon it as well, please. Then they will just need to verify the validity of the mine."

"Of course." Cassandra glanced at Theo, giving him a curt nod.

He inclined his head to her.

Watching Cassandra exit the room, Violet glanced back and forth between the two of them. She waited until

Cassandra's footsteps retreated down the hallway before looking to him. "What did I interrupt?"

"Nothing."

"I thought Cass was going to trip and shatter into a thousand pieces she was so stiffly rigid."

"She is ensuring my sister's usual role is fulfilled."

"Which role is that?"

"Protecting her friends. And Cassandra is doing a sufficient job at it."

"People tend to underestimate Cass, mostly because her voice is so soft." Violet's look went to the doorway Cassandra had disappeared from. "But she is made of steel."

"I just found that out."

Violet's gaze swung to him, a grin playing on her lips. "Did you convince her you are worthy of me?"

"No." He met her violet-blue eyes. "But I have yet to convince myself of that fact."

She chuckled, dismissing his words as she slipped her hand into the crook of his elbow. "Posh. I don't think you truly believe that. I know I don't believe it." Tugging at his arm, she started walking toward the office.

He followed along. "How was your meeting with Mr. Olston?"

"Good. Many questions were asked, but I think they believe me about the validity of the mine. They were most impressed that I was below ground and saw the vein with my own eyes—though I left out the part about my complete loss of sanity." She gave him a smirk over her shoulder. "They do want to meet with you or your solicitor before they sign the note."

"They?"

"Mr. Olston has an associate—a woman—who has been eager to invest in an opportunity such as this. She may be quite useful in the future for the Revelry's Tempest. The worth of my bank can be volatile, depending on the action on any given night. So I am beginning to see the advantages of having several sources of credit." Stepping inside the office, Violet spun in front of him, settling her hands onto the ridges above his hip bones as she looked up, her eyes sparkling. "But even more important, how did your meeting go with Baron Telliton?"

A smile came to his lips. "You were right. He is a slippery eel. He attempted to dance his way around it, claiming it was such a long time ago and he was sure he paid it in full. But because you warned me, I pressed, and he looked at his books, and, lo, to his utter surprise, he hadn't paid the debt."

"Remarkable, Theo." She hopped a gleeful step, squeezing his waist. "I am so relieved that was discovered. Did he say how long it would take to gather the funds?"

Theo scoffed. "Two months."

"You did not let him get away with that?"

"No. I told him two weeks would be more than sufficient."

"I would have demanded one."

"And I am sure you would have gotten it." His hands wrapped along her shoulders. "But two weeks is fine. The funds will come in at the same time as the gala—from which I plan to steal you away at the end of the evening."

"Steal me away to where?"

"My bed. With the utmost discretion, of course. And then we can wake up in the morning with no pressures upon our shoulders. Just you and I, and whatever we decide we want for the future."

Her eyes opened wide. "That…that sounds like a dream, Theo. Like a dream I could have never concocted for myself."

He grinned. "Not a nightmare, I hope? Waking up next to me?"

She pinched his side. "No. Don't be obtuse. A fantastic dream. A particularly wonderful dream."

He leaned down, a taste of the curve of her neck too much for his lips to resist. How had he ever walked away from this neck last night? "I have missed you in my bed, Vee. I don't care for the fettered access I have to you here in London."

She pushed slightly on his chest. "You are far too adept at diverting my attention, Theo. So before you make me forget every task I have set out for the day, I have a question for you about the ledgers we brought back from Glenhaven."

He reluctantly released her, and she went to the bookcase that fully lined a wall of the office. She had asked to borrow Theo's most recent set of ledgers so she could go through them more closely. She thumbed through a number of volumes on a shelf, finally pulling free a red leather-bound ledger and turning to set it upon the desk.

"I found them in this ledger." She flipped open the cover and thumbed several pages inward.

Looking over her shoulder, Theo could see this ledger held the most recent accounting records of the estate.

She stopped flipping the pages and the tips of her fingers ran down a column of entries. "These names. I did not recognize them as their purpose is not noted, and I could not find them in earlier entries, but then I saw them in another book."

Her forefinger stopped under a name. *Louise Macintosh.*

Theo froze.

"This one and this one." She pointed to a name six entries down. *Gerald Heltren.* She looked over her shoulder to him. "But the other book is so odd. It gives no indication as to who these people are, and it uses odd markings and symbols I don't understand."

Theo stiffened, taking a step backward as he attempted to keep his voice even. "What book is it, Vee?"

"Oh. Let me get it." She turned and stepped to the bookcase. Bending slightly, she looked at the spines of the books on the shelf at her waist. She pulled a small, thin book with a worn black leather cover from the shelf.

The edges of the book were tattered, bent inward as if it had been flipped through endlessly.

Unmistakable.

She set the book on the desk next to the ledger and untied the leather strap holding it closed. Opening it, she splayed her fingers wide on opposite pages to hold it from closing. "I remembered the names from in here, and then I mat—"

"You have it?" The growl in his voice was uncontrollable. "Who in the hell said you could take this book, Vee?"

Her hand snapped away from the book as she jumped. Released, the pages of the book fanned in a wide arc. She spun to look up at him, her hand flattening against her belly. "I—I found it at Glenhaven with the other ledgers and I thought it may be important so I had it brought with the set. It looked recent and I—"

He pushed past her, making her stumble as he snatched the book from the desk and slammed it shut. "You had no right to it, Vee."

"What? Why are you snapping at me, Theo? You asked me to look again into the ledgers to see if I could find anything else that was missed—"

Turning from her, he tucked the book into an inside pocket of his tailcoat. "I didn't ask you to snoop into things that are not your business, Vee." He pierced her with a glare.

"Not my business?" Her face crumpled as if he had struck her.

The obvious hurt did nothing to dissuade his anger. "You cannot just sneak around my belongings and steal whatever piques your damn interest, Vee." He took a step toward the door.

"Wait, Theo. Why are you yelling at me?" She reached out and grabbed his forearm. "What is in that book? Who are those people?"

He shook her grasp from his arm. "I said it was none of your damn business, Violet." He whipped from her, stomping out the office door.

Blinding red clouding his vision, he made it out the front door of the Revelry's Tempest and to the street within seconds. His legs shaking, running.

Away.

He needed away.

How in the hell could she take the book? Look at it? Who in the hell did she think she was to demand right to it?

Away.

He needed away.

{ CHAPTER 14 }

Twelve blocks passed before his lungs were near enough to exploding that his legs stopped.

Staggering to a brick wall for support, he bent over, clutching his knees as he gasped for breath.

Without thought, without even knowing he had been sprinting down the street, he found himself finally pulling his look upward. Where the devil was he?

He couldn't orientate himself with the dreary sky—clouds covering the city so thick he had no hope of finding the sun. Just buildings. Row houses surrounding him.

Rage still palpitating in his blood, he huffed, coughing, the air not making its way into his lungs fast enough.

What was Violet thinking, taking his book? What the hell was she doing stealing away the one tangible hold he had onto sins of the past?

A carriage roared past in front of him, a yellow phaeton with matching white speckled mares far too enthusiastic for the inexperienced young dandy attempting to control them. The horses swerved, one stepping onto the pavement and almost crushing a coal heaver busy with his work.

The coal heaver jumped, scampering out of the way as he shook his shovel, screaming unintelligible blasphemies at the fop.

Idiot man. Driving a team of horses he had no idea how to control.

Theo shook his head.

Idiot man.

The two words repeated in his mind. Taunting him. Turning on him.

Idiot man.

A third time, repeated.

Repeated for a reason.

He was the exact same thing. *Idiot man.*

He couldn't control Violet. Couldn't stop her curiosity. Couldn't stop her desire to help him. Especially when she didn't have a clue what that book meant.

It wasn't what the hell *she* was doing. It was what the hell *he* was doing.

Violet had taken one tiny step into his past, and he had needed to run. Away from her. Away from questions he couldn't bear to answer. Away from secrets that were his alone to bear. Away from admitting to atrocities he couldn't admit to himself.

She had ventured too close. Too close to his failings.

And he was a bloody coward.

He had seen it in her eyes as he had escaped the study. Her confusion. The turmoil on her face.

He was bloody well sinking a knife into the only thing that had brought him air in the last two years.

Violet.

An idiot—yes—he'd been that before. But a coward—never.

And he wasn't about to lose the last attribute he still possessed that held a modicum of honor.

He pushed off of the brick wall to stand straight, a breath hissing into his burning lungs.

Violet deserved more of him—expected more. And he wasn't about to disappoint her again.

If she became horrified at his words, if she cast him aside because of what he had to admit to, then he would suffer it. Truthfully, it was what he deserved. And he would walk into his fate with courage.

He started back to the Revelry's Tempest.

Fifteen minutes he walked, every breath bringing sanity back to his mind, every step buoying his confidence. At the end of the block that the Revelry's Tempest sat in the middle of, Theo's steps slowed as he watched an older man and a woman, both well-dressed, walk down the front stone stairs of the Revelry's Tempest and toward a waiting carriage.

A wide-brimmed black bonnet covered much of the woman's head, and just as she grabbed the hand of the footman to step up into the carriage, she paused, looking to the street, her face unobscured.

The devil take him to hell.

Not Fiona.

It couldn't be her.

Not the bloody ghost.

Theo broke into a sprint, but was too late to catch the coach. He veered up the stairs to the Revelry's Tempest instead.

Bursting through the front door before a footman could open it, he ran into Cassandra in the foyer, nearly knocking her over. Grasping for a limb of hers to catch before she fell, he managed to snatch a forearm and pull her upright.

With a gasp, she grabbed a hold of his wrist, steadying herself. "Theodore—"

"My apologies, Cassandra, but there is no time." Her feet steady, he released her. "Who just got into the carriage outside?"

"What? Who? I thought you were upstairs and—"

"Outside, Cassandra. They just came down the steps. Two people—who are they?"

"The creditor? Mr. Olston? I just finished meeting with him."

"No—the woman—who was the woman?"

"She is Mr. Olston's associate. She has funds readily available, and he thought she would be a good match with our needs."

"What was her name?"

"Lady Toplan." Cassandra's eyebrows drew together, perplexed. "Do you know her? They actually want to meet with you to audit the mine's output before we finalize the loan."

"When?"

"I do not know—"

Theo grabbed her shoulders, shaking her. "When, Cassandra, when?"

"Theodore, truly, you must calm." Her hands came up to knock away his arms, breaking his lock on her shoulders. "Today, tomorrow, they were not specific—they just said they would have an answer for us two days from now."

He jerked a step backward, realizing he was acting like a madman. "I apologize."

"What is amiss, Theodore?"

He shook his head. "Nothing. I need to talk to Violet."

Without waiting for a reply, he abandoned Cassandra in the foyer and ran up the stairs two at a time.

He stopped abruptly just outside the ballroom entrance.

He had to calm. He had to be sane.

Violet surely already thought he was addled after yelling at her about the book.

Three deep breaths to calm, and he turned the corner into the ballroom. Far to his right, Logan was in the connected drawing room talking in low tones with three of his guards. A quick nod in their direction, and Theo walked toward the office along the back wall.

He could hear Violet in the office, fingernails tapping methodically on her desk. She had to be looking at columns of numbers. She always tapped her fingernails when she was deep in ledgers.

His footsteps soft, he stopped in the open doorway. Her head was bent, her focus on the sheets in front of her, her left fingernails tapping, just as he had heard.

"I want to tell you, Vee." His words were rough, softly floating into the room.

He held his breath, waiting. It took her a long moment to look up from the desk.

She stared at him, her lips tight, silence thick in his ears.

"Not here, Vee." He looked over his shoulder, shaking his head.

"Tonight is a gaming night, Theo." Her voice was terse. "Guests will be arriving in a few hours. I cannot leave."

"Upstairs?"

Her blue eyes were waning, but her mouth remained set in a hard line.

He stepped forward as he fished his black leather book from inside his jacket. He set it gently on the desk, nudging it toward her with his forefinger. "Please, Vee. It is yours to study, if it makes a difference. I had no right to yell at you like I did."

She sighed, motioning with her hand to the door as she stood. "Let us go quickly, as I have much to attend to."

After grabbing the book from the desk, Violet stepped quickly around him, giving herself as much distance from his body as the office would allow. Theo turned and followed her, knowing full well he deserved her ire—her complete avoidance of an accidental touch from his body.

Up one flight of stairs, she moved to the left down the long hallway of private card rooms. At the third door, she turned into the room.

Walking into the card room, Theo recognized it immediately. The black fabric stretched tight over the large octagonal card table. The thick draperies along the far wall to match. Gilded gold sconces throughout the room for elegance. A full sideboard of the finest brandy. It was the room he had been gambling in—and losing horribly in—the night he ruined Violet's bank, decimating it with flips of his cards.

She stepped behind him, closing the door and locking it.

He turned around to find her standing with both hands behind her back, fiddling with the book.

"I am sorry, Violet."

Her bottom lip curved into a frown. She gave what looked like a quick nod as she moved past him, setting his book onto the card table. Her eyes lifted to him as she took a quick step backward, distancing herself from the table.

"Whatever is in that book, Theo, I want no part of it. I want to understand—but not at the expense of your anger. You yelled at me for no reason when I was merely trying to reconcile your numbers."

"You were trying to help. I understand that and it was unfair of me." His look darted from Violet to the book. It sat there, lonely on the table, a wart on the smooth surface for all to see. His fingers itched to snatch the book back, to hide it away, and he had to stomp down the urge.

He ripped his gaze away from it, his look landing on Violet. "So let me tell you, Violet."

Her arms crossed over her ribcage as her eyebrows lifted in question.

"Those names you saw—the ones that were in both books. They denoted payments to the families of men I owe debts to."

"What kind of debts?"

"The kind that I can never repay." His words came rough, dragging from his throat. "Those are the families of men that died under my command. Men that were killed for decisions I made. So the woman in the ledger you noted—she is one of the widows. The man—he was the father to one of the dead."

She pointed at the book with her head. "So this book—it is a book of amends?"

"So to speak."

"How many names are in here?"

"Many. The dead. Their relatives. Some of the men had large families they were supporting. Mothers and brothers and sisters and aunts and cousins. For many of those families, the death of their loved one and the loss of that income put them into bone-crushing poverty. I am attempting to rectify that. But I cannot do it all at once. I do not have enough. So I do it when I can, as it becomes available." He paused, shaking his head. "Always to them first."

She heaved a sigh. "Which is why you haven't had enough funds to reinvest in the mine."

He shrugged. "I have made these people destitute, Violet. It is what I can do. What I need to do."

"I understand, I think." Her frown deepened. "Yet why is this your responsibility, Theo? Thousands died in the war. All of those men knew the risks."

"Did they? Or were they looking to escape poverty? To support their families? Men are invincible when they are young and idealistic and there is nothing more noble than dying for crown and country. It is a nice sentiment. But I have sent too many men to be slaughtered to be able to hold tight to that idea of nobility. It is a hard thing to accomplish after hearing young men beg for life with their last breaths. Watch the horror in their eyes when they realize death has come for them. Men like Phillip."

Her lips parted, a slight gasp crossing her lips at his bitter words. Her eyes widening, she took a step toward him, her head angling to the side. "I didn't understand this before—but you think you're a monster, don't you, Theo?"

"I am a monster, Vee." His answer was immediate, leaving no room for forgiveness or delusion. "I knew time and again when I was sending a soldier into certain death—and I did it anyway. It wasn't on battlefields, masses of men scraping for life. It was one by one, man by man, my spies—friends, boys, fathers, brothers—into an inn, an alehouse, a stable, a market."

He paused, swallowing hard, forcing his words to continue. "Sacrifices had to be made. That was what I told myself as I would watch the heels of their boots disappear. That was always what I would watch—see last. Their boots. I would memorize their boots so I could identify them after the fact."

"And it has torn you in two."

His look dipped to the book. "So that—the book—those names—it is what I do. What I *have* to do. What I owe." His head shaking, his gaze lifted to her. "But you could not have known it—known the importance of the book. And I reacted. I had no control and you bore the brunt of that."

Her arms unfolded, her hands dropping to her sides. "You are not a monster, Theo."

His eyes closed, his head shaking against her words. "You do not get to decide that, Vee."

"No, but I do get to try every minute, of every day, to convince you of that fact."

He could feel her move closer to him.

"You are not a monster, Theo." Her hands went to his waist, slipping under his tailcoat.

"You don't know that."

She turned him, shuffling him backward as her hands moved up to slide off his coat. "Would I talk to a monster?"

The back of his thighs bumped into the card table. As much as he wanted to deny her, hold hard against her hands on his body, he could not do so. For he wanted even more so to believe her. To pretend that her words, her belief in him was warranted. Even if it was a lie he was allowing himself to be told.

"Would I talk to a monster?" she repeated, her fingers deftly removing his waistcoat.

"Vee…"

She pushed his white linen shirt up and off his body. "Would I touch a monster?" Her hands slipped down the front of his bare chest.

He shook his head, his eyes still closed.

"Would I press my body against a monster's? Let him touch me? Take him deep inside me?"

His head shook again, slow, fighting her words.

"Would I love a monster, Theo?"

At the corner of his eye, a tear escaped down the side of his cheek.

She moved upward, her breath dusting his chest, his chin, until she set her cheek alongside his, the wetness of the tear spreading between their skin. "Because I love you, Theo." She paused, her lips moving closer to his ear, her words wisps of air. "I love you, and I know in my soul you are not a monster. You are complicated and wounded and have the weight of unspeakable tragedies upon your shoulders—yes—all of that. But I know you. I know the man I once knew. The man before me now. And he is not a monster. He is the man that makes me feel when I had sworn to never do so again."

Her head slid backward away from his ear as her hands settled flat on his chest. "Look at me, Theo."

A deep breath lifted his chest, fortifying him against her words. He was a monster. He knew that. And it would only be a matter of time before she realized it as well.

"Open your eyes, Theo."

He opened his eyes.

She stared at him, the violet shards in her blue eyes darkened almost to blackness. "Hear me now, Theo. There was only one man that could have done what you did for me. Make me feel again. Real, heart gripping, soul rendering emotion. That man—all of him—everything in his past—everything that he now is—is the man I love. You are not a monster. You are the man I love."

Her fingers lifted from his chest, going to her hair to let the pins down out of her upsweep. Her hair unfurled, the long chestnut waves falling past her shoulders and down her back. Silently, her eyes never leaving his face, her fingers slipped under the edges of her dress, her chemise, and the mound of cloth puddled to the floor.

"You are not a monster, Theo. A man. Just a man." She took a step toward him, her fingers slipping under the band of his trousers, unbuttoning the flap and removing them along with his boots. "And you are going to prove it to me—prove it to yourself."

Her actions calm and smooth, only the ferocious brazenness in her voice betrayed what she needed from him. What she needed him to do. Do to her body.

His cock already straining at her naked body before him, her words lit the fuse she had laid when she stripped, no margin for feather kisses or sweet caress.

No. He understood this exactly as it was. As what it needed to be.

He rushed her, his right arm wrapping around her, pulling her backside up to slam her body into his. Her lips met his mouth with hunger. Raging, demanding hunger.

He spun, setting her backside on the octagonal card table, his tongue voracious in its appetite for her skin. Lips, neck, breasts, belly, and he went lower, tasting her for several strokes before she whimpered, yanking him upward.

Shifting her long onto her back, he moved onto the table, his knees pushing up on her thighs, opening her to him. He hovered for only an instant before driving himself deep into her wet body. Sliding in effortlessly, her body tightened around him only when he reached his hilt and started to withdraw. The core of her clasping upon him, begging him for the next stroke. Begging him for deeper.

Over and over and over. Her fingernails set hard into his back, savage as she provoked him onward. Faster. Deeper. Always deeper.

Her body arched upward, her breasts slamming into his chest as a garbled scream built in her chest.

He knew that scream. Knew it well.

He dropped his mouth to hers, capturing her as he rammed himself into her depths. The release, the contracting of her body was instant. The scream smothered in his mouth.

Her body clenched, seizing him, demanding he surrender.

Demanding he release.

Demanding he succumb to her words—he was just a man.

And the rest. The rest he had to let be.

He knew she was demanding all of that from him.

Begging it of him.

He let it go.

All of it.

He had to. For the one reason alone—she demanded it of him. Expected it of him.

And he would not disappoint her.

With a roar that expelled all of that from his body, he came, releasing himself.

Time, space, and his own body lost all meaning for long moments. Dead, alive, he could not decipher.

He hovered in the abyss until his breath suddenly sucked into his chest with a gasp, and his eyes opened. He realized he was squashing Violet into the table.

He instantly spun them, flipping her on top of him. "Hell, Vee, I crushed you." He forced the words out between frantic gasps for breath.

She lifted herself from his chest to look at his face. "It will take a touch more than that to crush me, Theo."

Her eyes searched him, studying carefully the pace of his breathing. Studying his soul, if he was to guess at it. It wasn't until his breathing slowed that her body eased from tenseness and she gave a slight nod to herself.

Her arms shaking with exertion, she dropped herself onto his body, her fingertips tracing the scars along his chest in front of her nose. "You have survived terrors I cannot even imagine. All these scars, and you were never broken, Theo. Not like I was. You humble me."

Watching her head bob up and down with each breath he took, he wrapped a strand of her chestnut hair between his fore and middle finger, staring at it as he curled and unfurled it over and over. "There are a thousand ways to break, Vee. And I did. I broke in ways that weren't obvious. In ways I will never understand."

"But you never sank…not like I did."

"No. But you also managed to do what I never could, Vee." The strand of hair slipped from his fingers and he snatched it back up, unwilling to free it quite yet. "What you did afterward, how you moved forth after your lowest moment—that was true courage. Courage most men would not have the mettle for. Courage I have lacked."

"I don't know if it was courage so much as a constant, gripping fear of ever being so numb, so distraught again, that I would believe my only option would be to give up." A shudder ran across her shoulders. "You must remember, I had Adalia and Cass to bring me back. To remind me of who I was. To force me to take each step until I could do it on my own."

His left arm tightened around her bare back. "And I thank the heavens for them every day for what they did for you."

"Theo, I know I said I couldn't be your anchor. But you must know I resisted it because I was afraid—afraid of everything with you. Of feeling again. Of wanting." Her face tilted up to him, her fingertips going to the line of his jaw. "If I remind you of who you are, who you can be, then I willingly take that responsibility. I will be your anchor. I had your sister. I had Cass. They were my anchors until I could be my own again. I will do that for you. I will remind you of who you are."

"But I don't want only that from you, Vee."

Her brow wrinkled. "No?"

"You said love, Vee." A smile curved his lips. "You said you loved me and now you cannot strike that from the world."

She chuckled. "I don't want to strike it, Theo. I want to live it." Her fingers slipped from his jaw to rest along his neck as she tucked her head back onto his chest. "What you said about the night of the gala—I want that more than anything. To wake up in your arms with a world of possibilities open to us."

The gala.

He stiffened slightly, kissing the top of her head in an effort to cover the motion. His hands casually settled flat onto the slope of her lower back. "Vee, that woman that was with your creditor, Mr. Olston—I don't want you to do business with her." He attempted to step lightly into it.

She perked up, setting her right fist on his chest and balancing her chin atop. "You saw her? You know Lady Toplan?"

"Lady Toplan, that was her name? Cassandra said that, but I wasn't positive I heard correctly."

"Yes. Lady Toplan. Do you know her, Theo?"

He didn't care for the concern that suddenly etched Violet's brow. He wanted it gone. Maybe he was wrong. Maybe it wasn't Fiona he had seen. He exhaled. "No. No, I guess I do not know the lady. Do not mind my imagination."

"Your imagination is bringing you into the past?"

"Yes." He shook his head. "Forgive me, Violet. I fear I will never be able to escape the past—I will always be drawn back to it—to the ghosts of the past."

"Ghosts?"

He sighed. "Of people long dead."

She moved herself up higher, balancing on the length of her forearms along his chest. "Theo, know what I ask of you. I do not need to know all that has happened to you in the last five years—nor will I demand to know."

She drew a long breath, her head dipping downward for long seconds, hiding from him. She lifted her look to him. "But I don't want you to live in the past that cannot be changed. I want you to live here, now, with me. Yet I also know you cannot forget the past. So if it creeps into our lives, into your voice, your actions—all I want is for you to tell me. Tell me it is not me. Tell me it is a ghost that has set your face to darkness and I will wait—wait for you to come back into the present. Just tell me you will not bow—not break under the weight of the past—and I will wait."

His throat constricted, a hard rock against any words he had, not that he could manage any.

He lifted his hand, wrapping it around the back of her neck and then drew her down onto his chest. It took a long minute before he could push words past his tight throat. "I need you, Vee. I need you with me tonight."

She nodded, her cheek rubbing against his skin. "I can get Cass to handle the gaming tonight."

"No. I don't want to come between you and your responsibilities. I will wait. Here. In your office. Upstairs in that mouse hole of a room if needed. I just don't want you in an empty bed. I don't want me in an empty bed."

His arm around her bare back tightened, a tremble going through his hand. He knew the hours alone in sleep—in the vast, dark lands between sleep and consciousness—offered little mercy to imaginations that could so quickly turn ugly. He needed her to ward against that. Needed to hold her. Needed to assure himself he was not imagining this—she was truly his, accepting him, scars and all.

She tilted her head on his chest to look at his face. "Yes. I think I overreacted when we first arrived here in London. The reality is no one bothers to monitor my whereabouts. I imagine a hood and cloak will get me in and out of the back entrance to your townhouse without issue? I will stay here through the first half of the evening, and if all is well, Cass and Logan can handle the rest of the evening's affair." Her hands slipped down to the sides of his torso, her light touch near to tickling as she lifted herself up to look at him straight on. "Theo…I don't ever want you to question this. I want you. And if demons come with you, ghosts of the past, then I accept them as well. You—all of you—is what I want."

"You have me, Vee. You have me." He lifted his left hand, cupping the side of her face. "And I will wait all night if I have to. Just as long as you are in my bed."

"I will be there."

{ CHAPTER 15 }

"I have been waiting for your appearance, Fiona."

"I imagine you have." Fiona Van Halverstin, now Lady Toplan, set her tea cup down and stood from the settee in the front drawing room of Theo's townhouse. She had helped herself to the tea he'd had readied for his meeting with Mr. Olston.

Turning to him, her green eyes, canny as always, swept across Theo where he stood in the doorway.

She had been a dead woman. Or so he had thought. Her neck for the noose, last he knew.

By the time word had gotten to him, she should have been dead.

Too late to save.

A ghost. One of the ghosts that had been haunting him for far too long.

He should've known she'd escape that fate. Fiona had always been able to escape anything. One of his best spies during the war.

And he'd been waiting for her since he verified hours ago just who Baron Toplan had married a year ago.

The three years since he'd last seen her had done her well. Her light blond hair swept softly into a sweet chignon under a tidy cap of black, she looked the part of the innocent. Heart-shaped lips that pouted on cue. Big green eyes with long dark lashes that could flutter, dripping of sexual innuendo.

That had always been her forte. Sex wrapped in innocence.

One of the most effective weapons in the wartime arsenal he commanded.

Maybe all of this was innocent. Maybe Fiona had moved on with her life after the war. Maybe it was happenstance that she was in his drawing room, drinking his tea.

Maybe.

For their past, for what she had suffered, he had to give her that benefit of the doubt. He owed that to her.

She took a step toward him, a cunning smile playing along her rosy lips. "I saw you on the street, Alton. I saw the second you recognized it was me coming from your lover's adorable little gaming establishment."

"Fiona—"

"The moment"—she shivered, her shoulders shaking in glee as her smile went wide—"let us just say it gave me chills. Old friends such as us—together again."

"Was it you by the coaching inn in Northampton as well? You at the Vandestile ball in Derbyshire?"

Her wide smile stayed in place, feigning confusion. "Me, in the countryside? You do know how I hate the countryside."

"I thought you were dead, Fiona."

"It is quite certain I am not."

"How did you manage to get to the Vandestile estate?"

"By carriage."

Theo held back from gritting his teeth. Once one of his closest confidantes in the war, Fiona knew each and every way to drive him to madness. Sweetly talking in circles did that very thing.

He spun around to shut the door of the drawing room, his eyes purposely avoiding the bottom step of the staircase where Violet had stopped to kiss him before she had left hours ago. Kissed him with such wanton prowess, he had been forced to carry her back upstairs—laughing the whole way—and delay her departure.

He pulled the door closed, the latch clicking as he paused to steel himself. He turned back to Fiona. "You know very well I could care less if you walked there. Tell me how you made it into that ballroom in Derbyshire, Fiona."

"I was invited."

"Were you stalking me?"

"Stalking you?" She laughed, her black-gloved hand landing on the flat expanse of her creamy chest. Her black dress was cut low, highlighting the long slope of her ample bosom. "Why do you imagine I would even know if you were alive, Alton? Last I was aware, you had disappeared, captive to Boney's Band of Vipers. The ball in Derbyshire was coincidence, nothing more. In fact, once I saw you there, I excused myself to my room. I did not want to chance bumping into you on the dance floor."

His right hand balled into a fist. "I don't believe you."

"Why is it always about you, Alton?" Her hand slipped off her chest, settling to her side. "Just as it was during the war—always about what you wanted—what you needed—what you ordered."

She took another step toward him, her green eyes searing into him. "Why do you believe you are still that important?"

In that moment, Theo knew without a doubt Fiona's appearance was anything but innocent. She had found him—sought him out on purpose.

Relaxing the fist at his side, he set an easy smile onto his face. "You don't make a move without a motive, Fiona. That is one of your outstanding traits—it always has been. How did you manage to procure an invitation to the Vandestile ball?"

"Are you asking how they could have possibly allowed a poor girl from the Cornwall countryside to walk into a ballroom of the aristocracy?"

His jaw shifted to the side and he nodded.

"I married well, Alton, after I made it back onto English soil. It was quite simple, actually, after all I learned in the war. Learned from you. Identifying the right elderly, rich baron to marry was the most difficult part of the process. But Baron Toplan turned out to be a gem of a man."

"I assume by your widow's weeds the baron is dead?"

"Nine months, now. He was a dear." A touch of sadness flashed across her face—sadness Theo would have believed if he didn't know Fiona so well. "And he did a healthy amount of business with the late Lord Vandestile, which was why I was invited to Derbyshire for the ball."

Theo stared at her, unwilling to speak, unwilling to add fodder to her tales of happenstance.

She gave an exasperated sigh, flitting her hand in the air between them. "You must get over yourself, Alton. I never knew what happened to you. You disappeared on us. Abandoned us in the middle of the war. So no, I was not stalking you. It was merely coincidence that we attended the same affair in Derbyshire."

He took a step toward her, using his height to his advantage as he glared down at her. "And now? How much of the past day has been a coincidence, Fiona?"

"Whatever do you mean?"

"The Revelry's Tempest."

"Ahhh." She nodded and then spun on her heel and went back to the settee. Settling herself on the edge of the cushion, the straightness of her back was faultless in its gentility. She picked up the tea cup she had set down on a side table and took a sip. Her look went to the front window, taking in the movement of the street for a long moment before her gaze shifted to Theo. "She is an interesting woman, Lady Vandestile. Resourceful. Smart. I enjoyed meeting her. I would actually admire her spirit were we in different circumstances."

Her words dripped with menace.

It sent Theo stomping across the room and he stopped in front of her, his fingers shaking, aching to throttle her. "Don't you even dare to speak her name, Fiona." His voice went vicious, his return threat just as explicit.

Unruffled, she took another sip of tea and met his eyes, a smile forming on her face. "Why not? I have been waiting an excruciatingly long time for you to care about something again, Alton."

Hell.

He had known it. Known it in his gut when he walked into the drawing room. Even though he wanted to deny it. She was here for him. Here for revenge.

"What in Hades are you about, Fiona?"

She looked up at him, her eyes narrowing as a wicked smile carved into the corners of her mouth. "Oh, I know you care about those twin nieces of yours and your sister—but they would never do. I don't hurt children. I don't hurt mothers." She nodded to herself. "So I had to be patient. You taught me that, Alton. You never thought I learned that lesson—at least to your standards—but I did. How to be patient and then deadly. And my patience has finally been rewarded with Lady Vandestile."

Theo's voice went deathly calm, not the slightest tip to any emotion. "That is where you are wrong, Fiona. You misunderstand my relationship with Lady Vandestile. The woman means nothing to me."

She chuckled, a coarse, bitter laugh. "Truly, Theo, you think to lie to me? Of all people?"

He shrugged. "I think you will need to be more patient if you intend to truly hurt me, Fiona."

"Hurt you? Did I give you that impression?" Her face went suddenly serene, innocent. "Well, then it is as you say. I will have to be more patient."

A knock came on the door just before it opened.

Theo's butler looked into the room, his eyes widening. "My lord—I apologize. I did not intend to interrupt. I believed Lady Toplan was alone in here awaiting the arrival of her partner."

Theo waved his hand. "It is fine, Fillmore. Mr. Olston has arrived?"

"He has. Shall I show him in?"

"Yes."

Fillmore disappeared, arriving back with Mr. Olston within seconds.

Fiona jumped to her feet, scooting in-between Theo and Mr. Olston with a bright smile on her face. "Mr. Olston, I have just introduced myself to Lord Alton. It appears I was early and I know it is not done, but I have been so excited about the opportunity to invest with Lady Vandestile that I must have confused our meeting time with Lord Alton." She stepped to the side, motioning to Theo. "But Lord Alton was incredibly gracious with me and entertained me until you arrived."

Mr. Olston smiled, smoothing the side strands of hair along his balding head as he nodded. "Very good, Lady Toplan." He looked to Theo. "I apologize if my associate has taken more time of your day than necessary, my lord. This is her first investment and she is eager for it to go well. I have cautioned her against acting without proper research."

"As you should, Mr. Olston." Theo's look landed on Fiona's profile—the woman once more a picture of innocence. "Lady Toplan would do well to properly research her next move."

"Yes, well." Mr. Olston glanced between the two of them. He motioned to the settee and side chairs. "Let us then review the documentation we have on your mine in Derbyshire, my lord. Lady Vandestile assures us it is currently undergoing exploration and a new vein has been found that will bring substantial income—her portion more than enough to satisfy the terms of the loan shall it become necessary."

Theo stepped back and extended his hand toward the settee with a slight bow to Fiona. "Of course. Let us review what is necessary, and then each of us can move on with our respective days."

He watched the grace with which Fiona went to her seat. Grace he himself had taught her.

A monster he had created. A monster he pitied. A monster now come for him.

A monster he owed.

That one thing repeated in his mind. He owed Fiona. Owed her his life on two occasions. Owed her for her unfailing loyalty to the crown during the war. Owed her for all she had given up during those days.

How truly addled was her mind? She always had danced on the line of sanity. He couldn't assume she would actually do harm. Yet he couldn't dismiss the very real risk.

And he couldn't break the code. Never reveal a fellow spy. The one thing that kept all of them safe.

Theo exhaled a seething breath. Above all, he couldn't chance the possibility that Fiona would go after the one thing sure to destroy him. Violet.

And Violet he would protect at any cost.

{ CHAPTER 16 }

"This one." Violet's eyes closed, pure bliss spreading across her face as her head tilted backward. "This is the one."

"That one? Which one is it?" Cassandra stretched over the round table in the empty ballroom of the Revelry's Tempest, picking up one of the seven silver platters that held a variety of twenty different bite-size tarts. "Did you pull it from here?"

Violet opened her eyes and pointed to the row of sugar-dusted berry tarts in the middle. "The three-berry ones. They are tart and sweet and melt like no other in your mouth. Raspberries, blackberries, blueberries and her crust is exquisite on this one."

Cassandra popped one of the tarts into her mouth. Her eyes went wide.

Violet chuckled, nodding. "I know. How has Cook never made these for us before? Plus, they are perfectly in theme with the three berries."

"I told her no expense was to be spared in coming up with the latest creations—maybe that was the key. It apparently allowed her to procure some ambrosia and grate it into the tart," Cassandra said. "I need another one to believe what I was tasting was real." She plucked another tart from the tray and slipped it into her mouth. "What spice is that? Not cinnamon…"

Violet took another berry tart from the tray, eying the remaining three of its kind. "Before we eat them all, we have to have Logan try one."

"Or not." Cassandra smirked. "Truly, Violet, he won't appreciate them—not like we will. He will swallow it without tasting it and then grumble a response, never acknowledging that heaven just fell onto his tongue."

Violet nodded. "I think you're right."

"Right about what?"

Violet spun in her chair at the sound of Theo's voice, an instant smile coming to her face. He was walking through the adjoining drawing room toward them. "Tarts Cook made for us to try—we are deciding upon what will be served at the gala. You need to try this three-berry one."

"Or you can refuse, and I can eat it instead," Cassandra said, grinning.

He looked to Cassandra as a strained smile came to his lips. "My tart is all yours, Cassandra." His gaze shifted to Violet. "Can I steal you away for a moment?"

Violet's smile faltered. Theo's face had not looked like that six hours ago when she had left his townhouse. No, she had left him in his bed, thoroughly devoured and with a thin sheen of sweat covering his skin. She had left him happy. Intoxicated in his exhaustion. She could barely move her own legs enough to carry herself down the stairs and to the waiting carriage in the mews.

She nodded, brushing her fingertips together to loosen the crumbs before she quickly wiped them on a napkin. She looked to Cassandra. "You will tell Cook she has exceeded any and all expectations?"

"Gladly," Cassandra replied as she picked up an apricot tart. "I will just make certain there are no other contenders to that berry masterpiece. Hopefully not, as I am already near to bursting."

Standing, Violet followed Theo out the main entrance of the ballroom. He glanced over his shoulder at her. "In the garden? There is too much activity in here at the moment."

Violet shrugged, foreboding settling heavy in her chest. "Let me grab my cloak on the way."

Within a minute, Violet was stepping into the gardens at the back of the Revelry's Tempest, watching Theo's back with wary eyes. She tugged the front of her dark cloak tight around her chest, a chill settling into her bones. A snap of springtime cold had descended in the past day, and she was already missing the sun they had been granted in the countryside.

"They will bet on anything here, won't they?" Theo asked.

"What?"

He pointed to the plant box on his right as he moved past it. In a row, the early sprouts of beans stretched upward in a straight line. Each sprout was marked with a name and a wager on how many beans would eventually grow on the plant.

"Yes. That one was Cass's idea and it was a splendid hit last summer. Grasshopper races will be the new garden game this year." Violet shook her head, dismissing the silliness of it, and her look centered on the back of Theo's head. "What is it, Theo? I don't think you brought me out here to discuss bets on beans."

He kept walking silently, only stopping once he was in the far back right corner of the garden, tall evergreen hedges creating a nook about them. As secluded as one could get here at the Revelry's Tempest without going into a private room.

He wanted to talk to her privately, but not so privately that he was willing to go into an upstairs room with her.

Her heart started to thud hard, even as she tried to slow it. This was silly. She was imagining the worst—going directly to catastrophe when Theo probably just wanted to talk to her about the mine, or the loan, or something else of minor consequence. There wasn't anything they couldn't overcome together—it had taken a tremendous battle within her own mind on that front—but she was now sure of that one fact.

Slowly, he turned around to her. His light blue eyes looked dull, his movements slow. Was he drunk? No. His gait had been normal. Or had it?

She attempted to force her most optimistic smile onto her face. "What? What is amiss?"

"I…" The one word slipped out of his mouth, rough, dissolving into nothingness.

She took a step toward him, grabbing his forearm. "Theo, what is wrong?"

Her words jarred him, a quick jolt running through his entire body. It focused his eyes and he looked at her chin, avoiding her eyes. "I cannot continue this any longer, Violet. This farce between us. We must stop what we have so foolishly started."

Her fingers tightened into the muscles on his arm, his words filtering into her brain, seeping their way past instant disbelief. "What is wrong, Theo? Why—what are you saying?"

"We are done, Violet." The brisk words snapped into the air between them. His blue eyes lifted to meet hers, steel resolve vibrating in his look. "That is what I am saying."

Her hand jerked off his arm, her body reacting where her mind would not. "No—what has happened, Theo? Something must have happened." Her hand lifted to touch him again, but halted in midair, hovering in the space of nothing.

"Not a thing has happened, Violet. I now have clarity. Clarity that has previously eluded me."

"Clarity?"

"How every step I've taken in my life has nudged me, bit by bit, further away from you. I was a third son. Not worthy. Nudge. I left for war. Nudge. Atrocities I committed in that time, again and again. Nudge, nudge. I ruined your bank. Nudge. I yell at you. I disappoint. Nudge. Nudge. Demons that refuse to release me. Nudge." He shook his head. "It is unfortunate that I let us believe in this for even a moment. But I cannot fight it anymore, Violet. How many nudges, how many steps away from you do I take before I can finally admit that I am not worthy of you? While the one that suffers from my weakness is you."

"Do not even think to say you are not worthy of me, Theo."

A chuckle escaped him in a brittle guffaw. "That is a lie I want to believe. So I do—I did. You said it, so I believed it. But no more. It is a lie I cannot cling to any longer. I am stopping this—us—now."

His last words—so vehement—made her gasp and stumble a step backward, her slippers crunching into the granite gravel of the pathway. "You…you cannot. Not after you…you said you loved me…you wanted the future." She shook her head, her gaze dropping to the ground between them as her chest tightened, painfully seizing her next words before she could speak them.

"Just because I love you, Violet, does not mean I should have you." His black boots shifted on the gravel, his stance widening. "I have faced the harsh truth of it. A truth I was attempting to deny." The harsh timbre in his voice softened, his words going faint. "I have lost the will to change, Vee. To want more. The last fortnight with you—it was a dream I was touching, hoping for. But that's what it was, and I realized it today."

"When? What happened? I left you this morning—happy—you were happy. So…when?" The effort it took for her to lift her eyes to him exhausted every raw fiber of pride within her, for she knew her soul was bared at the moment—that he could see the destruction he was manifesting.

But she had to look at him. Had to see it in his face. She wouldn't believe it otherwise. A tear—fat and rude and despised—rolled from the edge of her left eye without warning.

"Right before you woke up in my bed this morning. I watched you. And you…you were beautiful, Violet. You were everything I ever wanted in life and knew I could never have." He stopped, taking a breath, his chest rising high.

For a brief moment, she wondered if he would go on.

His mouth set into a grim line. "Sleep had you—and peace was on your face. I knew it then. You possessed a peace that I would never have again. It was so clear in that moment."

"Don't say that, Theo."

"Say that I will never have that peace? That my pain will always hold you back—drag you under with me? It is the truth, Violet."

"But I never asked you to be at peace, Theo. I only asked you to be with me—demons and all. And you are letting them break you. Break us."

"I am already broken, Vee."

"No." She stepped toward him leaving no space between them. "Don't make me give up on you, Theo."

Pulsating with defeat, but unwavering in conviction, his blue eyes met hers. A sad smile curved the edges of his lips, his voice a whisper. "Give up, Vee. Give up. Don't try to fix me. You cannot do it. Just give up."

His words stole her breath. For long seconds, she could only stare at him.

Stare and let his words hang between them.

And then she snapped.

"Bastard." She took a breath deep into her lungs, vile taking a hold of her tongue as she lifted her chin and stepped backward. "Good riddance to you, then. I actually only wanted the guarantee of the mine from you, Theo. I knew I would have to trade myself for it. And since I now have it in writing, you are correct. Now is as good a time as any to break ties. You do me no good with your morose ramblings."

He cringed, her words cutting. "Don't do that, Vee."

"Do what?" Her shoulders snapped back, her right hand smoothing the front of her peach dress. "You were the means to an end, Theo—nothing more. You served your purpose well. I do thank you for that."

His head lifted and then dropped in one slow nod, his eyes flickering away for a second, and then landing hard on her. "Then you have exactly what you need, Violet. I wish you the best of luck."

She gave him a curt nod, her hand flinging out, motioning to the back gate.

Without another word, Theo turned from her, walking along the back pathway and out the rear gate.

And then he was gone.

Gone.

Violet stood in the back corner of the garden, still, her hand frozen to her belly, for long minutes.

How could she have possibly let this happen to her again?

She was so happy hours ago, minutes ago. And then this, out of the depths of nowhere.

It was the one thing she had sworn—to never allow herself to be in this position again. To let a man take a hold of her so hard that she could be destroyed so easily.

She had failed again. Miserably.

And the devastation happening within her—her body seizing up, piece by piece crushed, smashed under the weight of the pain—was her reward.

She fought to stay upright. To keep the shell of her body from crumbling.

How?

How could she be so very wrong again?

How many times was she going to be a fool?

{ CHAPTER 17 }

Violet glanced up from the list in her lap to Cassandra. Her friend had been pacing, but now stood still with her arms folded over her ribcage as she stared out the front window of the second level drawing room at the Revelry's Tempest.

Cassandra had been standing there for minutes, looking down at the street as they went through a final list of things that needed to happen in the next four days before the gala. Cassandra's attention had only been half on Violet as she had been ticking off the list, line-by-line.

Violet sighed to herself. "Is he out there again?"

Startled, Cassandra spun to Violet. "You know?"

"I do." Violet shrugged and set the list down next to her on the cushion of the ivy-embroidered settee. They were nestled into the nook by the front bay window, the space too small for a gaming table, but large enough for two settees and four side chairs offering proper respite from activities. "Logan asked me if he should remove him from that open property across the street."

"What was your answer?"

"I told him we didn't have time for such nonsense." Violet's hand swooped through the air for effect. "We have only days until the gala. And I refuse to waste another thought on that man. There isn't a spare moment."

"Not a moment?" Cassandra's eyebrow arched.

"No. Not one." Violet ignored the disbelief in Cassandra's eyes—ignored everything that had to do with emotion, just as she had since she had pulled herself together and come in from the gardens eight days ago. "Does he look as though he is just passing by?"

"Why?"

"I have something to return to him." Theo's book of names still sat in her office. Left here more than a week ago when he yelled at her about it.

"I have no idea on his intentions out there." Cassandra looked back over her shoulder out the window. "After what you told me happened in the garden, I don't understand why Theodore has been down there, on and off, for the last eight days now."

"Days?"

Her face cringing, Cassandra looked back to Violet. "Logan didn't tell you that part?"

"No."

"Well, it has been days."

Violet shook her head, dismissing the news. What Theo now did with his time was none of her business. He had been clear on that fact.

She reached to the side table to pick up her cup of tea. "His actions seem most unnecessary."

"They do." Cassandra nodded. "Is he hoping for a glimpse of you?"

"He would do far better to hover around the alley if that was his goal, as he knows I always come and go by way of the mews."

"So why do you think he hovers?"

"I don't think anything on the matter. I cannot afford to." Violet took a sip of her tea, eyeing Cassandra above the rim.

"Well, just four more days, and then you can repay the loan to Mr. Olston and cut the last tie to Theodore. But still…his current behavior is odd. I thought he would stop after the first few days. Do you think he is worried about the portion of the mine he signed as the guarantee?"

"I have no idea what Theo hopes to accomplish out there. Nor do I care."

Cassandra offered a half-smile and turned back to the window to look down at the open property across the street. "I just don't understand how he could do this. That man loves you."

"What?" Her hand suddenly unsteady, Violet set the tea cup clattering to the side table.

"When we were young—Theodore adored you like no other man I had ever seen look at a woman." Cassandra's attention stayed on the empty property below. "It was never when you were talking or dancing with him—how he looked at you—it was when you didn't know he was watching."

"How? How did he look at me?" Against her own good sense—she acted the idiot by continuing the torture of the conversation—the question slipped out of her mouth.

Cassandra glanced over her shoulder at Violet. "Like you were his air."

Violet had to catch her breath. She shook her head. "That was five years ago, Cass."

Cassandra shrugged. "Yes. But it was also a week and a half ago, as well." She unfolded her arms, her right knuckles tapping on the lower frame of the window before she turned away to Violet. She walked toward Violet and sat on the wingback chair next to the settee.

"I never understood why he left five years ago—left you, Violet." Cassandra set her elbow on the arm of the chair, her fingers picking at the rolled edging of the indigo chintz covering. "Yes, his brother died. It was a tragedy. But to leave you at the same time…it just never made sense. You should have been the one he turned to after that."

A lump instantly formed in Violet's throat. She picked up her tea cup and took a sip. "He was…he was trying to protect me then."

"Protect you from what? You were an heiress. You were adored. A soon-to-be bright light of the *ton*. What did you need to be protected from?"

"Myself." Violet sighed. "He was a third son and he didn't want me to have to make the wretched decision my uncle was going to force upon me—Theo or my money."

Cassandra's nose wrinkled. "Your uncle is an arse."

Violet nodded.

"But Theodore—a fool. I know you well enough to know what you would have chosen if only he would have given you the chance."

Violet set her tea cup down on the side table. "But maybe not then—maybe Theo was right—maybe I wouldn't have chosen him. I was young. He was young. Neither of us knew what we were doing. Who we were."

Cassandra's eyebrows lifted in serious disbelief of her words.

Violet threw a hand up. "You are right. I would have chosen him." She shook her head. "And I lie to myself—we still don't know what we are doing—who we are."

Her head slanting to the side, Cassandra's look softened. "You flog yourself unnecessarily, Violet. Whatever Theodore's issues are, you are not to blame."

"But he is? As much as I blamed him all those years ago for leaving me when we were young, it turned out he was only trying to protect me."

The words were not out of her mouth for but two seconds before Violet jumped to her feet, rushing to the window. She scanned the barren property across the street, nestled between two townhouses. Construction on a new home had started eight months ago on it, and then had been abandoned before they had finished the foundation. She searched into the nooks and shaded corners. No Theo.

Why had she not considered this before?

She closed her eyes for a long breath. She was a fool for even thinking it. Or was she?

She opened her eyes, her look landing on the corner of the building next to the property where Logan had seen Theo leaning a day ago.

Theo had protected her all those years ago.

Was it possible he was protecting her today, as well?

If so, from what?

And did it even matter?

~~~

Of all the places Violet needed to be at the moment, standing outside a milliner's shop and waiting for her new friend had not been on her agenda.
~~~

Lady Toplan had stopped by the Revelry's Tempest earlier in the day, so excited about the upcoming gala that she asked if she could help with the preparations in anyway.

Violet was on her way to visit her goldsmith on Bond Street to give final approval on the souvenir markers she had commissioned for the gala, and Fiona had jumped on the offer to accompany her.

Aside from her generous loan, Fiona had become fast friends with Violet and Cassandra and had visited them regularly at the Revelry's Tempest during the past weeks, always willing to help in the fun of planning the gala.

The woman was fascinating to chat with. She had lived in numerous places all over the continent, and every story she told brought out a wanderlust in Violet that she didn't know she possessed. Location after location Fiona would expound on—all sights Violet would love to see someday, if she could ever find her way to leave the Revelry's Tempest for a spell.

But for as much as Violet liked her, Fiona was currently impeding on the hundreds of tasks she needed to complete that day.

Violet leaned to the left, searching past the display of hats in the front window of the shop to find Fiona. Fiona had promised it would be a quick stop to pick up her headdress for the evening of the gala, but now she appeared to be looking through a collection of feathers the milliner was showing her.

Foot tapping, Violet turned to watch the busy street, the people darting in and out between carriages and jostling down the pavement, and debated on whether she should dart in and excuse herself from waiting. Fiona did have a sizable investment in Violet's bank at the moment, and could make life extremely difficult for Violet if she chose to pull her funding two days before the gala. For Violet to gather the funds needed for her bank in the last hours before the gala would be near to impossible.

Violet glanced back into the shop.

No. Better to wait with a smile on her face. In all of her visits to the Revelry's Tempest, Fiona had always been more than respectful of Violet's time. She would be out soon.

A sudden hand gripping her arm and yanking her to the side made Violet yelp.

She stumbled a step before she could look up.

Theo.

Of course. No one else would so rudely manhandle her. She hadn't seen him. Hadn't heard word from him since he left her in the garden. There had only been the reported sightings of him hovering about the Revelry's Tempest.

And now he thought to accost her on Bond Street?

He hadn't shaved in a day or two. Dark circles were etched under his eyes. His clothes sat slightly rumpled on his frame. Heaven help her, he wasn't drunk and about to make a scene on the street in front of all of London to see, was he?

She jerked her left arm away, trying to escape his hand. His grip only tightened, tugging her along.

Her look swung around. He had pulled her away from the milliner's shop and a step into an adjacent alley.

"Violet—you cannot trust her." Theo's voice was gravelly, as though he hadn't spoken in days.

"Trust whom?"

"Lady Toplan."

"What? What are you talking about, Theo? Lady Toplan is a perfect dear—somewhat outlandish, but she makes me laugh and is fascinating. We have become fast friends and she is nothing but a sweet—"

"I need you to trust me, Vee." He shook her arm, emphasizing his words.

"Well, I don't." She reached up with her right hand, her reticule swinging, and tried to pry away his fingers. "You have absolutely no right to grab me in the middle of the street and make demands of me, Theo. I don't trust you at all."

"Vee." He paused, growling to himself as he shook his head. "Dammit, you have to listen to me—"

"I have to do no such thing. You ended us, Theo—you." Her hushed tone turned into a hiss. "So don't you dare try to insert yourself into my life now."

Theo suddenly jerked backward, dropping her arm as he drew himself to his full height.

For a moment, she couldn't figure him, but then she followed his look over her shoulder and turned around. Fiona had exited the milliner's shop and was looking back and forth along the street for her.

Fiona's head turning, she spotted Violet, and with a quick wave and a smile, came toward her. "There you are. I had thought for a moment I had been abandoned."

Violet tucked up under her bonnet a stray lock of hair that had fallen when Theo had yanked her along the pavement. She knew she was a sudden disheveled mess but did her best to set a calm facade onto her face. "I would not abandon you, Lady Toplan." She took a step backward, motioning to Theo. "I understand you met Lord Alton when you and Mr. Olston went to discuss the mine with him."

"Of course." Fiona inclined her head to Theo. "Lord Alton was very gracious in answering my many questions that day. I know very little about mines, but I was anxious to learn."

Violet chuckled, still trying to calm her clothing and rapidly beating heart. "Mines are not nearly as interesting as one might think they are. Suffocating to be exact."

Fiona's look swung to Violet. "Oh, now I remember you went down into Lord Alton's mine. I had forgotten you told me of that adventure."

"Adventure is a kind word for it." Violet dared a quick glance in Theo's direction. Whereas he had been brimming with fire and alarm a moment ago, he was now the picture of bored nonchalance. Remarkable. He was an expert at lying. How had she forgotten that fact?

She shook her head, stretching her smile wide as she looked at Fiona. "You are done? The milliner has your headdress ready?"

"He will. I wanted to change out several feathers, so it took a touch longer than anticipated. I apologize." She glanced back and forth between Violet and Theo. "And I apologize for this as well as I did not mean to interrupt a conversation."

"No. There was no conversation." Violet took a quick step to place herself between Fiona and Theo. "Lord Alton was just wishing us the best of luck on the gala. He is anxious to get his full title to the mine back."

"I imagine he is." Fiona nodded, her green eyes moving past Violet's head to look at Theo as a bright smile came to her heart-shaped lips. "Well, not to worry, Lord Alton. I am positive it will all be over in a few days' time." Her gaze shifted to Violet. "Shall we?"

"Yes." Violet stepped to the side, offering a tilt of her head to Theo. "Lord Alton."

He mimicked the motion, his blue eyes blank. "Lady Vandestile, Lady Toplan."

Violet was walking before he finished. She had never wanted to escape awkwardness as badly as she needed to in that moment.

Being in Theo's presence, his hands on her. It had turned her stomach upside down and sent her chest into spasms almost as horrific as she had suffered in the garden eight days ago.

She was done with him.

She had to remember that.

He was done with her. She was done with him.

Done.

Even if her body was intent on having a very different response.

~~~

Theo walked to the end of the block and then turned around, sliding into the inset open air vestibule of a butcher's shop. He watched Violet and Fiona walk away. Fiona jabbering on, her hands animated. Violet laughed.

He had made a drastic mistake.

Fiona hadn't believed him. She had seen right through his lies. She always had.
~~~

Even with proof—even though he had broken everything between him and Violet. Even though he had left her. Again. Proved that she meant nothing to him. Proved that harming Violet would not concern him in the slightest.

Fiona knew.

It had been a desperate gamble on his part—cutting Violet from his life—but he'd had no other option to deter Fiona. A gamble he had lost.

And the second he had removed himself from Violet, Fiona had swooped in. True to form. True to her expertise. True to everything he had taught her during the war. She was a spy of the highest order. A deadly spy.

And he had just inadvertently set that spy on the one person that meant more to him than anything.

His fist jammed into the brick wall behind him, drawing blood.

He had believed he was doing the right thing by leaving Violet. It was the best way to protect her from Fiona and the revenge he now knew she was after.

But he'd been wrong.

And now he was in no position to protect Violet.

He sighed, looking down at his bloody knuckles. Fiona had done it masterfully. Made him distance himself. And then wonder. Worry. Hover. Follow. Until he finally showed his hand on Bond Street.

Fiona had done all of it without a direct threat on Violet. And until she actually did threaten Violet, she was untouchable. She would always own the upper hand, for he had nothing to accuse Fiona of. He couldn't very well throw her into a cell for making a new friend. And Violet would never believe him about her. At least not until she trusted him again.

Such beauty in how Fiona operated.

His choices had dwindled to one.

There was no other way to protect Violet—truly his only chance to even possibly keep her safe—than to convince her to take him back. To convince her he had been wrong. That they belonged together.

Because they did. And not just because her life was very possibly in danger.

They belonged together, come what may. Come the fury of the damned.

But convincing Violet of that fact…convincing her to trust him again…

Now he just needed to accomplish the impossible.

{ CHAPTER 18 }

No. Not this.

Not when the night had been perfect.

Perfect on all counts.

The food. The entertainment. The fun. The betting. The mirth. The plump coffers. The laughter.

Success on every front.

Success Violet hadn't been able to enjoy.

She had been positive something was going to explode, upsetting the entire night. A performer not appearing. Undercooked food. Heavy losses for her bank at the tables. Out of tune music. Bitter losers. The newly concocted games of chance falling to disinterest. Wild accusations of cheating.

Then, of course, there was the one worry that had topped the hundreds of things that could go wrong.

Theo showing his face.

But he hadn't. And none of her other worries came to fruition. It was success beyond all her imaginations.

She had just made a sweep of the private card rooms and all were now empty. There were only a few stragglers left below in the ballroom, so deep into their cups of the delicious gala concoction of pears, lemons, oranges, sherry and cognac that they could not find the door and the early morning rays of spring sun.

All had been perfect. A resounding success.

So no.

Not this.

But there was her arm twisted high in the air beside her. It was yanked, pulling her body along with it and making her slippers slide haphazardly across the hallway floor as she was dragged into a private card room.

She wasn't even surprised by the manhandling anymore. She knew exactly who she would see when she looked up.

For not wanting anything to do with her, the blasted man sure did love to grab her and toss her about at will.

The door to the private card room slammed shut in front of her.

Jerking her arm from his grip, she spun to him. "How did you even get in here, Theo?"

He shrugged, apologetic grin in place. "I slipped in the back past two of Logan's new guards. It's hard to deny entrance to someone you don't know the appearance of."

Her fists went onto her hips as she glared at him. "I will have to speak to Logan about how he trained those new guards."

"So I was not wrong." His grin faltered. "You would have denied me entrance."

"I would not have bothered—but Cass, Logan—well, I cannot account for their actions."

"Logan? What did you tell Logan of us?"

"Nothing." Her hand flicked out to wave in-between them. "It is not that hard to discern, Theo. He knows I was embarrassingly happy when you were around, and then… not so much."

The grin retuned full force to his face. "You look beautiful, Vee. The dress matches the violet in your eyes."

Her head snapped back. "No… No…"

What was he even thinking? To accost and then compliment her after how he tossed her aside weeks ago?

She shook her head, sighing, weariness hitting her. "What are you doing here, Theo? Why do you insist on hovering? It has been a long night and I am exhausted."

He took a step toward her, his hands lifting, moving toward her upper arms, but he paused before grabbing them when he saw she was ready to spring away. Instead, his palms flipped to her, both pleading and calming. "Hovering is as close as I have dared to come to you. Believe me, Vee, I have been trying to get you alone since seeing you on Bond Street."

Her head cocked to the side, her right eyebrow rising in suspicion. "You have? Why?"

"Because I cannot stay away, Vee." The weight of his words transformed his face, his light blue eyes suddenly fierce, the line of his jaw tensing. His hands inched forward, slipping onto her shoulders. The straps of her gown not offering nearly enough cover, his palms instantly heated the bare skin he touched.

Violet stiffened, her arms wrapping around her torso as she took a step backward. He stepped forward with her, not letting her escape.

She flipped a hand upward, setting it on his chest to stop him. "You cannot do this to me, Theo—please—not tonight, of all nights. The gala is finally over and I should be celebrating downstairs with Cass and Logan and the guards and the dealers and the staff—people who like me, love me. *Want* me."

"I want you." The line of his hard-set jaw flickered. "Never mistake that, Vee."

"Never mistake that?" A laugh, half a scoff, half a gurgle, bubbled from her throat. "I have been a fool to your words before, Theo. I don't intend to repeat it."

His head dropped forward, yet he didn't release her shoulders. "I made a mistake, Vee. I convinced myself that if I left you—you would be the better for it. Safe. Happy in a way that you could never be with me. Because I will drag you down. Because you deserve so much more than what I can offer you." His head lifted, his ice blue eyes burning with intensity. "But I cannot do it. For as much as I have tried to stay away, you are an impossible flame to deny."

She drew a deep breath, trying to dislodge the air that had wedged into her lungs, making it hard to breathe. "Why in heaven above should I believe you, Theo? Believe that you will not decide a month from now to cast me aside again?" Her palm left his chest to thump onto the bare slope of her breastbone. "Because I'm an idiot? Is that what you think? You can disguise what you did anyway you like—convince yourself you were doing it for me—but it was you, Theo. You. You were the one to cast me aside. You were the one that did not want me. Why would you think I would ever allow myself to be in the position to suffer that again?"

"Because it is me, Vee." His voice was low, measured.

"You are not enough, Theo."

He nodded, a pang of pain running across his face. "I know I am not. But I have no other answer, Vee." His fingers along her bare shoulders pressed into her skin. "Because I am begging. Because I made the stupidest mistake in my life—not once, but twice. I left you because I believed you would be better off without me. Twice I did that. And I am twice the bloody idiot. That was made perfectly clear the other day when I saw you on the street."

"Why then?"

"Because I realized you need me. Because for all I cannot offer you—you need me."

"What?" Her word came out shrill, her entire body jerking, trying to escape him.

He held fast and closed his eyes, his lips drawing inward with a breath that lifted his chest. He opened his eyes to her. "Because there is a sadness in you, Vee. It permeates your being, your soul. You had it when we were young, after your parents died. I saw it in you again that morning in the servant's room upstairs when you kicked me awake a month ago. And it was there, in you, on the street a few days ago."

He paused, shaking his head. "You need me because I take it away, Vee. That sadness. I am not so arrogant as to think I make it disappear, but when you are with me it is lessened. You are lighter. Your soul is not mired in darkness. I had it wrong all this time, Vee. I don't drag you down. I lift you up. And I finally realize that."

Her eyes widened at him, shock mixing with instinctive denial.

He was wrong. She wasn't sad—a constant, permanent shadow hovering over her that she could not set herself free from.

Was she?

"Theo, no…"

Her words trailed as thousands of tiny lies—lies she told herself every day in order to make it to the next minute, to take the next step, to not descend into the darkness that had almost killed her once—started to explode in the back of her head.

Tomorrow would be sunny…There would be no scandal during the next event…The breakfast biscuits would be fluffy next time…She would soon have enough funds to limit the gaming nights to twice a month…Her bed wasn't cold…The maid only need to lift the top hem of her bodice so her breasts would attract less attention…The birth of Adalia's babe would go well…If she talked long enough at him, she could persuade Mr. Olston to respect her prowess with numbers, rather than just ogle her body…The rain would ease, it always did…Her smile was believable…She was a lady, even if gentleman didn't always respect it…She would be fine without Theo in her life… She would find happiness, someday, if she just kept moving, kept searching.

She would be fine.

She would be fine.

She would be fine.

Her face dipped downward, her eyes closing as the lies overwhelmed. Lies she'd had to tell herself because he was right. She was always fighting against that one fact.

She was sad.

And she never would have admitted it to herself.

"I thought I was helping by leaving you, Vee. After the book—after my reaction to it being missing. I didn't want to see your sadness resurface. I didn't want my demons to be the cause of it. But that was my mistake—I knew it when I saw you on Bond Street."

His hands moved up along her shoulders to settle along her neck, his thumbs tracing the line of her jaw. He lifted her face to him, even as she refused to look at him.

"You need me because I make you happy, Vee. Deep down, soulfully happy. I don't know how I do it. But I know I do. Are there others that can accomplish that? Yes, I imagine there are. I am humble enough to recognize that." His fingers tightened along her neck, punctuating each of his raw words. "But no one—no one—is going to love you as much as I do. That—that I know. I know it above all. So I am begging you, Vee."

Her eyelids heavy, stones of the greatest weight, she had to fight to lift them and let her eyes go to his face. For a moment, her breath left her. She had never seen him as serious, as fiercely fervent as he was in that moment. She had to force a whisper. "Begging me for… what?"

"For you to believe in me. To trust me. I have gone down this path before, and I will not make the mistake again." His hands moved to cup her face. "I will not break, Vee. You asked me not to bow under this weight, and I will not. I want this. I want you, Vee. I want us. And that was what I did—I cracked. But I didn't break—I know it because I cannot accept my fool actions as the end—the end of us. I am refusing to be broken like that. If we are to be finished, then I am fighting it—fighting for us until the end."

His hands on her face shook, the intensity sending tremors through his fingers into her body. "I just need you to believe in me, Vee. Like only you can. You see me—what I am capable of—like no other. And for as much as you need me, I need you a thousand times fold."

His words stopped, his look desperate. Desperate for her response. For a chance. For her.

She was a damn fool.

Again and again and again.

So what was one more time?

She sprang onto her toes, her lips meeting his hard, her hands wrapping around his neck.

The only response she could muster. The only response he needed.

His arms locked around her, dragging her fully onto his body, the pulsating heat between them both undeniable and unquenchable.

His head slanted to the side, demanding further access to her mouth, his tongue plundering, exploring, starved from days without her body.

His right hand slipped below her backside, teasing, as his left hand found its way to her right breast, seeking out her already hardened nipple. His lips slid downward, tasting the skin along her neck.

"Theo, I want…" Her words dropped, the exquisiteness of his lips along her neck stealing her breath.

"What, Vee?

"I want you for hours in your bed. I want to fall asleep in your arms. And I want what you said—I want to wake up with you with no pressures upon us, just a world where we can carve out whatever happiness we can."

"Then that is exactly what I want." His lips on her neck didn't halt his devouring as he spoke. "Can you leave?"

She nodded, clutching his head to her neck. "I just have a few more tasks to handle tonight. And then I am yours."

"Mine?"

"I am." Her fingers deep in the thick of his blond hair, she pulled him from her neck, finding his clear blue eyes. "Yours."

~~~

Smoothing the front of her amethyst-hued gown, Violet stepped into the mess of the ballroom. If she had thought her patrons could make a mess on a regular gaming night, she had grossly underestimated the disaster they could concoct on a night such as this. Food and drink spilled, discarded haphazardly throughout the space. Glass shattered on the floor. Paper scraps in all colors from the betting slips dusted every surface. Chairs overturned.

A whirlwind of wreckage.

She hoped the gardens had fared better. Much of the entertainment of the night had been outside, since they had been blessed with unusually clear skies. Even though Theo would be waiting for her in the mews, she dreaded having to walk through the back gardens for she would have to see the destruction in the plant beds. Adalia would have a fit if she knew her precious roses had been broken and mangled. But there would be time to revive them, time for new leaves to grow before Adalia made it into London again.

Walking across the ballroom, Violet picked her way around broken glass scattered on the wooden floors, not wanting to gouge the shards into her floorboards even more. Cassandra must have cleared out the last of the gala's attendees, as the maids were already busy cleaning, the four of them in opposite corners, working inward.
~~~

Spotting Logan by her office, she went over to him, her neck craning upward at his height. "All is well?"

"It is, my lady." He offered a curt nod, per his usual limited replies. For as handsome as Logan was, for as much as his dark eyes were mesmerizing, and for how one wished for him to talk at length, he never did. She liked that about her head guard.

"And the proceeds were as expected?"

"They were. Double the goal as of a half hour ago."

Her hand flew to her chest. "Double?"

He nodded.

"I had not imagined that. Are there any more patrons still here playing?"

"A few with the roulette wheel in the garden."

"Is there any chance we will lose anything substantial?"

"No. The scrubs of coin purses is all that is in play. And Walters has already been dispatched with the bank of the evening."

"Excellent. He is delivering to Mr. Olston as well?"

"It is his first stop."

A relieved smile overtook her face. "Thank you, Logan." She looked around the room and then glanced up at him. "You are positive you do not wish to officially take over in managing this place?"

"I enjoy my position as it is, my lady. It is more important for my men that I remain in my current station."

Her right cheek lifted high in deviousness. "That does not mean I cannot double your salary, Logan."

The slightest bit of red tinged his forehead. "I would prefer any increases go directly to my men, my lady. I am in no need of more."

Violet exaggerated a sigh. As much as she knew Logan would always put his men—all maimed but perfectly capable ex-soldiers—first, she wished for once he would think on his own future. "You have been saying that for two years, now, Logan. Your men are already better paid than you."

"As it should be, my lady." He inclined his head. "I must excuse myself to the gardens and the encouraging of the last guests to be exiting."

"Of course. Thank you, Logan."

Logan left her, and Violet turned, scanning the mess. She walked into the drawing room, halting in surprise as she spied Fiona sitting in a tall wingback chair, facing the front street. With the angle Fiona sat in, Violet had missed her earlier.

"Fiona, you are still here."

Fiona sat straight, turning to Violet. "I am. I am just so in awe of the night's events—all that you managed to procure for the masses. And those nighttime pigeon races with each bird marked as a patron—brilliant. Did you see Lady Buntton took her winning bird home to keep as a pet?"

Violet nodded with a quick smile. "I had a lot of help—yours included." She moved to stand in front of Fiona. "And you must know I am eternally grateful for your assistance, Fiona."

Fiona stood, smoothing the front of her dark gown. Gold fibers woven into the black satin shimmered in the early morning sunlight streaming in from the front window. "I am just happy I could be of help. I have been searching for purpose since my husband died, and this has occupied my time quite nicely. I thank you for including me."

"Of course. I have so enjoyed spending time with you." Violet's smile tightened. "But I am afraid it can be no more."

Fiona's head jerked to the side, startled. "No more—why ever not?"

"How is it that you know Lord Alton, Fiona?"

Her forehead scrunched, the slight wrinkles making Fiona look much older than her sweet face usually revealed. "Lord Alton? I don't know the man at all, Violet. I only met him with Mr. Olston when we discussed the vitality of the mine."

A frown set onto Violet's face. "Yet, I believe you do know him. I saw how you stiffened when we ran into him on Bond Street."

Fiona twinkled her fingers in the air, her voice light. "Well, that is silly, Violet. You must be imagining truths that do not exist. That was only the second time I have seen the man."

"And do not lie to me, Fiona. I am not a blind idiot." Violet's stance widened. "Van Halverstin. That was your name before you married Lord Toplan, correct?"

Fiona's smile faltered. Only a moment, but a definite hiccup in her facade. She redoubled her efforts, and her smile slid easily back onto her face. "It was. How did you know that?"

"I researched you, Fiona. I do not do business with people I know very little about, especially when there is an alarming incident such as there was with you and Lord Alton on Bond Street. So I researched you during the last few days." Violet took a tiny step forward, her voice lowering. "And when I learned your birth name—I recognized it."

"From where?"

"From another list. A list Lord Alton possesses. I could scarcely believe it to be true, but then I checked to verify, and your name was in his book. Your name."

"Violet, truly, there must be many Van Halverstins. Clearly this is a mistake."

"No. And next to your name was that of your mother. Letty Van Halverstin. She lives in the Devil's Acre."

Fiona glanced around the room, her smile faltering, spiraling downward. "I…I don't have a mother, Violet."

"You do." Violet kept her voice even. "I visited her. And she described you perfectly. She does not know you are alive."

"Violet—"

"Why would she think her daughter is dead, when the truth of the matter is that her daughter is merrily going about town, spending an unending well of coin while she is living in squalor?"

"You misunderstand."

"No, I do not think I do. And I fear I cannot afford to hear your explanations. To this very moment you have lied to me about your association with Lord Alton." Violet's hands drew to her hips, her words scorching. "So whatever game it is that you have been playing with me—with Lord Alton—it ends here, Lady Toplan. Today. I have already sent the loan repayment, your portion included, to Mr. Olston. And I thank you for your contribution to the success of the evening. But there is no need for our paths to ever meet again. We are done."

The last remnants of the smile evaporated from Fiona's face, a twisted frown overtaking her lips. For a long moment, she seethed. But then in a burst of restraint, she inclined her head, stepping to the side and out of Violet's direct path. "As you wish, Lady Vandestile."

Without another look, Fiona spun on her heel and walked toward the drawing room door.

The graceful swing of Fiona's black satin gown glittered under the morning rays of sun, and Violet stood rooted in her spot, watching, wary, until Fiona vanished out the doorway.

It took Violet a long moment to draw air into her lungs.

Unpleasant as that had been, it had needed to be done.

The woman had lied to her. And Violet gave no margin to liars—especially when a liar's motives were clearly suspicious. That Fiona's motives appeared to be aimed somewhat against Theo was worrisome.

She would have to ask Theo just what exactly his history was with Fiona. Not that he would necessarily answer her. And she was not about to push for more. Fiona was in his book—apparently thought dead by Theo—which meant she had ties to him from the war. Beyond that, Violet accepted that was all she may ever know of the woman.

A shame she'd had to cut her, for how delightful Fiona was.

Maybe it was all a misunderstanding. Maybe Fiona and Theo knew each other from the war, but had agreed to go about their lives without ever mentioning the past again. It was possible. Theo did avoid the past when he could.

Her right fingers tapped on her hip bone. Maybe she was wrong. Maybe she had just cut Fiona for no reason. But until she knew the truth of their association—why Fiona was in Theo's book—she could not afford to have the woman in her life.

Ask Theo. She mustn't forget.

But first, she had to close out the ledgers for the night.

{ CHAPTER 19 }

The gardens were just as she feared. Gravel strewn into the flower beds. Cracked branches, dangling in death. Spring sprouts ground into the dirt, long leaves already wilting at the tips.

Violet sighed. A double thank goodness Adalia wouldn't be back in London for months. Longer if that babe in her belly continued to be stubborn and not make a timely appearance.

Even with the unusually bright sun, the air hadn't warmed in the last hour and she tightened her shawl in front of her chest, covering the last bit of skin open to the brisk morning air as she weaved her way through the garden beds.

Reaching the center of the back wall of tall evergreens, she opened the wrought iron gate, stepping through the arbor to the mews. Directly in front of her, an unmarked black carriage waited with a footman at the ready by the coach door. She would have to commend Theo on his discretion.

"My lady." The footman bowed his head, opening the carriage door and then holding his hand out to her.

Violet's look ran over him. Theo must have hired a new footman with Baron Telliton's repayment of his loan, as she had never seen this servant before.

She set her fingers in the footman's hand for assistance and moved to the iron carriage step.

In that moment, before her eyes had lifted to the coach's interior, a hand jabbed out and grabbed her arm, yanking, heaving her into the coach.

This was not Theo's manhandling. This was pain.

Her shins banged hard into the lower lip of the carriage, shots of agony vibrating up her legs and sending a weak squeak from her throat. Instantly trying to twist from the grip, she was jerked, dragged forward and then thrown onto the bench of the carriage.

Her feet clear of the door, it slammed shut, locking her into the interior darkness of the coach.

A hand, cold and thick, wrapped around her throat as a rag was stuffed into her mouth, cutting her scream. The coach surged forward.

Frantic, Violet blinked again and again, forcing her eyes to adjust to the dimness quicker than they wanted to. Squirming, her fingers attempted to pry away the harsh fingers squeezing her neck. Her sight came into focus.

No.

Not Fiona. It couldn't be Fiona sitting across from her. Sitting in absolute calm, watching Violet claw at the man's hand around her throat.

Not Fiona. Fiona was sweet. Funny. Attempting to play a mischievous game with Theo, yes, but not capable of this. Not capable of kidnapping.

The hand at her throat tightened and Violet's eyes swung to the man next to her. So large, the brute's neck curved, craning his head downward so he didn't risk hitting the roof of the carriage with every rut the wheels hit.

She started to talk, to plead, giving no mind to the nasty rag stuffed in her mouth. The brute would understand something—something of her desperation. Coin—she needed to offer him coin.

Her tongue tangled in the cloth, muffling all words. So much so, her own ear didn't understand her garbled sounds.

"Stop. Don't sink to pathetic, Violet. I respect you far too much for that." Fiona waved her hand in the air, seemingly to clear it of Violet's desperation.

Violet's frantic tongue stilled against the cloth in her mouth.

Fiona pointed to the brute still pinning Violet by the neck to the back cushion of the bench. "And don't bother with him. The man knows exactly who is paying him. And he cares far more on that than any sympathy you might possibly conjure." Fiona leaned forward. "There is no room for those with honor in my employ. Do not make that silly mistake."

The carriage tilted, taking a hard corner. Fiona's hand fell from midair to brace herself on her bench.

Yet the brute's grip on Violet's throat didn't falter. If anything, it held her securely in place.

She looked across the carriage at Fiona. How had she ever thought Fiona was sweet? A friend?

How could she possibly be this gullible—again and again and again?

Fiona nodded to the brute and he lifted his free fist to bang on the roof of the carriage. Clomping hooves slowed, angry nickering coming from the front of the carriage.

With an ear-piercing squeak of the springs, the coach halted.

"This is where I leave you, dear Violet. You have been a delight and I thank you for that." Fiona pointed at the brute as she stood from the bench. "My man will be delivering you to your new quarters."

The carriage door opened. Picking up her skirts, Fiona stepped down and out of the carriage. Her feet on the street, she stopped to look up at Violet, her cherub mouth curling into a dazzling smile.

A smile Violet knew, without a doubt, came from the bowels of hell.

"God speed, dear friend." Fiona nodded to the footman and he slammed the carriage door closed.

The brute's fingers tightened around her throat.

~~~

Not bothering to knock, Theo banged open the heavy oak door. Nearly impossible to track down, why the head of Violet's guard even had—or could afford—a room at Brooks's was beyond his curiosity at the moment.

The door slamming open, it crashed into the wall and bounced back at him as he stormed into the room.

A scream, and then a woman scrambled from the large bed, yanking a sheet with her to cover herself.

Hell. So much for the strict rule of banning women at the club.

Already to his feet and naked except for his right boot, Logan advanced, his fist swinging three steps before he reached Theo. His blow—knuckles of steel—landed square on the side of Theo's jaw, cracking him two steps backward.

Squelching the visceral urge to retaliate—he had just walked in on the man in bed with a woman, after all—Theo threw up a desperate hand before Logan could land another
~~~

blow. "Stop. My apologies, Logan. But where in the hell did she go?"

Logan's hand froze in the middle of his next swing. "She? Lady Vandestile?"

"Yes, man. For blasted sake, where the hell did she go?"

Logan's head swiveled to the woman standing next to the bed, her eyes wide, her cheeks pink. She held no alarm at the scene—only an admiring look as she studied Logan's backside. Logan motioned his head to the door.

With a remorseful look that lingered on Logan's rear, she set her head down and scurried out past the two men clad only in the sheet. She resisted glancing at either one of them as she passed.

Logan lowered his right fist, his left hand reaching out to slam the door closed.

"Again, my apologies, Logan. But I need to find her."

Logan looked at him. "I am not her keeper, Alton. I am her employee."

"No. But you must know where Violet is—or where she left to."

Logan threaded his arms across his bare chest, not even slightly abashed by his own nudity. "Nor am I going to tell you a single thing. You are an ass and have walked into the wrong den of depravity if you think to gain my cooperation."

Theo's hands curled into fists. "You know nothing of the matter between Violet and me."

"I know that you crushed her."

"Yes, I did. And I bloody well did it to protect her."

Logan's eyes drifted down to Theo's fists, but he made no motion of defense, his look merely traveling back up to meet Theo's glare. "From what? I have Lady Vandestile more than well protected."

Theo had to forcibly unclench his fingers. "Something—someone—that was out of your viewpoint."

"Nothing is out of my viewpoint when it comes to Lady Vandestile and the Revelry's Tempest."

Theo bowed his head slightly in deference. "I don't imagine so. But this—this is."

Logan shook his head. "I'm not telling you a thing."

Theo took a step forward. He would beat this out of Logan if he needed to. "She was supposed to be with me. She was supposed to leave the Revelry's Tempest this morning with me. Before you even left there."

Logan's left eyebrow cocked. "She was to leave with you?"

"Bloody well yes, man. She told me she had just a few items to take care of after the night—an hour at most—and she would be out to my carriage. I went out to wait for her but she never came out."

"Have you checked her townhouse?"

"Of course I have." Theo's hand ran through his hair. "She's not there. Her staff has not seen her. We checked every room. I went to Lady Desmond's townhouse. Nothing. We went back to the Revelry's Tempest. The maids have not seen her—we checked every room there as well."

"Did you check with Lady Toplan's household?"

Theo froze, a cold snake of ice curling down his spine. "Lady Toplan?"

"Yes. I watched Lady Vandestile walk out through the gardens to the mews. I believe she entered Lady Toplan's carriage."

"Shit."

A frown set onto Logan's face, the first signs of true concern etching his brow. He turned from Theo, reaching for his trousers strewn over the back of a wooden chair. "We go there now."

Theo grabbed his upper arm. "We cannot."

Logan ripped his arm from Theo's grasp. "I don't take orders from the likes of you, Alton."

Theo attempted to beat back the frenzied rage pulsating in his veins. Logan was not the enemy. He had to remember that. He took a step backward, his voice calming. "I recognize your dislike of me, Logan. And frankly, I deserve it. But you need to heed me on this—I know we cannot just go over there."

"Why not?" Logan shoved his right leg, boot and all, into his dark trousers.

"You were in the war."

"So?"

"So you know the atrocities that happened on the continent."

For a second, Logan's dark grey eyes flickered unmistakable pain. "Yes."

"So imagine a woman in the midst of that—Lady Toplan. She knows the atrocities more intimately than most—more intimately than the average soldier. And she is no longer sane because of it." Theo ran his hand over his eyes, rubbing. "I thought…I thought she had managed to hold on—to escape it. To come out unscathed. I wanted to believe that. Give her that chance. But I was wrong."

Theo's hand dropped, forming into a fist that beat into his thigh. "Lady Toplan is after me. And I stupidly thought the best way to protect Violet from it was to cut things with her. If I had nothing to do with Violet, Lady Toplan would want nothing to do with her—could not use her against me. I thought I could protect Violet that way. I thought I could protect Lady Toplan from herself that way—I owed her that margin of mercy from all that happened during the war."

His trousers buttoned, Logan looked at Theo as he grabbed his white linen shirt. "You owed her from the war? This was some sort of benevolent comeuppance?"

Theo nodded. "I had hoped. But I was wrong. Lady Toplan is too far gone—she cannot be redeemed. And I was stupid for believing in that hope."

Logan grunted. "Know that I don't give a damn about whatever atonement you think to achieve, Alton. What I give a damn about is Lady Vandestile. She is the only reason I haven't pummeled you already." Logan put on his shirt, his glare landing on Theo. "So what do you propose?"

"Lady Toplan is brutally intelligent."

"So?"

"We step carefully. Or Violet is going to get hurt."

~~~

Her body prone, flat on her back, Violet lay in the cold swath of muck, shock choking her—choking into stillness the shivers that had racked her muscles for hours.

She stared up, her neck craned awkwardly to the side so she could concentrate on the few stars she could see through the wispy clouds.

Two days straight and through the night they had traveled.
~~~

And this was where the brute had dropped her.

She had stopped screaming for help hours ago. Or what she thought was hours ago. It was still daylight then, her only guide to time passing. Her voice, along with her hope, had faded with the light.

Only the stars now. Only the thin sliver of stars she could see from her angle up through the opening of the mine shaft.

She couldn't move closer to the mine opening. Stretched as she was, the shackle around her ankle prevented her from getting any closer. But at least she could see it, the opening. The hole in the ground.

He had destroyed the ladder on his way up, hacking at the wooden rungs with an ax. Even if she could free herself from the iron shackle around her ankle, she couldn't escape up the shaft.

Trapped.

As much as she tried not to think on it, dwell on it, that one thought weighed on her, second by second suffocating any hope she had in her chest.

Trapped. Trapped underground. Trapped in a coffin of rock and mud.

It was an hour before she realized the stars couldn't help her. The stars could do nothing but twinkle, silent, far-away witnesses to her horror.

The last vestiges of hope dwindling in Violet's chest, she snatched at them, holding onto them with all of her being before they vanished out of her grip.

She had to get out of there.

She had to not crumble.

Not break.

She had far too much to live for.

Her arms heavy, she pushed herself to sitting. In near blackness, she ran her hands along the wet, muddy stone beneath her. Her forefinger bumped into a rock, her knuckle scraping against a sharp corner of it. It would do.

Back and forth, back and forth. It took time. Lots of time. Clawing at the dirt. Wedging the rock. Until finally, she freed it from the muck and picked it up. Her muscles strained, the rock hefty enough that she needed both hands to lift it. She set the rock to the side as she lined up the shackle's iron chain between her bent legs. Grabbing the rock, she lifted it high over her head, bringing it down with as much force as she could muster.

A sharp spark flew through the darkness. Her fingers dove down, running along the slick iron links. No impact. Not even a notch in the metal.

Again. Harder. Spark.

Again and again. More sparks.

But the metal would not yield.

No matter. She would do this over and over until she broke the damn chain.

Clawing the rock, her fingernails started to tear off as she beat the chain, swinging without mercy. Sharp ridges cut through her skin.

She could feel the blood on her fingers, slippery. Making her grip impossible.

The rock flew from her hands in the next swing, slamming into her shin, her skirt only marginally softening the blow. The pain shocked her body, the horror of the situation magnified once more.

Blackness tightened around her, swallowing her, wrapping around her neck, her chest.

She pushed back at it. Pushed at the air around her.

She knew it was just air, yet her hands lifted, pushing, shoving just the same.

She was losing it—losing her mind—losing it fast.

She had to get out of there.

Had to, before she had no sanity left to save.

Her fingers dropped to the ground, sifting through the mud, searching for the rock.

She had to be smart. If she couldn't break the chain, maybe she could break it free from the rock it was attached to.

She had no other choice.

She had to get out.

{ CHAPTER 20 }

"Where the hell is Violet, Fiona?"

The wretched woman didn't immediately turn from the fire she was standing and staring at, and Theo had to resist the urge to lunge across her drawing room and choke the answer out of her.

Where once, not but days ago, he had pitied Fiona, now only a feral hatred ran through his blood as he looked at the back of her perfectly coifed blond hair.

Fiona turned from the fireplace. Her eyes ran over Logan, assessing him as he stood behind Theo. Dismissing him, her gaze settled on Theo's face. She smiled. The serene smile. He recognized it well. The one that held a stopper on the numerous monstrous schemes that ran rampant in her head.

"I am surprised it has taken you this long to come to me, Theo. I expected you to show early yesterday morning to make your demands of me. It is like old times, no?" She took a step toward him, her fingers clasping meekly in front of her black skirt. "Do you remember how demanding you were of me? How demanding you were of *everyone*?"

She was directly to the crux of it, then. Theo's jaw tightened. "George made his own decisions, Fiona."

"No." She took another step toward him, her serene smile fixed on her heart-shaped lips. "You made the decisions, Alton. You made the orders. George followed them."

"I had hoped you would be past this, Fiona."

"No. You had hoped I would be dead."

Theo flinched, her words true to the mark.

Her look dipped to the floor as her fingers unthreaded, her palms flattening the front of her dark skirts. Her eyes lifted to him. "You told me George would be fine, Alton. You told me he would survive, that there was no need for me to accompany him—but the whole time you knew—you knew he was about to die on that mission into that arsenal and you didn't let me save him."

"No, I didn't. I was too intent on saving you. I wasn't about to let you die in that hellfire as well." Theo's look hardened at her. For as many times as he had told her this, she never heard him. Never believed him. *Refused* to believe him. "That is what would have happened if you had gone in with George. You would have been killed. It was an easy decision to make."

"Killing George was an easy decision?" She scoffed a bitter chuckle. "You truly are a cold one, Alton." She paused, her head shaking as her smile curled into a snarl. "You took that choice away from me. It was my decision to make—to go in with George. I was ready to die if it meant saving him."

"That is exactly why I did not let you go. You were far too valuable to lose to a stupid sacrifice such as that."

"To die for the man I loved? That would have been stupid?"

"Yes."

Her head slanted to the side as she stared at him. Ever so slowly, the serene smile fell back into place on her lips. "How do you feel now about love, Alton?"

Reacting without thinking, his savage charge forward was stopped by a heavy hand on his shoulder.

Logan. Thank the heavens he had enlisted the man's help.

Theo stilled, his glare piercing Fiona. "Your grievance is with me, Fiona. Take me. Leave Violet out of this."

Her hand lifted, forefinger tapping on her lower lip. She shook her head. "No. That hardly seems fair. You made the choice for me once. Killing the man I loved. Not giving me the chance to save him." She met his glare with serenity. "Now I make the choice for you."

"Fiona—that was war. War. A war now over. The men in the war—you, me—we were all guilty. We all played the game of it and we knew it. We knew death was a part of it. I knew it. George knew it. You knew it. You played the game the same as the rest of us." He stopped, drawing a breath to calm the tremor in his voice. "But Violet is innocent. She had nothing to do with that time. She does not deserve this and you know that."

"Do I?" Her left hand went to her hip. "Life is war, Theo. Death, suffering will always be a part of life whether we are in the middle of a war or not. I have had to suffer under the decision you made three years ago, Alton. So now you will suffer under the decision I make."

Logan's fingers tightened on Theo's shoulder, stopping him before his muscles coiled into action. Theo hadn't even realized Logan's hand had remained on his shoulder, holding him in place. His respect for the man increased a hundred-fold.

Theo took a long breath and then nodded, conjuring his own mask of indifference. Practiced, masterful—the detachment settled onto his face, the same as it had during the war. That the remnant of who he once was came so easily stung, searing him down to his soul. Stung because it was a remnant of the atrocities he had committed during the war—the atrocities he had witnessed—the atrocities he had manipulated into place. A callous reminder of the past he had thought to never have to revisit again.

But for Violet. For Violet he would drown himself in any hell that he needed to.

"I have something that will persuade you otherwise, Fiona."

"You have nothing that could sway me, Alton."

Theo looked over his shoulder to Logan and gave him a nod.

Logan's hand dropped from Theo's shoulder and he disappeared out into the front foyer of Fiona's townhouse.

Theo stepped to the side, clearing the space of the drawing room doorway. It only took a few seconds and Logan reappeared, his hand clasped onto the arm of a man that he dragged along with him.

Logan stepped into the room, pushing the man—clad in rags of clothes, with flea-infested hair and beard that had not been cut in years, and his wrists bound in front of him—forward.

"No…no…no." Fiona's desperate whisper filled the room as she clutched her chest, her head shaking, shock sending her eyes wide in disbelief.

She stepped backward, almost into the fire. Theo jumped forward, grabbing her shoulders and jerking her away from the fireplace before the flames could lick the back of her skirts.

She looked up at Theo, then back to the man, her words haunted. "Geor…George?"

The man nodded.

"What…how?"

"He didn't die in that arsenal explosion, Fiona," Theo said. "No. Instead, George turned traitor."

Her gaze shot to Theo. "No—he—he wouldn't have—never."

"He did."

Her look crept to her lover. "George?"

His face pained, emphasizing the sallowness of his cheeks above his ragged, unkempt beard, George offered one nod.

"He has been a prisoner since that time," Theo said.

Fiona had to tear her eyes off of George to look at Theo. "But why—why did you not tell me?"

"Would you have believed me? Or would you have joined him, Fiona? It was easier that he was dead. We could protect his family. They did not deserve to pay for his sins. And I could protect you—protect you from yourself. I know how much you loved him. What he would have made you do."

Her head shook, disbelief still shining in her eyes as she searched George's face. "So he died a hero instead?"

"Yes."

"Yet the whole time he has been…" Her look whipped to Theo. "Where? Where has he been?"

"Newgate."

"All this time…" She gulped, her eyebrows drawing together as she took a step toward George. And then another step. And another. "All this time and you were here…so close." She stopped directly in front of him, her hand slowly lifting, her fingers shaking as they reached to touch his cheek.

A soft cry escaped her mouth as her hand flattened against the side of his grizzled face. Tears streaming down her cheeks, her green eyes shifted to belief. "You are alive."

George nodded, his pained eyes reflecting hers. "I am."

Theo audibly cleared his throat.

George's look tore away from Fiona to glance at Theo. His eyes hardening, he sighed, his look dropping back to Fiona. "You need to tell him, Fiona. Tell him where that woman is at." His voice crackled dry over the words, a throat not accustomed to talking.

Fiona's head jerked back, her eyes snapping out of shock. She looked over her shoulder at Theo, and then back to George.

"You have to tell him, Fiona," George said. "Tell him where Lady Vandestile is."

"But you—no—I cannot—"

"He promised we could be together, Fiona. He swore it. But you have to tell him."

Fiona's head dropped forward, her body sagging as her forehead rested onto the tattered cloth of George's shirt.

For a long minute, the room froze.

Patience.

Patience.

Patience.

Theo repeated the word over and over in his mind as he stared at the side of Fiona's head.

Patience.

Don't mind that she was taking her blasted sweet time about it. That Violet could be in hurt, in pain.

Patience.

If he pushed Fiona, Violet could very well be lost to him.

A quick intake of breath, and Fiona lifted her head, her gaze rising to look into George's eyes. Her look not leaving her love, her mouth opened. "She is in the mine."

"What?" Theo's yell filled the room.

"Your mine in Derbyshire. She is there. Shackled below. I knew you would stumble upon her…eventually." Her calm eyes refused to leave George's face.

Theo's breath, his chest, his heart, dropped to the floor, his legs almost giving out. No. Not the mine. Not Violet in the terror of what that mine did to her. Hell. Pure hell. No.

Theo stumbled one step forward, fully intent on choking the life out of the blasted woman. But then he veered just before Logan intercepted him.

He wasn't going to waste one minute. Not one second.

Violet would not be forced to spend one more moment in that mine than necessary.

He ran to the door, passing Logan.

"Alton—you swore it," George called out after him.

Without breaking stride, Theo looked back to Logan. "Put her in a cell next to him."

Logan nodded. "I will follow as soon as it is done."

Theo barely heard his words, as he was already out Fiona's front door.

He slammed it behind him.

Blast it to hell that it had taken a full day to find George in that unearthly jail. If it hadn't taken so long…

Dammit. He could already be pulling Violet from the mine.

He ran down the street, shoving people out of the way, no time for anything other than getting on a horse and riding like hellfire all the way to Glenhaven.

~~~

Theo's boots splashed into the muck at the bottom of the shaft, his palms stinging from the burn the rope caused on his quick descent.

He had arrived at the mine with rain pouring and daylight waning, only to find the ladder down into the mine had been destroyed—hacked to pieces. That he'd had to find a rope to descend had driven him to near insanity—especially when there had been no response to his bellowing Violet's name down the shaft.

His burning hands were reward for not taking care as he should have as he dropped into the mine.

He turned, spotting her instantly just past the open shaft, a huddled lump against the wall of the mine just before the first curve. A lump buried under folds of cloth. A dull shard of light twisted into the darkness, revealing a heavy iron chain curled out from under her chemise, snaking its way to a flat iron plate pounded into the granite. An odd trough into the granite ringed the plate, bits of smashed rock smattered all around it.

No words. No blasphemes. No scream.

Not one thing loud or long or hard enough to express the numbing rage seizing his body.

His feet lead weights in the muck, he walked to Violet slowly, barely holding back the need to run to her and grab her and smother her in his arms. No. He had to restrain. He
~~~

had to move slow—slow, so he didn't surprise her. Slow, so he didn't upset whatever balance she had left in her mind—assuming she still held to sanity.

He remembered too well her reaction the last time she was in the mine. It was the only thing in his mind the entire ride to Glenhaven. Her fear, her unyielding terror had been brutal to watch once, and his obsessive imaginations did him no favors as he thought of Violet below ground, in the dirt, alone, wet, cold.

He stopped at the plate hammered into the granite, kicking at it. It didn't shift, the nails still embedded deep in the rock.

The tip of his boot mushed into the mud by the chain as his eyes fixated on the mess of cloth over her torso, searching and praying for her chest to rise in a breath.

"Vee." His voice cracked, the whisper barely audible to his own ears. He swallowed hard, then opened his mouth again as he dropped to balance on his heels. "Vee."

He reached out, his fingers landing softly on her knee, her thin wet chemise the only barrier between his hand and her skin. He looked at the mess of silk about her body, realizing what she had done. She had ripped the skirt off her gown at some point, using it to wrap around her upper body for warmth.

Theo had to shove back boiling rage. She had been dumped here in her gala gown—a flimsy little affair that offered no protection against the cold.

No food. No water. No way out or in. Only her gown.

The harsh truth of what Fiona had truly intended shook him.

Violet was never supposed to survive this.

A cold, miserable death.

That was what Fiona had intended for him to find.

The cell he had sent the witch to was far too generous.

His trembling hands went down to Violet's ankle, searching for the shackle attached to the chain. Finding it, he pulled her leg straight. The iron around her ankle had a heavy lock on it. A lock that was never meant to open.

With a shudder, he squeezed Violet's knee, gently shaking it. "Vee."

No response.

His hands traveled upward, shifting the cloth, now black with dirt and mud. Tugging the silk downward, he could finally see her face. Her left hand was curled into a ball, limp in front of her nose.

He searched through the jumble of cloth until he found her back, rubbing it. "Vee."

A breath.

A jerk.

He rubbed harder. "Vee—Vee, wake up."

A moan.

He pulled away, tearing off his coat and then setting it about her body, lifting her to slide it underneath her torso.

In that moment, he saw the blood. He had thought it dirt covering her hand at first, but now closer, he knew it was blood. He dropped the jacket to pick up her hand, uncurling her fingers from the cocoon they had been folded into.

Her fingertips were bloody, nails nearly gone, worn down to scabs, her skin torn with blood and pus in a mess all the way to her wrist. His look scurried about the ground and he spotted the rock, instantly understanding. She had been trying to pound her way free from the granite.

For days.

Making her hands a bloody mess in the process.

The rage in his gut multiplied beyond what he thought possible.

"Vee." His voice was hard now, no longer under control. "Vee, you have to wake up." He found a shoulder and shook her, no longer gentle. "Wake up, Vee. Now."

A moan. Her eyelashes slowly fluttered as a long exhale left her lips. "Theo."

"Yes—yes." His hands went to her head, grasping her face between his palms. "That's it, Vee. Wake up. I am here."

It took an agonizing moment for her eyes to open fully to him. She blinked hard several times, unable to focus. "Theo?"

"Yes. I'm here, Vee. Right before you."

She nodded in his grasp, her eyes closing. "I am stuck. I couldn't break the chain. But the granite I am almost through."

"I know. You did good. And I am going to speed this up and get you out of here."

The faintest smile came to her lips, her words a whisper. "I knew you would find me."

He leaned forward, kissing her forehead hard. "I always will, Vee."

She nodded again. "Let us go. I…I don't know if I can walk. I am so…weak."

"I have to free the chain, Vee."

"The chain…it is still on me?" Her head shifted forward so she could look in the general direction of her feet. She couldn't focus on it.

"Can you not feel it?"

"No."

"I have to go to get tools, Vee. I can't get it off of you without them."

Her eyes lifted to him. "Just get it off of me, Theo, so we can go. I want to go. Leave."

His hand went to her forehead, pressing back matted hair from her face. "I want to Vee, I would give anything to have a way to get the blasted iron off you in this moment. But I have to go to the stables. I have to get tools to get it off of you. I can wedge the plate from the rock if nothing else and we can deal with the rest at Glenhaven."

She gasped, the quick influx of air in her lungs causing her to cough. "You…you are leaving me down here?"

"No, not leaving. I will be back in an instant. Just to the stables, and I will be back."

"Don't leave me." Unmistakable panic spiked in her voice. "Theo, you cannot leave me down here."

"I have to, Vee. Only for a few minutes so I can get tools—help. I have to get ropes, a ladder. I cannot get you out of here by myself."

"But you can. Just get it off, Theo." She grasped the front of his shirt, tugging. "Don't go. Please, please, don't leave me down here."

His fingers went over the back of her hands, clamping onto her. "You have to trust me, Vee. It will only be a few moments. I swear I will not fail you. I will be back."

He started to peel her hands from their iron grip on his shirt.

"Theo, I cannot—this coffin—I cannot—cannot—"

Her hands free from his shirt, he clutched her face. "I will be back before daylight fades. I swear, Vee. I will be back."

"No, you can just carry me out, we can leave together right now."

"I cannot break the shackle—the chain—without tools, Vee."

"But the test—the test."

"What test?"

"The test—I didn't give up. This was a test and I didn't give up—I never stopped trying to get out—never gave up on you—never. This was the test and I didn't fail it. I did not fail. I had faith. So you cannot leave me now."

"I have to, Vee. Only for minutes—only minutes."

Her head jerked between his hands, her voice going shrill. "So you don't want me to leave? You want to keep me down here? Forever in the coffin?"

In that moment, Theo realized how tenuous her grasp on reality was. What her mind must have suffered during the past two days.

Her breathing turned into gasps, hysteria setting in with tears she couldn't afford starting to stream down her face. "Don't leave me, Theo. It is death, death this is. They are all around me and talking to me and I am trying not to listen but they are there. Everywhere. Don't leave me."

Forcing his voice calm, his hands tightened along her face, trying to pull her back into reality by sheer willpower. "I will be back as soon as I find tools and someone to help,

Vee. I swear. Just hold on. Just a little longer, Vee. Can you do that? I will be back before you know it."

Her head dropped forward without a response, her breath slowing, her body slumping.

"Vee, answer me. I will be back in minutes."

No response.

"Violet, I have to leave. Just close your eyes. Close your eyes and imagine us in the garden at Glenhaven. Imagine the night air on your skin. The scent of budding boxwoods. The heat of my body next to yours. Imagine that. That night. And at the end I will be back. I swear it, I will be here."

No response.

Brutal terror seized him.

Her panicked begging was far better than this—the disappearance of her voice, her eyes, her mind.

Fighting the need to hold her—for he needed to get her out of there far more than comfort her—Theo tore his hands from her face.

He stood, turning to the mine opening before all strength to leave her left him.

There was no doubt that he was utterly destroying her by leaving her in the mine.

He ran to the rope, starting upward and using the footholds offered by the few bolts still in the wall from the destroyed ladder. Pulling himself up and out of the mine, he gave his left arm no possibility to fail. Not when he needed to get back down to Violet.

He yanked himself up over the edge of the shaft and then stood and looked down into the mine.

Not a sound was heard.

He afforded himself a quick moment to pray that he had not just broken Violet.

Broken her by leaving her.

Again.

{ Chapter 21 }

"I can't fix her, Sprite. I need your help."

His sister hurried down the last three steps of the winding staircase in Dellon Castle, her newborn babe clutched to her chest. She rushed across the stone floor of the foyer, skidding to a stop in front of Theo as the heavy front door was closed behind him.

"Theo—they just told me you arrived—an emergency?" Adalia's eyes ran up and down his body. "What in heaven's name—"

"She is in the carriage—Violet is. I didn't want to shock you. Had to prepare you." He stopped, rubbing both of his eyes with the butt of his palms.

"Violet? Cass's last letter said you two were together—in love—but that it ended abruptly. Had I been in the position to come to London I—"

"We *are* together, Ada, that is not up for debate, nor is your scolding necessary. I am here for your help with her—help she needs—I need."

His sister looked to the side and spotted her butler quietly stepping away. She sprang to him, thrusting her bundled babe into his arms and ignoring his look of mortification at having to take the babe. "Take him upstairs to Miss Lawson, Jenson."

Holding the babe securely, but slightly away from his crisp black jacket, the butler did as bade, awkwardly navigating the steps upward while holding the babe clear of his clothing.

She turned back to Theo just as he pointed at her butler. "Are you sure he isn't about to drop my newest nephew?"

Adalia flicked her hand in the air. "It is just a show. Jenson loves holding the babes when no one is watching. He is only making a production of it because you are here and it is so far beneath him." She grabbed his upper arm. "Theo, now what are you saying? What are you doing here? You look beaten to Hades. And when was the last time you slept—your words are slurring."

"Stop. Let me talk, Sprite," he growled. "It's not about me. It's Violet. She's broken and I cannot fix her."

"Violet? Broken?" Her hand tightened on his arm, fear striking her eyes. "What has happened?"

"She was in a mine. Captive for days."

"What?" The shrill word echoed in the cavernous four-story foyer.

"I will tell you every detail. But Violet is more important right now. It broke her. Being in the mine. It broke her." He paused, shaking his head, his voice cracking. "I broke her."

"What? How could you do that to her?"

"There was a shackle around her ankle, and after I found her I had to leave to get tools to free her. Ropes to lift her out of there. And it broke her when I left—I broke her, Sprite. I broke her."

"Wait." She tugged on his arm. "What do you mean, how is she broken?"

"She has been numb since we got her out of the mine. She is going through the motions—she will take baths. Eat. Always silent. And between those things all she does is sit and stare into nothingness for hours at a time. She does not speak. And she jumps every time I am near her. She jumps and scampers away from me if there might be the slightest brush of my hand. I tried. But I cannot reach her. Cannot help her."

"How long has she been like this?"

"Nine days."

"Why did you not come earlier?"

"I was waiting until word that your babe was born."

Her face crinkling in fear, Adalia pushed him to the side and went to the door, heaving it open and running out to the carriage. Without waiting for the footman, she jerked wide the carriage door and stepped up and into the coach, closing the door behind her.

Theo stepped out through the front door of the castle, standing on the top step, staring at the coach. The curtain on the carriage window drawn, all Theo could do was stare at the mud splattered up onto the sleek lines of the carriage, hoping against all hope that he had made the right decision to bring Violet here to his sister.

The days after pulling her from the mine had sent a spike through his heart. Her vacant stare. Her inability to answer even the simplest question—to even talk. And she had been getting progressively worse. Sleeping longer. Sitting in his drawing room for less and less time. Eating less and less.

A shell, nothing more.

He didn't need her perfect—even the smallest indication that she was still in there, could still recognize a world around her, he would gladly take.

But there was nothing.

As much as he didn't want to admit it, he realized everything he was doing to try and bring her back, to engage her, he was failing at. Failing at all of it. Failing miserably.

The coach shifted on its springs and the carriage door opened.

His sister stepped down from the carriage and he looked past her into the dark depths of the coach. He couldn't see Violet. Not even her legs.

She had ridden to Dellon Castle scrunched in the corner of the coach, her legs drawn up under her skirts on the bench. A ball—a small little ball that was attempting to disappear.

Adalia closed the carriage door and walked to Theo, motioning him to move inside the castle. Tearing his eyes away from the motionless carriage, he turned and followed her in.

"Did she talk to you?" Theo asked as his sister clicked the door closed behind him.

She glanced at him, her eyes flickering away, avoiding.

"Tell me, Ada, did she talk to you?"

Her look met his, the green in her eyes pained. "Yes, she did."

"And?"

She sighed, her brow crinkling. "And you need to go, Theo."

"No. I am not leaving her." The words came out harsh, almost a yell.

Adalia grabbed his forearm, not backing away from his flash of fury. "Yes. You need to leave. I am not saying forever—but now, in this time, you need to be gone."

Theo's eyes closed for long seconds. He didn't want to hear it. Didn't want to acknowledge that he couldn't fix her. That he wasn't the one she needed.

His eyelids cracked open, his gaze landing on his sister's face. "I…I need her, Sprite."

"Yes." Adalia nodded. "And I suspect she needs you as well. But she doesn't know that yet. She can't know that. Not with what happened to her."

Her other hand came up, and she grasped his shoulders, squaring herself in front of him. "You need to leave, Theo. She needs to not see you. Not be near you. Please."

"Can you promise me it will end?"

His sister's mouth clamped shut, her lips drawing inward. A slight shake of her head, and she shrugged with a long exhale. "I cannot. I don't know what will happen. I don't always understand how her mind works."

Brutal honesty.

But that was why he came here, trusting Adalia above all others.

Slowly, Theo nodded.

There was nothing more he could do.

He was a failure.

~~~

Violet sat on a small round stool, plucking ambitious weeds from around the base of Adalia's pink dwarf Centifolia roses. A long bout of midsummer rain during the past week had invigorated all the plants in the rose garden at Dellon Castle—including the weeds.
~~~

The tips of her fingers wrapped around the pointy leaves of a chickweed and she yanked. It was good—satisfying—to be in control again. Even if it was only control of a small little patch of land. The weeds kept sprouting, but she had control. She could pluck each and every one of them from the ground, destroying them.

If only controlling the people in her life had been that easy. Uncle Demetrick, Mr. Nullter, Malcolm, Fiona. All weeds. All people that played with her life—regarding her as a simpleton puppet on strings. All people that she wished she had plucked from her life far before they could do harm to her.

The gravel on the path next to the square rose bed crunched, and her head popped up from the crouch she was in.

"Oh, Violet, I did not realize you were out here." The duke stopped, clippers in his right hand. "You were hidden between the bushes."

Violet smiled at Adalia's husband. "Did Adalia send you out here to gather some buds?"

He looked down at his hand, seemingly forgetting what he was carrying. "She did. She wanted a few flowers to set by the bassinet, so Edward would have the scent of roses locked into his mind forever. But she was specific—she wanted a strong, noble scent. Maid's work, clearly, but Ada thought I would do a better job of choosing a manly scented rose than her maid."

Violet stifled a chuckle. "There is such a thing as a manly scented rose?"

He shrugged with a smile. "Ada believes it, so I suppose there is. And I am apparently the only one that can deliver strong and noble."

Violet looked down, hiding her smile as she dropped the weed in her hand onto her pile of refuse. The man did love his wife.

She stood from her stool, careful not to snag her dress against any of the thorny branches. Brushing the dirt from her gloves off on her apron, she looked up at him, sincerity in her eyes. "You are a good husband, Duke."

It gave him pause, as theirs had not always been the most cordial of relationships. A slight smile crossed his face as he offered a nod of acceptance. "And I would be a better one if I had a clue which one of these varieties was strong and noble and manly." He waved the clippers in a sweep above the forty square plots of rose beds, each holding eight thriving plants.

"Well, I have no clue either on which holds the essence of vigor and strength, but I am more than willing to help you sniff it out."

"Thank you."

Violet stepped carefully past the rose bushes and onto the gravel of the pathway. She motioned down the row. "I will take this side and you take the other?"

He nodded, and they started. Walking slowly, she bent occasionally at open blooms, sniffing. Rose after rose held the most feminine of notes to Violet's nose. The duke appeared to be having the same luck.

They were onto the next row when the duke sneezed three times in quick succession.

He looked out at the sea of roses, shaking his head. "Theo always enjoys saying I am a slave to my wife, and this current scene would, apparently, prove it beyond a doubt."

Violet's look whipped to the duke at the mention of Theo.

She had thought of Theo constantly during the past two months. She had driven him away—she knew that. But at the time—in the horror of how her mind had twisted after being captive in the mine—she had been incapable of doing anything but that.

And since she had arrived at Dellon Castle—and Theo had left her there without a word—no one had dared to mention his name to her. Not Adalia. Not Cassandra when she had visited four weeks ago. No one.

But the duke. The duke would dare just such a thing.

He was oblivious to her stare as he bent to a pretty rep-tipped yellow rose and inhaled.

"You speak of Theo. Have you heard from him?"

The duke shrugged.

She bit the tip of her tongue, debating on whether to say any more. "I worry on him. I worry about his book."

The duke glanced up at her, his eyebrows arched. "You know of his book?"

"I do. The names of the fallen, their families. Fiona's name was in his book. He thought she was dead. I figured that out before she stole me and threw me in that pit—that she was alive and had ill designs toward Theo. But I was stupid. I never imagined what she was capable of."

The duke stood straight, pulling himself to his full height. "He failed you on that threat, Violet, and he will not forgive himself for that." He scratched the side of his jaw. "Yet, from what I understand of your time together, Theo wanted nothing more than to prove to you what he was made of. To prove to himself he was worthy of you. But even more so, I think he was trying to prove to himself that he was worthy of living his own life."

"Why would he need to do that?"

"I don't imagine he would have told you everything of his actions during the war."

She eyed the duke, suspicious. "What did he not tell me?"

"You know of his book, yet I guess he would have only told you of those men he had caused the deaths of. Those were the ones that weighed heavily upon him—heavier than a hundred stones." The duke started walking again, pausing at the next set of roses before looking to her. "But if I know Theo, he would not have told you of all those thousands of people he saved in the war."

Her jaw dropped. "He saved thousands?"

The duke nodded. "And not just soldiers. Women and children, whole villages we were able to defend because of the information Theo and his men gathered."

"No, you are right. He did not tell me of that."

"No, because he has never reconciled how one side of it—death—could outweigh the other—life. He struggles constantly with that argument. And he can't change the past. It is hard to find peace when one only remembers the bad."

"And you tell me this why?"

"Did he tell you of the torture?"

She nodded, solemn.

"He believed he deserved it. Every strike of it. Every cut. Every drop of blood." The duke leaned over for a quick sniff of a simple pink rose. "But he didn't—not by far. Because Theo proved what he was made of—proved it a hundred times over in the war. Honor is all to him. Loyalty. But those deaths—they cost him—it changed him from what he was."

"Yes." She nodded. "That I have seen."

He looked up to her without straightening. "Did you know him well before the war? When you were young?"

"I did. We probably would have married, had it not been for my inheritance and a meddling uncle."

"I did not know that. Theo was….lighter back then."

"Yes. A rascal." The mere thought of the long ago twinkle in Theo's blue eyes brought a smile to her lips.

"Yes." The duke took another sniff of the pink rose and then shook his head with a chuckle. "The things he made me do in those days."

"Me as well." She shrugged. "I was different then as well. Lighter."

"Here. Smell this one." The duke pointed to the pink flower just below his face and then stood and took a step away from the bush to give her space. "I wish I had known you then."

"And not only after I learned to despise…well…men?"

The duke shrugged. "It would have made our initial conversations more pleasant."

She chuckled as she stepped in front of him. "Maybe. Maybe not. I didn't initially know if Adalia needed to be protected from you."

"You will always land on the side of Adalia, I realize that."

"I will." Violet leaned in to reach the rose he had indicated and inhaled.

"I also admire that."

She pointed to the pink rose, a smirk playing about her lips. "I think you are right. That is the one. It is by far the most manly of roses I smelled."

A grin twinkled in his eyes. "Are you just giving up as I am?"

Her left eyebrow cocked as she looked to him. "I will not admit to it if you won't?"

"Agreed."

"Excellent. My nose could take no more. A few of those and Adalia will be happy." She pointed to the pink roses, pausing a moment, her throat choking on the question she really wanted to ask the duke. Her look skittered up to him. "Theo…have you…" Her voice trailed off as her cheeks warmed.

She found she couldn't force the full question onto her tongue. Where was Theo? So instead, she shook her head and offered an awkward smile. "Forgive me—questions I have no right to." She wiped her fingers on her apron and took a step backward. "I will leave you to this—Adalia will love your choice." She started to move past the duke and along the path.

"Oh, before I forget, Violet."

She turned back to him.

"My stable master has reported you've exhausted all the trails on the western side of the estate ten times over. If you are going to ride today, you should try something on the eastern side. Inquire with Valence about the path. The cherry trees are starting to fruit in the orchard and might be a pretty sight."

She nodded. "Thank you for the suggestion. I will ask him on it."

{ CHAPTER 22 }

Violet leaned forward, patting the glistening brown neck of her mare. She had just slowed the horse's gait, the wide-open trail they had been flying along now narrowing to a winding trail into the thick of the woods.

This eastern trail she had enjoyed—far too much. So much so that she had lost herself in this side of the duke's estate, the side she wasn't familiar with, and now the light of the sky was quickly waning.

She looked up through the canopy of the trees and frowned. She had a half hour, maybe less, before sunset. If she wasn't back to the stables soon after nightfall, Valence would have a fit. As would Adalia. Probably the duke as well.

But it was worth it. It always was. It had been her salvation, the riding.

If it hadn't been for these horses, for the solace the duke's vast estate offered, Violet would still be inside, a quivering mess, her mind lost to her. But the exercise did her well. For as hard as it had been to crawl out of bed those first days here—and she had fought with Adalia for hours against doing so—the riding did her well. She knew that the first day she had ridden.

She had pushed the horse for hours that day—far too long—and had gotten a scathing look from Valence for it. Since then, she had asked very specifically for the horses with the most stamina, and ones that would enjoy the hard ride.

So it had been day after day. Adalia dragging her into the light of the morning. Setting her feet one in front of the other. Making her move, eat, talk. It had been grueling, gradual, but Adalia had tenacity like no other, never once even considering giving up on her.

And then one day Violet got herself out of bed. Got her mind back.

High-pitched chattering broke through the quiet of the forest and two red squirrels ran across the path. The first with a nut in its mouth, the second with a high tail on the chase for that nut. They scurried down the path, kicking up twigs and leaves until one dove onto a tree, ringing the trunk upward. She grinned at the madcap scene as her horse went by the tree.

Another look up at the sky through the thick branches, and she started to debate on retracing her steps. Valence had said the trail would circle back to the stables, but she had no idea if she was even still on the trail he spoke of.

She craned her neck to the side, looking ahead. The path looked like it curved soon, the trees appearing to thin. If there was an open space approaching, at least she could fully see the sky and get her bearings about her enough to head west.

It was twilight before her mare made it near to the edge of the woods and Violet could see that the clearing she was moving toward actually held a small lake.

Along the surface of the water, something moved. An otter cutting through the glassy reflection.

The otter moved upward. And upward.

Violet pulled on her reins, stopping her horse just within the last line of trees.

It was no otter in the water. It was a man.

A man standing up in the lake, his head the only thing poking from the water. He moved languidly through the lake away from Violet's direction, his arms just below the surface.

She watched the back of his head for a long moment, debating on disturbing him. On the one hand, the man probably knew which way to point her. On the other hand, she had the odd sense she was witnessing something intimate, something purely peaceful that she shouldn't disturb.

Just as she started to tug on the reins to move back into the woods and give the man his peace, his head turned toward the shore, showing his profile.

"Theo?"

The word spurted, loud, from her lips.

Splashing, he spun in the water and had to rub his eyes clear as he searched the edge of the woods. "Violet?"

He took several strokes and then started walking toward her, still swiping droplets from his face. His chest rose above the water…ribs….stomach…waist.

Her hand flew up. "Wait. Stop."

Theo froze, his fingers in his hair, halfway through pushing his wet locks from his forehead. Confusion set onto his face before he glanced downward. A slow smile, wicked and knowing, curled onto his lips as his eyes travelled to her. "You cannot show up here—on the tip of this pond, at the edge of darkness, out of nowhere—and expect me not to come toward you, Violet."

"But you are—you are naked."

"I am."

"So I would prefer you to stay in one spot for a moment."

"How long a moment?"

"This is just as much a shock for me as it is for you, Theo. So please, a moment."

He nodded, his fingers moving from his hair and flicking the wetness away. Droplets splattered, sending spreading rings throughout the surface of the water. His hands settled at his sides under the surface of the water.

Half hidden behind a tree, she watched him as he stared at her for long seconds in silence, his face unflinching, not belying anything he was thinking.

Her horse flicked its head, nickering. It broke Violet's stare and her hand tightened on the reins.

"How long do I wait, Vee?"

"How long have you been here in the middle of the woods?"

"Since I brought you here to Adalia."

She gasped. "You…you have been here all this time?"

"I will always be at your side, Violet, whether you know it or not." He shrugged. "Albeit a bit further away than I would have liked. But I was not about to show myself to you."

"Where have you been living?"

His hand lifted out of the water, pointing to a break in the trees to the left of the pond. "The east hunting cottage is down that trail."

"For two months you have been there?"

"It is all I need. I was not about to leave you, Violet."

"And this"—her hand lifted, motioning out toward the water—"is there no tub there to bathe in?"

He chuckled. "It is a hunting cottage, Vee, so no. Men on hunts find their stench most enjoyable."

She laughed.

His left hand went down, cupping the surface of the water. "Besides, I like the lake, bathing in it. It was something I started during the war—we swam where we could, since proper baths were hard to come by. A lake is spacious—me moving within the water, instead it moving around me."

Violet nodded, a soft smile coming to her face.

"Your hands on the reins, Vee." His voice dropped to a low rumble as he motioned with his head to her hands. "Do you want to leave?"

The question danced through the twilight to her, soft, sneaking upon her.

She wasn't prepared for this.

Wasn't prepared to have to answer that question.

Earlier in the day with the duke, she had wanted to ask on Theo's whereabouts. She had wanted to know, even if she wasn't sure what to do with the answer.

But to have Theo standing in front of her. Living, breathing, his ice-blue eyes staring at her like they always had—with the heat of barely bridled desire, with pure visibility straight into her soul.

She wasn't prepared for this.

But that didn't mean she didn't want it.

"I understand if so, Vee." The low rumble was tempered from his voice, replaced with restraint on his words. "Two months is not long enough. I accept that and I will not push you to stay."

Two months was not long enough?

Of course not. Not to Theo. Patience. The man and his patience. That was Theo's forte. Of course he would wait.

She closed her eyes, her head dropping forward. She inhaled, feeling the breath roll deep into her chest. It did nothing to calm her heart. Did nothing to settle her belly that had begun to flip over and over and over.

She had been wrong about so many things—so many people over the years.

But Theo.

Theo was not one of them. She knew that. Knew it all the way to the marrow of her bones. He was a part of her, if only she could accept it—admit to it.

Her head lifted, her eyes meeting his.

"Two months has been plenty, Theo." She loosened her boot from the stirrup of the sidesaddle and slid down the horse's side, knowing full well Theo's stare was searing her, waiting with caution to pounce, lest she try to escape him.

Silently, she tied the leather reins to a low-slung branch at her left and then walked forward. It wasn't until she stopped, her heels on the rough sand, her toes licking the edge of the water, that she lifted her eyes to him.

His stare searing her had been an understatement. His look had turned ravenous, ready to devour.

It stole her breath. That one look that said everything. That banished any lingering doubts she had about what had happened, what she had suffered, and how she had reacted—how she had lost her mind.

He didn't hate her for her actions. He hadn't given her up for Bedlam. He wanted her—more than ever. All of that burned in his eyes, begging her to know, to understand the depth of how he needed her.

"Strip, Vee."

The heated request—the command—wrapped around her, seizing a hold of her body. Her limbs started to move without thought, without her mind reacting to bristle against his order.

Tugging off her kidskin gloves, she then untied and pulled off her compact riding hat, the ribbon of it slipping through her fingers as she dropped the hat and gloves to the sand by her boots. Her fingers ran down the row of shiny gold buttons along the center of her cobalt blue riding habit. One by one the buttons popped free, her look not breaking from him.

She peeled back the jacket of her habit, letting it slide to the ground behind her.

She would strip for Theo any time, any place, and she knew it.

He knew it as well.

For all that had happened, his confidence in this had not wavered.

A smile played on her lips. She would, however, make him pay at some point for ordering her about.

She lifted off her white linen shirt and unclasped her skirt, letting it drop to puddle at her feet, partially in the water. Bending, she unthreaded the laces of her tall boots, stepping out of the leather and rolling down her stockings. She stood, letting one shoulder slip out from the strap of her thin silk chemise, then the other.

The silk dropped, falling to the ground, and she was bared. Full and vulnerable.

Theo swallowed hard, his intense stare layered with both lust and relief. His voice, impossibly rough, skipped across the surface of the water to her. "Swim with me, Vee."

She lifted her right foot, stepping clear of her clothing and letting her toes sink into the water. Cool, but holding just enough heat of the summer to not shock her skin. Her left leg followed, and within seconds she had waded into the water.

He needed her to come to him. To want him.

And there wasn't a thing in her way.

She moved forward in the water, her breath held, lodged in her throat. Her hands dipping down into the water, she didn't stop until she was before him, the top half of her body rising from the surface. Close, within arm's reach, but she had to pause before she touched him. Had to look at the entirety of his body. The hard lines, the scars of the past.

She accepted all of it. Things she would know, things she would never know.

Because he was worth it. Worth entrusting her life to. Her heart. Her soul.

Her mind had left her for a spell. But when it had returned, this was the one truth she knew above all others.

"I failed you, Vee." His words drew her look upward to his face.

"No—do not." Her head shook. "Do not ever say that. I deserved it. It was just."

"What? Why in Hades would you think such a blasphemy?"

"Because fate has been waiting for me." Her look dipped to the water. "I tried to kill myself once. I threw it away. Life. It was why I was punished. I didn't value life, and so what happened to me was just." Her look lifted to him. "A test. Fate needed to right the scale and it did."

His eyes closed, pained as he shook his head. "It wasn't just, Vee." His eyes opened to her, fire melting the coolness in the blue of his irises. "It just was. It was a woman that is crazy. A woman that had lost all sense of honor and loyalty and right and wrong. I tried to protect you—tried to stay away—but I was weak. I cannot be without you in my life, Vee."

"What happened to me, Theo, it proved to me, in the most brutal way, that I want life. I did everything I could in that mine to escape, to survive another minute, because I wanted life." Her right hand moved forward under the surface of the water. "I wanted a life with you, Theo. But when you left me, I broke—it tore my heart out and shattered it."

"Vee—"

"It didn't matter that you were back in minutes. That you carried me out of that hellhole with your left arm." Her right hand lifted, water dripping as she set her fingertips along the slick biceps in his left arm. His skin tensed under her touch. "Your left arm, Theo. You weren't about to fail me. I knew that. I know what you did. I know you saved me. But my heart was shattered. My head was. And it has taken this long for my mind to put all of the shards back together."

She paused, swallowing hard, her voice drifting to a whisper. "And I have been afraid since then that I have lost you."

"You will never lose me, Vee." His voice hoarse, he reached out, pulling her toward him, his muscles shaking with the need to have her skin touching his. "I have let a lot of things go that I ruined, that I should have fixed—but you—never."

He wrapped his arm around her back, setting the full length of her against his body as he buried his hand into her hair and clasped her head to his chest. A deep breath shook his torso and he buried his face into the top of her head.

"I only wanted to be your sanctuary, Vee. Your sanctuary against all that had beaten down your soul." He stopped, swallowing hard. "Hell, I wanted that. Needed that. That I was your sentence to horror…"

A shiver ran through his body, yet the heat of him cut through the cool of the water, warming her.

"It just was, Theo. It is the same for both of us. It just was." She threaded her arms under his so she could clasp the back of him. She had wondered if she was ever to have this again. To be able to touch his skin, inhale his scent, hear the low rumble of his voice.

By the grace of stars aligning for her, she had been granted this. She wasn't about to let it slip through her fingers again.

She tilted her head back, pulling away from his chest so she could see his face.

His blue eyes blazed with unconditional love, the intensity both startling her and warming her soul.

"Theo."

"Yes?"

"I am ready."

His eyes closed to her words, and for a long second, he held no reaction, his body stilling.

"Tell me those words are exactly what I am praying they are." His eyes remained closed, his words slow, each said with care.

"They are." Her hands tightened against the muscles in his back. "As long as what you're praying for involves a clergyman and me being by your side until the end of days."

A smile formed on his lips as he slowly exhaled the deepest breath. He opened his clear blue eyes to her. "You are mine, Vee?"

"I am. And you are mine."

He nodded, his smile turning wicked. "Then I have two months' worth of lost adoration on your body to catch up upon."

She laughed, moving to wrap her hands around his neck as she pulled her legs upward along his thighs under the water. "Then let us commence with the adoration."

"I am at your command, my love."

{ Epilogue }

The gardener dug his shovel into the rocky soil, wedging it under the stone. Pressing downward on the tip of the handle, his weight and leverage on the wooden pole was a weak force against the marble. Undeterred, he pulled his shovel free and dug into the ground in various spots, repeating the action four times before the marble stone loosened.

He and the boy he had brought with him each took a side and rocked the stone back and forth for several minutes. With hefty grunts they managed to free it and then lifted it out of the ground, setting it into a wheelbarrow.

The gardener paused to look at Theo.

His gaze lifting from the fresh black dirt, Theo gave the man a nod. The gardener and the boy started off down the path on the hillside, wheeling the tombstone away and leaving just Theo and Violet to stand alone on the hill.

The whole of it took ten minutes.

Violet stood quietly beside Theo, her hand clutching the nook of his arm as she stared at the empty rectangular cut of dirt where the stone had been.

Theo cleared his throat. "That was remarkably undramatic."

Her fingers tightened into his arm muscles and she chuckled, looking up at his profile. "It was. I thought…"

He met her dark blue eyes as a wry smile came to his lips. "That the earth would open up and swallow me? That lightning would strike down upon me?"

She nodded. "Something akin to that."

"Well, those were the two specific possibilities running through my head. And I am immensely grateful neither one came to fruition."

She smiled, her hand reaching up to settle along the side of his jaw. "I as well."

She stared at him for a long moment, her smile fading. Her hand dropped from his face as the shards of violet in her eyes turned serious. "Truly, Theo…tell me."

His look dropped from her to the shallow hole. It took several long breaths before he managed to center his own thoughts in his mind, and his mouth opened. "Truly? I am relieved. It…that that slab of marble existed out here. Day after day. It has weighed upon me. It has for a long time."

Silent, his wife's hand slid down from the crook of his elbow to squeeze the muscles in his forearm.

"After I came back from the war, I wanted to be dead for so long." His gaze lifted to her. "But now…not now. Not since the moment you kicked me in the Revelry's Tempest."

A soft smile played on her lips. "I must have kicked you hard."

He chuckled. "You did. The finest kick I ever received." He turned fully to her, his hands lifting to capture the sides of her neck. His fingertips played with the few loose strands of her chestnut hair escaping from her upsweep. "Life—you—all of it is too precious to leave a stone like that in the ground."

His look dipped downward to her protruding belly. "And I would never forgive myself if our child stumbled across it one day and it scared him."

"Or her."

He inclined his head, a grin playing on his lips. For how little he truly cared if it was a boy or a girl, just so long as it was healthy, he did love to goad Violet when he could. "Or her. Or him. Or both."

Violet's look lifted to the sky with an exasperated smile as her palm settled on the top of her stomach. Her gaze dropped to him. "You have done this well, Theo."

"What?"

"Life. The mine producing, securing the future of the Alton estate. Impregnating your wife. Finding your way forward. Helping families of the fallen. Finding peace." She stepped as close as her belly would allow, threading her hands along the sides of his stomach as she looked up at him. "I always knew you were strong enough for it. Smart enough for it. Had the will for it."

"I'm glad you knew it, Vee, because I surely had a difficult time finding it."

"But you did. And that is what matters." Her eyes twinkled. "You even paid off that bothersome debt you owed me."

He chuckled. "I did, didn't I? Who says gambling is a losing game? That was the best money I ever lost."

She shook her head, and before she could scold him, his hands moved upward to cup her face and he kissed her. Long and lazy, but simmering with the fire he always had for her.

He pulled up, satisfied to see the blush warming her face and the plump of her lips. "I do believe we are done here." He nodded toward the house. "So then, let us move on with this life of ours."

"Gladly." She turned, nestling herself into the side of his body as he wrapped his arm around her shoulders.

They started down the hillside.

Their bodies melded into one.

~ About the Author ~

K.J. Jackson is the author of the *Hold Your Breath, Lords of Fate, Lords of Action, Revelry's Tempest,* and *Flame Moon* series.

She specializes in historical and paranormal romance, loves to travel (road trips are the best!), and is a sucker for a good story in any genre. She lives in Minnesota with her husband, two children, and a dog who has taken the sport of bed-hogging to new heights.

Visit her at www.kjjackson.com

~ AUTHOR'S NOTE ~

Thank you for allowing my stories into your life and time—it is an honor!

My next story in the *Revelry's Tempest* series will debut in winter/spring 2018.

If you missed the *Hold Your Breath, Lords of Fate,* or *Lords of Action* series, be sure to check out these historical romances (each is a stand-alone story): ***Stone Devil Duke, Unmasking the Marquess, My Captain, My Earl, Worth of a Duke, Earl of Destiny, Marquess of Fortune, Vow, Promise, Oath,*** **and** ***Of Valor & Vice***.

Never miss a new release or sale!
Be sure to sign up for my VIP Email List at
www.KJJackson.com
(email addresses are precious, so out of respect, you'll only hear from me when I actually have real news).

Interested in Paranormal Romance?
In the meantime, if you want to switch genres and check out my Flame Moon paranormal romance series, ***Flame Moon #1***, the first book in the series, is currently free (ebook) at all stores. ***Flame Moon*** is a stand-alone story, so no worries on getting sucked into a cliffhanger. But number two in the series, ***Triple Infinity***, ends with a fun cliff, so be forewarned. Number three in the series, ***Flux Flame***, ties up that portion of the series.

Connect with me!
www.KJJackson.com
https://www.facebook.com/kjjacksonauthor

CPSIA information can be obtained
at www.ICGtesting.com
Printed in the USA
BVHW031302280520
580497BV00001B/74